JUST DYING
TO TELL

By Neil Patrick

For Linda, Adele, Lauren and Keir

JUST DYING TO TELL
First published by Touching Tales 2014

Publisher address: 484 Oundle Road, Peterborough, UK PE2 7DF
neil.patrick1@ntlworld.com

ISBN 978-0-9576083-2-0

Front cover photo © Chris Munden Back cover photo © Stephen Orsillo/Shutterstock

A dark night in November

When the man pretending to be a psychiatrist and the woman posing as a social worker had left the ward, Robert began to concentrate hard on the instructions coming through loud and clear within his head.

He was to hurry to Norwich Cathedral where he would receive a message that would save humanity from the invaders.

Good to get the go-ahead, he said to himself. But communications were so tricky. It was like a madhouse in here.

The invaders were proving to be a determined lot. They'd even injected him, thinking it would put him out - unaware, of course, of the protective power he had been given.

Their tactic was to say he was wrong in the head - and they'd gone to a lot of trouble with the set-up. First there was the 'psychiatrist' and the nosey woman he had brought with him; then it was the 'nurse' who kept coming with the suspect tablets, which he dutifully took - and secretly spat out into a tissue, feigning a cough.

Surely they'd twigged that his training as a doctor meant he knew all the dodges?

That nurse's face had been a picture, Robert thought to himself - smirking with pleasure - when she'd come with the meds, and he'd said: "I hope that's not clozapine. Danger of drug-induced agranulocytosis. Anyway, shouldn't I really be on olanzapine?"

Just testing her.

"It's only what the doctor asked me to give you," she'd said, all flustered.

Of course it wasn't medicine. It was some poison or other, to foil the mission. And, fair enough, he had to admit they'd certainly succeeded in frustrating progress.

But things would be underway soon. Robert had already started a log. It was in code, of course - well, who could you trust round here? And the drawings were nearly finished. He was especially pleased with the felt-tip picture showing how the world would look if he didn't get to Norwich and the entire shebang went up.

He'd noted that the nosey woman had glanced at the drawings and then nodded knowingly at the 'psychiatrist'.

But what did she know? He didn't like her, and he didn't like that smile. In fact, if he'd got the right weapon to hand – a pair of scissors would have done – he would have wiped her out then and there. One advantage of all that training was that he knew where the arteries were.

But heigh-ho, no scissors – not even a nice sharp ballpoint pen.

Robert opened the letter that had been on his bedside tray since morning. Someone had done quite a passable imitation of his mother's handwriting but he curled his lip dismissively at what they had written...

"Darling Robert,

I'm so very sorry to hear that you have become ill again and I will be coming tomorrow to see you. I phoned twice but they said you were asleep.

Please love, don't be frightened, it will be all right, trust me and do everything the doctors say and stay safe till I get up there..."

So Mum sent this, did she? Yeah, right!

He liked the way they'd put "trust me" in there – nice touch.

Robert went over the next lines laboriously. He was definitely drowsier and began to fear that he'd absorbed some of the toxins from the tablets...

"Ally and Isla will be visiting too at the weekend. They send all their love and have told me to make sure you rest up..."

Well, well. They'd got the family names spot on, so maybe he'd underestimated them. In fact, this was beginning to appear like quite a sophisticated operation. But then they couldn't have travelled to earth without being phenomenally clever.

The voices were fading now and Robert, propped up in his bed, lost his fight against sleep.

When he awoke, the TV set up near the ceiling was on and, although his limbs felt heavy, he swung his legs down and began to listen. He heard the newscaster say something about budget cuts and then, very loudly, "…but first Robert must leave for Norwich."

He still felt exhausted, just as he sometimes did after a busy shift in A & E. Yesterday had been so demanding, what with all the walking, warning people about the threat. Then there was the fight with those invaders dressed as Goths, then the endless questions at the police station.

After such a long time out in the cold, the bed was so comforting and he was so sleepy.

But he had been handpicked for the mission. He mustn't forget that. It was not every day that you were called upon to save the world.

He gave himself a little lecture: If you'd rather sleep Robert, fine. Go ahead. But just think of the consequences of them winning, and the world ending.

Think of Mum being vaporised, and all the Yeovil players, and the loving friends all over the world.

"Also, Robert," he said to himself out loud, "don't forget all the sick little kids you have pledged to help. Just think of them being snuffed out."

He suddenly shouted: "Go and do it, go to Norwich, Robert!," shaking a fist and startling a woman nearby.

She was carrying a clipboard. He could see by her expression that she was another one of the invaders pretending to be a nurse.

o o o o o o o

Kath McGill was looking out for the taxi. The drivers always had trouble finding the cottage, tucked away behind next door's beech hedge.

Her overnight case was at her feet and she had checked she had her keys, that there were no gas rings burning, and that the heating was off; she was surprised how the house had cooled down so quickly while she was waiting. But then winter was here, even though it was barely November. Of course, she said to herself, she might be feeling the cold because of the shock…

It would all seem better when she could hug Robert, and have a good talk with the doctors. By now they should have a fair idea about the poor boy's condition. She felt a tremble in her bottom lip but fought the urge to cry.

She dreaded the journey, not because of having to change at Castle Cary to get to King's Cross, then, at Peterborough, to get a taxi to the unit, but because she was impatient to see Robert. No, not impatient – desperate.

But he would be all right, she decided; he had been fine after that first, terrible episode before his A-levels. Quite well for years, really. True, there had been that worrying period at the end of his first year at medical school but since then he had been the same loving, loveable Robert.

The train was half empty and so she chose a window seat; she tried to breathe slowly to ease the tension, to gain some inner peace by gazing at the distant woods and the empty fields, black and wet beneath the morning haze.

It was at times like this that she drew on the spiritual capital she had hoarded. It was also at times like this that she missed Eric most. Dear Eric would have made sure she had a coffee and a crossword and would have buoyed her up with a continuous flow of encouraging words until they were there.

Robert, bless him, had inherited that caring nature from his father. He was certainly not goody-goody. Just good.

Once she had told him how little trouble he had been in childhood, and how eminently reasonable he had been as a teenager. He had rolled around laughing and said: "Yeah, Mum – I was perfect… until I got that very naughty idea that I had to slaughter the headmaster and his family!"

"OK, a slightly worrying notion," she had chuckled, warmed by the way they could be comfortable talking about what had been a terrifying time all round. As she'd topped up Robert's wine glass she'd added, "But you have to admit, Rob, that chap was thoroughly unlikeable…"

"True, Mum – but not unlikeable enough to deserve what I was planning in here at the time," he'd said, tapping a temple and grinning.

It was all a now-distant nightmare that had involved a bread knife and a crazy all-night vigil with Robert hidden in a clump of laurels in the head's garden.

When what they both called 'the illness' struck again after his medical exams, Robert had come home for cosseting during the long, slow healing process. Once she had gone up to his den with a cup of coffee and found him on his bed, curled up in a ball and cowering under cushions, as if he was under attack from some invisible force.

It was then that she understood her limitations as a mother. Even laying down her own life for him – which she would have done without a moment's thought – would not silence the demons in his head.

o o o o o o o

An announcement from the train guard, and sudden shafts of sun slanting through the window, brought Kath back from that dreadful time to this new challenge. In half an hour she would be at the unit seeing for herself how Robert was. At least until then he was safe, in good hands.

She reminded herself to ask whether work pressure might have triggered this new crisis. Robert always gave everything – in his studies, to his friendships, to sport, to her.

He adored the job, despite the cruelly long hours. That's where the caring nature came in, Kath said to herself.

When they last spoke he had mentioned his plan to specialise in paediatrics and he had hardly got the sentence out of his mouth when she had shouted: "Yes, Rob – that would be just you!"

He was gentle, funny. She could imagine him finding ways to get children to allow the most terrifying procedures, or explaining distressing situations in a way that made youngsters feel that this awesome, high-fiving footie fan was going to make things right, or at least do his best.

The taxi dropped Kath outside the unit in the November gloom. The building was characterless and depressing; she didn't like the idea of Robert having to be in such a place.

When she identified herself on the intercom, a matronly woman in a vivid floral dress, making her larger than life, looked myopically through the glass wall of an office to the left of the main door.

Her brow was furrowed, her glasses pushed back into her haystack of grey hair. The woman seemed to Kath to be preoccupied, stressed.

She put an arm round Kath's shoulders and mechanically inquired about the journey and then asked a colleague whether they might have some tea, then took Kath into the glass-walled room. Kath sensed that something was not right.

The woman described how the day before Robert had become challenging in the shopping centre. His knuckles were bleeding suggesting he'd already been in a fight, and there was a large bump on the back of his head.

"Fighting? Robert?" Kath said. "I must see him."

"Maybe he had just fallen. But we had to act for his personal safety. Hence the need for us to keep him here…"

It was clear to Kath that the story was incomplete. There was going to be an ending.

They both took a sip of tea as if bracing themselves.

"Mrs McGill, we'd made Robert quite comfortable and he seemed to be settling down nicely."

Seemed. The past tense felt like a hammer blow.

"Quite calm, once we got him stabilised. But I'm afraid… well, he seems to have left."

Left? But they'd told her this was a secure unit…

Kath held her breath and waited, in case there was more.

"We're looking into the circumstances of course. But I'm sure

10

that's less of a concern to you than Robert's whereabouts. To that end we've notified the police and been in touch with his friends and colleagues."

Kath rarely let her anger out but her fury took her over. She heard herself saying: "There is absolutely no excuse! Robert had been sectioned. You have let my son down and perhaps even put him in danger. He could be on a railway line at this very moment."

The woman reached for Kath's hand but she drew it away.

"I do understand. But Robert will be OK, I'm sure," the woman said. "The police are already out there looking. We've never lost anybody for long, Mrs McGill. He'll be back, you'll see."

The Indian Summer, two years later

1

When without warning Sniffer stood up, leaned on the bookcase and dropped his pyjama bottoms, his wife and brother were only mildly disconcerted.

They had seen it all before.

Sniffer had always shown a disregard for everyday niceties. In his forty-seven years, most of them as a grown-up who really ought to have known better, he had never, ever looked before he leapt, never erred on the side of caution.

Sniffer never thought before he spoke, had never taken counsel, never trodden carefully. His brother Terry had once summed him up – "When most people put the brakes on, Sniffer will tickle the accelerator." Sniffer had always been an absolute bugger.

Viv had grown to regard the infuriating aspects of Sniffer as the price of the fun and the sometimes-delicious uncertainty that came from living with him. But often the price seemed too high. That's when the play fighting got out of hand and blood was drawn.

The two visitors were a little ruffled by Sniffer's lapse in manners. They averted their eyes and didn't respond when Sniffer demanded that they take a good look at the extent of his rash.

Dusty gamely tried to normalise things – "Well, when I married Sheryl I knew I'd be seeing more of you Sniffer but I didn't think it would be as much as this!"

This did little to break the tension that had crackled in the air since Sniffer pulled the ripcord, so to speak.

Viv's irritation was tempered by the sudden thought that perhaps they all ought to start making allowances because of the health business.

With Sniffer it was hard to tell where the "normal" left off and the "ill" Sniffer began.

Untameable was the word a mutual friend had used about him to Viv when, ten years before, she had been poleaxed by his charm, dazzled by his spirit and his grey-green eyes.

She had been warned. In fact, when the subject of marriage had come up, at a time when Sniffer's mother was on her last legs, she had said: "If it was me, Vivienne, I wouldn't."

But despite everything, Viv would not have missed the Sniffer Experience. She could never say that it had been boring. Stressful – yes, often. Shaming, sometimes. Insecure, always. Explosive, occasionally. And once, a couple of years ago, truly heartbreaking.

On the very night she met him, to her astonishment Viv had surrendered, teetering on over-high heels in the rain in a darkened pub yard, a night that had become more memorable for the rubbish bin that had rolled backwards as he devoured her, than for the head-spinning passion.

When they were reminded of their meeting she would say playfully: "I thought it was the earth that was supposed to move, Sniff, not the bloody wheelie bin!"

In fact there had been no playfulness lately, not since the affair, and the tests, and the devastating prognosis. Now the memory loss thing was making her fear that the essence of the man would slowly leak away before the cancer got him.

So the charity ride had seemed such a good idea, something positive for Sniffer to focus on. But now they were all gathered, and considering this latest episode, she knew that she would have to tell him that he would have to stay behind.

So damned ironic, she said to herself: Here I am, try to stop a dying man biking because he might hurt himself.

2

Sniffer looked around, appearing to have forgotten that his pyjama pants were still round his feet. Viv hurried to his side and, kneeling, tried unsuccessfully to haul them up, grimacing at having her face where it was forced to go.

"Do yourself up man!" she chided. The pyjamas fell once more.

Dusty – Viv's very new, and very round, brother-in-law – coughed and Terry's solemn, slender friend, Malcolm, looked intently out of the dining room window.

Terry put his arm round his brother's shoulder and said gently: "Come on Sniff, it's not on..."

"That nurse said I might get rashes," Sniffer shouted. "But, bloody hell, look! Imagine that on a bike saddle!" He turned to the wall and stooped to display his scarlet rump, like an exhibitionist baboon.

This time, against his better judgment, Dusty did look, and noted with puzzlement Sniffer's tattoo – spindly letters, CHE, ending abruptly at the angry red cleft of his buttocks.

"Sniffer! Make yourself decent won't you!" Viv shouted. She propelled herself backwards on her knees and pleaded: "Dusty and Malcolm haven't come all that way to see your backside."

Sniffer remained motionless, outstretched arms against the wall, as if about to be frisked. The room was silent.

As Sheryl arrived with mugs of tea, she stopped in her tracks, the tea slopping onto the tray. Viv had mentioned that Sniffer had been behaving even more unpredictably than usual.

Here was the evidence.

The static scene before her suggested some Bible illustration. Viv on her knees might have been Mary Magdalene, with three of the disciples, all fixated by the florid bottom with its mysterious coded inscription.

"Everything all right?" Sheryl asked brightly, blushing and walking crab-wise to the corner of the room to get as far away as possible from Sniffer.

Teaspoons tinkled against mugs, above whispers. Sniffer, restored to decency, sat impassively now, eyes forward, looking at nothing.

Terry brought tea to Sniffer's chair. He had always looked up to his older brother, even when the things he'd done had made him ashamed to share the name. Calling him "Sniff" reflected a proprietorial pride. Only Viv and him called him Sniff. And only Sniff – and very occasionally Sheryl – called Terry Tel.

"Look Sniff – I've been thinking. Maybe it's best if you don't do the ride. We'll do it for you. Me, and Dusty and Malcolm."

Sniffer took time to pretend to weigh his brother's words but his answer was ready instantly.

"I'm coming, buh," he said, looking hurt and sticking out his whiskery blue-black chin.

That's just the face he made when he was little and being stubborn, Terry thought. That look has come back after all those years...

So had the "buh," a description that dated from when they lived in Clench; back then all males from eight to eighty were boys, with the confusing variation over truly young boys, who were always called ol' boys.

"Look matey, Viv's worried sick and the doctor's washed his hands of the whole thing," Terry said appealingly. "Being ill and riding bikes don't mix."

"I'm doing it, Tel," Sniffer insisted. "And the tenting."

"But Sniff, time's moved on. You're not 19 and fit as a butcher's dog. Sleeping out could kill you. On top of it all, you've got an arse like a forest fire!"

Sniffer stared hard into his brother's eyes. Terry knew that look.

"You'd be barmy, Sniffer," Dusty chipped in, nervously. "You could fall under a lorry."

Sniffer glared at the new relative, despising his second chin and his girlish curls. There was also that hint of a smile that never left his podgy face, no matter what he was feeling or saying. There was no feeling behind that smile. And then there was that bloody Lancashire accent

"Not barmy yet, Dusty, but getting there. Look. The ride was for me. Get it?" he said sharply.

A year before, when Dusty had married Sheryl, she'd been transformed from a lonely divorcee to a love-struck teenager of forty. But Sniffer found it hard to accept someone who was so quick, too quick, to integrate with the family, and he was still uneasy that Terry, a good fen boy, had chosen to settle "up there," to teach.

It was only two or three hours away but "the north" was beyond the pale, a place where rival football teams bred their talent, a place where people like Dusty came from.

Sniffer was proud to have remained true to his origins.

OK, Viv and him had finally moved out of the wilds but it was only to Peterborough, still a fenny sort of place and in fact "The Gateway To The Fens." So he hadn't exactly sold out, not like Tel. Actually he was still in the country really, out on the edge of the city, where everything still had a bit of a fen feel.

He'd acclimatised, in a manner of speaking, but he sometimes pined for the true Fens, the space, the straight roads to bomb along, and for his past homes, all over, in Clench and Whaplode, but especially the little place near Ramsey with a barn for a workshop, where he had been happiest.

It had been nearly two years already since the move.

Two years? Where did the time go? Time was something he thought about a lot, now there might be so little of it left.

The great thing was that he could still get out at night when he wanted. There were still a few good pubs in Peterborough. But if he was honest he still missed the piss-taking regulars in The Webbed Foot, and the practical jokes, and the fact that at any time he dropped in, he would know someone, usually, everyone.

Sniffer had always liked his late nights. It was the buzz from the music, the feeling that anything might happen; the way drink made women talkative, daring, easy, ready for a laugh.

He had never really settled in that way.

After a couple of years of domesticity with Viv he had grown restless at weekends.

"For God's sake sit, Sniff!" Viv would say when he couldn't settle. "You're like one of those caged animals that pace about all day."

There had been a phase when he'd escaped from what indeed sometimes felt like a cage, broke free for a while, and tested the marriage until it hung by threads.

He remembered the night when, at his mention of the word "home," Viv had run at him and screamed: "What do you know about home? Home is where you get ready to go out, and come back to with your hangover."

Of course, with all the recent trouble and Viv's vigilance, lately he'd rarely ventured out.

Maybe it was the illness as well. He just hadn't felt up to it. He'd even put Mad Mick off a couple of times, and the very best nights of his life had been with Mad Mick.

Yes, it was probably the illness and the treatment.

Also, he wanted to be with Viv a bit more than before. He had begun to feel grateful just to have her around and, when he thought about it, ashamed that it had taken a doctor's diagnosis to show him how much he had taken her for granted.

3

Dusty was convinced that Sniffer shouldn't ride but now he was wondering about himself, questioning whether he was up to it.

The old bike he'd brought had been his son's, and when he had put it on Terry's car rack he'd realised it was ridiculously small for a long trip, and it weighed a ton.

Not only that, there was the niggle about his fitness. Obviously marital contentment was calorie-rich. He hardly had a shirt that fitted now, or trousers that fastened. Proof came on cue as he was forced to rock to and fro to get out of the deep settee to move towards Sniffer.

Dusty hoped to get talking, without the usual friction, and maybe slip in a question about that tattoo, when the time was right of course. He couldn't stop puzzling over it.

Such an odd, secretive place to have the initials. People usually paraded their love, getting KAYLEIGH or SHAYDEN etched in Germanic script on their arms.

But what to make of CHE?

Then the answer came to him.

Chelsea!

Strange though – Sniffer had always been a Peterborough fan…

Posh-till-I-die – that was Sniffer. And anyway, why would the tattooist have stopped at CHE?

Surely Sniffer can't have been a Che Guevara supporter! Not Sniffer.

Dusty started out tentatively on his mission.

"To be honest Sniffer, I'm with Viv and Terry about the ride," he said, stooping so he didn't have to raise his voice. "Sheryl's all on edge about you. It's daft and it's dangerous."

"My decision. A grazed knee isn't going to make any difference what with the state I'm in," Sniffer said acidly, looking at Dusty with distaste.

Dusty took a confidential tone: "How about this: when you go to the game tomorrow, and they do the announcement, Terry can get them to say that owing to the illness, you're having to drop out but we're carrying on for who those who have given sponsorship money?"

Dusty was in marketing and could see the heart-tug potential there.

"Bollocks."

"Now then, Sniffer…"

"Bollocks."

"But Sniffer…"

"Don't you understand the meaning of the word bollocks?"

"No. It's a rather coarse term of endearment we don't use ooop north," Dusty retorted, with an exaggerated accent, switching from seriousness to laughter. Sniffer didn't laugh. He hated the way Dusty said "nor", in that Lancashire way, instead of "no."

When Dusty and Sheryl had come down last time Dusty had said: "Lovely smell, Viv – is that pork you've got cooking?" But what Sniffer heard was: "Is that poooerk you've got coooking."

There had been a bit of an atmosphere when he'd teased Dusty about his accent but – fair play to him – Dusty had gamely fought back.

"It's just like you lot round here saying compooter," Dusty had protested. "Or commoonity. Or foooneral."

Foooneral or funeral. No matter how you said it, it was a word best avoided when talking with a man with an illness that would probably see him off. Sheryl had pinched Dusty on the back of his arm where it really stung. Sniffer had seemed oblivious.

The group migrated to the kitchen where Viv washed up and cried simultaneously, gently massaging tears away with fingertips of her wet rubber gloves.

"It's in remission for now but they've said it's all looking pretty hopeless," she sniffed.

She paused at the sink, and said: "Sometimes he goes into denial, or forgets what they've told him. This forgetting thing is what's breaking my heart. He isn't the old Sniffer."

Viv believed the diagnosis had made Sniffer confront something dark inside, maybe something from the past, some buried secret. After the talk with the specialist, Sniffer had said: "Can't complain. I deserve it."

Viv looked perplexed. "It was as if it was, what do they call it, divine retribution?"

Sheryl, Terry and Dusty gathered round the sink while Malcolm stood apart, limply holding a tea towel, uncomfortable to be privy to intimations of death, and family secrets.

"They suspect that the new thing might be Korsakoff's," Viv confided. "Brain. From the drink." Then, laughing through her tears, she added: "Sniffer calls it Corsets Off."

"Korsakoff's – that's dementia isn't it Viv? *Dementia*, Viv?" said Terry. "That's settles it. He's not riding anywhere."

Viv tilted up her chin and offered her face to Sheryl, who wiped her eyes with a corner of the tea towel. They rejoined Sniffer who was lying in his recliner chair, with his head slumped forward, asleep, and continued to chat quietly and as if he were not there.

"They say the chemo might have triggered off the memory thing, or it could have been the cancer," Viv said.

Terry, Dusty and Malcolm sat motionless and silent. What was there to say?

"But it could be he's not been getting a certain vitamin so they've pumped him full."

Viv looked ruefully amused at another irony: "All those years trying to change him," she said "and here I am trying to get him back to what he was!"

Viv wiped her nose, shook her head as if to gather herself, and turned to Terry who had drawn up a chair to be next to Sniffer.

"So there we are. But there's another big change that you'd never have thought possible."

Everyone looked at her in expectation.

"I think Sniffer's found God. Well, not exactly found him but he's gone looking."

"Bloody hell!" said Terry, staring in disbelief at his sister-in-law.

"Fear, Terry. That's what's behind it, guilt, or whatever's been stirred up inside him."

A smile lit up her face once again as for a moment she tried to rise above it all.

"Not that my Sniffer has any reason to feel guilty. As if!"

Then a dark feeling of foreboding came over her. She was sure that she had a pretty good overview of Sniffer's deceits, the things he might be ashamed of.

But what if there was something really dreadful, something so awful that it would haunt him until he took his last breath?

4

Terry's face still registered surprise and bafflement. Sniffer had a spiritual side?

Viv raked back the dark curls from her cheeks and perched on a stool and took off her glasses. She looked eager to share news of this mystifying turn of events.

"It was after the tests that showed that he'd got secondaries," she began. "He was reading stuff like 'Does Hell Exist?' that kind of thing.

Terry scratched his bald patch and murmured: "I've never, ever known our Sniff care a monkey's about anything remotely religious. Never even heard him mention God except as part of swearing."

He paused a moment to come to terms with this new aspect of someone he knew better than anyone else; better even than Viv, he supposed.

"Come to think of it though, we all went to Sunday school, didn't we sis?" he said to Sheryl.

Sheryl scoffed: "When Sniff didn't run off to play with Gary, that farm kid, was it out Walpole Marsh way? But then they were very religious, weren't they? Some odd… well, a cult I suppose."

Viv said pensively: "He doesn't know it but I've seen him writing stuff, stuff about the past, places and people. Including some people he knows I don't like to hear mentioned."

Terry knew that Viv was thinking mainly of the Egg Woman.

He remembered that messy business all too well.

25

He'd picked up Jess from work that afternoon, and driven down like a bat out of hell. Viv had been so distraught, they had feared what she might do.

Strange, he hadn't felt at all disloyal to Sniff by being supportive to Viv. What was wrong was wrong, even if your brother was the villain of the piece. And he was.

Talk of Sniffer's spiritual awakening gave Viv the ideal prompt for her story of the women who had called the other day offering religious tracts.

"Yes, drab women, oldish, came saying that they had a message and it wouldn't take long. Sniffer shouted to let them in. It wasn't long before they were wishing he hadn't!"

Everyone laughed. They each pictured Sniffer playing these women like hooked fish.

"He gave them a right grilling. Wanted to know about life after death, and resurrection."

One of the two ladies, Viv said, had been telling Sniffer that Jesus had once brought some bloke to life after he'd been dead four days and Sniff made some crack about jump leads.

Viv was a skilled raconteur, a talent that she had put to use in her amateur dramatics. She was shy about venturing an impersonation, but Terry and Sheryl laughed out loud when she imitated Sniffer's voice.

"So Sniff says 'Now, tell me this. What happens if I'm resurrected and I end up with a load of Lithuanian lads? Will we have a resurrected interpreter? And what if the chap next to me says: Hello Sniffer, nice to meet you, I'm Adolph. Worse than that, what if I end up in a bunch of resurrected Norwich supporters giving me loads of chelp about Posh?'"

Sheryl, who had been subdued, suddenly slapped her knees with delight and Terry laughed until he was red in the face. Viv noted how his laugh was identical to Sniffer's, the even teeth prominent, the little tiny furrows round the cheeks and the eyes narrowing.

As they were leaving, Viv said, Sniffer had harangued them at the front door. "Now… come on girls. Straight John Bull. Is there such a thing as hell? Plain yes or no."

"The women looked at each other," said Viv and, adopting a nervy, high-pitched voice added "'Well, sort of, would you say Irene?' and then this Irene dived into her handbag for leaflets."

Viv brought down from the mantelpiece a flimsy folded sheet, held it up and proclaimed: "For freedom from a morbid fear of death turn to Hebrews 2:15…"

She replaced the leaflet and, as she did, the face of the performer fell away, leaving just plain Viv, pained and bitter.

"No more morbid fear?" she said, the tears coming again. "So why's my Sniffer upsetting himself so, when he could just bloody well turn to Hebrews and rest easy?"

No one answered because there really wasn't anything to say.

○ ○ ○ ○ ○ ○ ○

Sniffer slept on. Viv studied his face and then whispered: "I've decided, Terry. He'll get on that bike over my dead body."

Sniffer made a moist slobbery noise and seemed to plunge even deeper into sleep.

"We need to sort things out though," she whispered. "He had a couple of special wishes, things he wanted to do."

"What sort of things?" Terry asked, glancing to check that Sniffer was still asleep.

"Well, he wanted to take your mum's notebook about the Fens and give it to that new museum. And there's a few other old bits, old clothes that were handed down through Great Aunt Nancy."

"No bother," said Terry. "We'll be going that way into Ely. Haven't seen Mum's book for yonks but I remember the bit she wrote about the ghosts, and the big flood and all that stuff about the Fen Tigers."

"Oh yes…" said Viv, suddenly. "And you're not going to believe this Terry," Viv murmured, striving not to wake Sniffer. "He wanted to light candles along the way. Imagine. Candles. One at Ely, one at Clench, one at Norwich and the last one here in the cathedral."

There was a snort from Sniffer. Without opening his eyes, he said, very deliberately: "Wanted to? Look. I'll be riding, Viv."

Viv left the room shaking her head as Sniffer cleared his throat and said: "Used to love tents. It's just you and the elements. Makes you feel alive. Yes, lovely. Tents and summer mornings! Anyway, you can't beg for sponsorship and then take the cushy way out with B and Bs can you?"

He looked at Terry, Malcolm and Dusty in turn and announced with an icy cheeriness: "By the way, did Viv tell you all that I might have Corset's Off as well as the bother with the lumps?"

There was not a sound and eyes were averted.

"Don't worry. It's not all bad," said Sniffer breezily. "If the memory does pack up at least I won't remember that I've got what I've got."

5

Sniffer stirred in his bed, then woke up when Viv bent to kiss him on his perfectly circular bald patch. One of Viv's hands was cupped around multi-coloured tablets, with the other she placed Sniffer's Peterborough United Play-off Commemorative mug on his bedside table.

Viv noted – now Terry was visiting – how Terry's tonsure had turned out the same, and she was reminded once more of how similar the brothers were. Same blue-black chins, same grey-green eyes; both always as brown as chestnuts whatever the season,

Last night, when Sniffer had gone to bed, Dusty had asked how Sniffer had got his nickname. It was a question he'd never remembered to ask but he was interested because he had been referred to by his own nickname since schooldays, long after his mother's idolatry of Dustin Hoffman had ebbed away. In fact it was only during the wedding ceremony, when he married Sheryl, that the family discovered that Dusty was really Dustin.

"I can understand me being landed with Dusty," he said, "but I mean, Sniffer. He sounds like a retriever…"

Terry described how it dated back to childhood when Sniffer had sniffed, instead of blowing his nose.

He said that in later life the nickname had been a blessing because it meant that his Christian name, bestowed by his mother in memory of her beloved brother Clarrie, a celery-grower out Wimblington way, was near redundant.

29

"He absolutely hates being called Clarence," Terry said, with feeling.

Terry said that when Sniffer was old enough to know it was regarded as an old man's name he would cringe every time the teacher called it out. Later, whenever he had to answer to it - in the doctor's surgery, to the custody sergeant, wherever formal naming was involved - he wished he was invisible.

What Terry remembered, but didn't voice, was that when his brother moved into his teens and began his relentless pursuit of women, the name Sniffer, with its connotation of the hunt, seemed perfect; it was a nickname he had grown into.

As it was, today he had woken confused, not only about where he was but also over who he was. The lustre had gone from his eyes and he looked around as if the surroundings were unfamiliar. But when Viv took hold of his hand and won his attention by staring hard into his face, his sense of time and place seemed to return.

"And how's you today?" she asked with a tenderness that surprised herself. She had put her guard down in the last few days and started to use simple loving language. There was just residual warmth now where there had once been fire.

He sipped his drink, washing down his tablets in twos and threes. That done, his mood seemed to brighten.

"Football today is it? Posh?" he asked.

Viv took off her glasses and began to tease her damp curls with her fingertips but all the time monitored Sniffer in the tilted side mirror of the dressing table. She seemed to spend her life watching, waiting, guarding now. She didn't begrudge this, despite all that had gone on, but sometimes she thought it was pretty unfair, the way things had turned out.

Sniffer had spent a lifetime not really caring about anybody really, while she had never stopped caring - first for her kids, then her invalid mother, and then for Sniffer. She seemed to have done all the hard work involved in keeping the marriage going.

But then she had been complicit in it all, gone into it with eyes wide open. She knew Sniffer's failings, even before they met. His reputation "went before him" but rather than heeding this, she was drawn by it.

She had stepped blithely into the web and become helplessly entangled, easy prey for the infuriating, lovely, selfish, funny, bloody Sniffer.

He had baggage. He brought virtual sacks of it with him into that register office and she knew there was lots more scattered elsewhere, stuff he had found it convenient to forget.

She had once come across a jokey threat people used to attribute to brides; perhaps it was on a seaside postcard. The message was "Aisle, Altar, Hymn." Over the ten years not a great deal had been achieved towards that goal.

There had been fresh starts but they had petered out. Maybe people couldn't actually be changed, she'd decided. Yet there was so much that needed changing. There were the lies (white ones and jet black ones), occasional boorishness, almost-cruel frankness.

Much worse, there had been if not affairs, disloyalties, Sniffer's "friendships that had started to go too far." He included the Egg Woman in this anodyne description, when they both knew it was something much more significant.

At the most testing of times, the music had saved her. The society shows took her out of herself; in fact, the only time she felt totally, sublimely free was when she was at rehearsals, or giving it her all on stage.

Singing carried her somewhere else. Reading a script transported her to the place the lyricist had dreamed up, a place that for a couple of hours was real.

Viv had often tried to assess the bad and the good that had come from meeting and marrying this man. If she'd been presented with one of those scales with chains and brass plates, and told to weigh up the pros and cons, there was no doubt that the Egg Woman would have made one of the pans clang down on the minus side. And that was before all the smaller but hurtful other negatives were piled on top.

But there were compensations to drop into the other plate. Lots of laughter, rare and clumsy kindnesses, ill-judged but welcome gestures of love, independent spirit, pride in the work he did.

She knew he would fight to the death for her, reserving for himself the right to treat her badly when he had won. And he would win. Sniffer always came out on top and it was only now, with the illness, that there was a question mark over his supremacy.

She gathered Sniffer's big, rough hand between hers.

"Right, Sniff," she said, "I'll tell you what's happening. Today you go to The Posh because they're going to announce the ride. More sponsorship money."

Sniffer's brow furrowed. "Did you say going to Posh? Posh?"

"Football. Peterborough bloody United! London Road – the club you've supported since before you met me! "

Sniffer looked as if he had retreated into himself. He had that baby look again.

"Remember the programmes on top of the wardrobe?" she teased. "Remember that big day at Wembley and poor old Terry having to go down to London to pay your fine and get you home?"

His face showed no understanding. This was the worst memory lapse so far. Sniffer forgetting that he was a lifetime football fan.

"Posh have actually invited you. Terry arranged it. You can wear your scarf and they'll all cheer when they hear about the ride. Then you go there again after the ride. You'll get more sponsorship."

"I'm off football. Most players are gay now."

"They're not gay! And what if they were? Come on Sniffer, you love football. It's me who hates the silly sodding game," she said.

She put her finger on the end of his nose. "You, you, went to see Posh on the afternoon of our bloody wedding! Remember?"

"Oh yea. Tommy Robson. Made two and hit the post two or three times. It was persisting it down and they were all slithering about but he ran rings round them. Lovely feet. Lovely player."

Viv stared hard at Sniffer. How could this man summon up, out

32

of his confusion, a particular football game from God knows when?

The recollection turned out not to be perfect but Sniffer finally arrived at the precise landmark of the many he held in his head –"No, I tell a lie. That was yonks before. It was Bournemouth and we smashed them 6-0."

"But do you remember our wedding?"

"It was sunny, like now. Could hardly see the match for the sun in our eyes."

"Yes, sunny, like now, but do you remember our actual wedding?"

"You've never let me forget." There was pride in his smile. He seemed pleased that he had managed to be light-hearted.

"Who is it today? Who's playing, Viv?"

"Ipswich. A friendly, Terry says. Things start properly next week."

Sniffer walked gingerly to the bay window, and looked into the far distance.

"Did you say I'm going on the bike? Well, I won't be riding the Triumph – the oil's pissing out of it."

"Sniffer, you sold the Triumph even before we got married."

Viv's face became clouded with worry. She paused to absorb this new, extreme moment in Sniffer's confusion.

"No, Sniff – Terry's driving you there. The biking's tomorrow. They're taking your candles for you, and delivering your mum's book to the museum on the way."

"Have you asked her for it?"

"No love. Your mum died. Remember?"

"Died? Well, bloody hell! Why didn't somebody tell me?"

Viv reached into the bottom drawer of the old bureau and pulled out a battered red exercise book on which was pasted a smudgy label. The title, written in fountain pen, read: FEN WATER IN MY BLOOD – a life on the Levels, with some history and first-hand memories.

The day before, Viv had found the phone number of the Fenland World Museum and Sniffer had rung to say that he wanted to donate the book along with a pair of rusty ice skates worn by his grandfather's brother in the fen races. There was also a reed-cutter, a christening gown and some ancient underwear Great Aunt Alice's mother had worn.

Viv glanced out of the bay window and could see Terry and Malcolm in the drive easing a tandem from the roof rack of Terry's 4X4, while nearby Dusty examined the connecting fitting of a lightweight trolley he had taken from the back.

They'd all been crazy to even think of letting Sniffer get on a bike. At least Terry and Malcolm looked like cyclists, although she did wonder whether Dusty, carrying all that weight round his midriff, would make it to Norwich.

Headwinds would test him, even though the forecast was for a week of sun. She remembered biking to school in "fen blows," walls of wind that bent trees, coming in thrilling gusts that scuffed up the water and sent birds hurtling, helpless, up and away. She loved to shout as she rode and feel the wind making her eat her words.

Sniffer was at her side now, asking: "What's their game?"

"Just your Terry and Malcolm, the friend who teaches with him, sorting a few things out. For the ride. With Dusty."

She led him to the kitchen for coffee and his tablets. "Dusty?"

"Dusty? Your Sheryl's Dusty! Her husband."

"Oh, I know him. The fat little one. Well, I'll have to start getting my stuff together soon," he said, and Viv braced herself for the battle to come.

6

As Sniffer's riders prepared for the trip, in a cavernous, sun-filled, pristine room at the Fenland District Hospital, two women worked listlessly, side-by-side at a solitary desk in the unbearable heat.

Doreen had just gone into what she described as her "bolshie mode." She had placed an opened umbrella and it lay behind her head, shielding her from the window, as a broad hint to any passing manager.

It was not like it had been, when they had been part of a team. Now only bits of work filtered through – random, impersonal work from the now centralised admin pool. Most files were marked Confidential.

Doreen loved confidential medical papers. She often tried to picture the people involved and was morbidly fascinated by the medical language and (if she were honest) loved trying to calculate the patients' likelihood of survival.

When Doreen returned to the desk, having trudged down three floors to the hospital shop, she put her thumbs under elastic hidden beneath her dress, let it snap and declared: "God, you don't half feel the flab on days like this. Roll on winter."

She put down the slimming magazine she had bought and slumped down into her chair, then passed one of two chocolate bars to Kathy who said: "Sod the diet!" and fell upon it as if she had not eaten in days.

For a time, they worked in silence, pecking away listlessly at the keyboard until Doreen picked up one of the files and said quietly: "Oh dear…Oh God."

Kathy reached over and read the name on the front of the file. "Metastasis. Secondaries," said Doreen under her breath. "Poor Sniffer."

Kathy put her hand on Doreen's and said: "Sniffer? Does he work with your Jerry?"

Doreen had gone red and looked unsettled. She didn't reply.

"Are you OK Doreen?"

Doreen tried to be dismissive – "No, it's just that I recognise the name."

Doreen looked so forlorn, Kathy wanted to offer some comfort.

"We get a bit of a one-sided view working here, love. Look at this pile of files and you'd think everybody in town was dying."

"But we are, Kathy aren't we?"

Kathy decided not to reply in case the conversation turned philosophical. It was a minute to home time. Kathy liked to get away on the dot.

She put away her glasses, gathered her car keys from the desk top, and bent over to read the name on the folder Doreen was holding.

"Clarence. A real old-fashioned name. I bet he's a lovely old boy…'

"He's not old, Kath. Like me, 47."

"But I bet he's a nice chap, too nice for that to happen."

"Yes."

"So. Are we off?" Kathy asked.

"You go, Kath. I'll just finish this one," said Doreen absently.

When Kath was sliding gingerly onto the baking hot seat of her car, Doreen, three floors up, was still daydreaming.

She wondered whether it was embarrassment, or maybe the nasty surprise, that was making her feel hotter than ever.

They were right, the friends who had turned on her just before she had married Jerry. She had been pig-headed. She remembered trying to tell them that Sniffer was not wicked, just misunderstood.

Of course, they were jealous, some of them. Sniffer had something of the roaming traveller about him that appealed to young girls. He was like those sun-tanned, slightly oily, boys working the waltzers at the fair, spinning the cars to make girls scream and hold onto their skirt hems.

Funny, Jerry and Sniffer were both Posh mad. At some time over the last twenty-five years they must have stood beside each other on the terraces oblivious of the common link – her.

Daft as it was, even now Doreen sometimes looked at her kind, pot-bellied Jerry and wanted to confess and ask him to forgive her.

But it was much too late. Life was short, after all. She re-opened the file, sighed, closed it. As she walked to the lift she was lost in herself, looking back to another time. Some old pop records did that to her.

It had been a wickedly wonderful time. It was as if she had been under a spell, with Sniffer the evil sorcerer.

She pressed the lift button and before turning to thoughts of Jerry's dinner and the strawberries she had bought for them to share she said to herself: "Shame on you Doreen. But you know damn well you wouldn't have missed it for the world."

o o o o o o o

Sniffer's name had been mentioned every day at Johnsons' building suppliers in the run-up to the charity ride.

Much of the talk had been about whether it had been wise to back his plan to ride all that way, from Peterborough to Norwich. The latest rumour said he was on the way out.

The dilemma for the Johnson family was that Sniffer had been a model customer for years. Old Man Johnson said it was only right to get behind him, come what may.

They all knew it was too late to call a halt now, anyway. Most of the money was in. They'd delivered the tee shirts to the house. The bike shop had set the tandem aside. Jo and Brian had even decided where they'd ambush Sniffer on his ride, to cheer him on.

The heat of the afternoon had invaded the showroom, bringing with it a torpid atmosphere, an ambient timelessness.

Jo was re-stocking, and after replenishing the racks of screws, she turned to Brian and said: "Did you see Sniffer's face, Bri? He looked haunted when he last came in. The spark had gone."

Brian could see that Jo was upset.

"Yea. You know what I think he looked like? An old, knackered lion. You know, when they lose their teeth and aren't in charge any more."

"Old lion, Bri? Hang on, Sniffer's not that old."

Brian quickly added a hopeful note: "Anyway, they can do wonders nowadays Jo. Don't let's write him off."

Jo never tired of Sniffer's flirtatious ways. The gulf between their ages made things feel safe for her, and the suggestiveness was almost always on the right side of decency. Just.

Old Man Johnson was now behind the counter on his special, deeply cushioned seat, a perch enjoyed each day after he had spent what little energy he now had on morning tasks.

The heat was making him even more soporific than usual this afternoon. He had been called Old Man Johnson for twenty-five years but he was now feeling his seniority in his bones.

He really felt extremes of weather and he had now fully accepted that he had been overtaken by the times. He was perplexed by the computerised stock-ordering and still suspicious of transactions that did not involve paper you could handle. His had been a world of cash – coins (often dusted with plaster), crumpled notes unearthed from pockets in overalls, and sometimes scruffy, discoloured cheques drawn from beneath layers of working clothes.

"Sniffer'll be OK," Old Man Johnson said languidly.

He had always had a soft spot for Sniffer; he liked his wildness. "He's a fighter that one," he said languidly.

"He's certainly been a fighter," said Brian. "Remember the state of him after that rumble outside that chip shop? His eyes were so black I thought he was wearing a Zorro mask."

Old Man Johnson's bubbly laugh turned into a cough.

"Before my time," said Jo. "But I was here when he got that call on his mobile from the horrible developer bloke he'd fallen out with."

Old Man Johnson's mouth gaped to reveal his entire set of false teeth and he held the pose throughout while Brian described how Sniffer had held the phone away from his ear and they could hear the diatribe throughout the showroom.

"Remember," said Jo, "how he whispered, mouthed it to me, 'Tell him I've just fainted.'

"I wouldn't do it but he nodded at me, didn't he, and pushed the phone at me. Eventually I said 'I'm very sorry but I'm afraid Clarence has just fainted. He's spark out. I have to see to him…'"

"That business wasn't about money," said Old Man Johnson. "It'd be about a woman, the bloke's wife. Or his daughter."

They spent a moment, each silently calling up episodes from the Sniffer biography.

Jo and Brian went to and fro fetching boxes of safety goggles and sanding discs. Old Man Johnson tilted his tea mug and, seeing it empty, decided to ward off boredom with another tale.

"The funniest thing I ever saw in my life was when him and Mad Mick came in that year, just before Christmas shutdown," he began.

"Mad Mick?" Jo said.

"He still gets in now and again," Brian said. "Fancies himself, does a bit of labouring for Sniffer. Drives a dirty great American thing on bloody great big wheels. Got some of those holes in his ear, lobes like squid rings."

Old Man Johnson chipped in. "They'd been in The Webbed Foot all afternoon and then called in here togged out in women's clothes. Going to a fancy dress do. Sniffer in fishnets and Mad Mick in a blonde wig and a bosom out here" - he made cups of his hands and held them a foot from his chest.

"Didn't Sniffer sit on your knee and kiss you on the lips Dad?"

"Best forgotten, that. Reeked of ale. Lipstick all over. And best forgotten that business with your mother. She wouldn't entertain him after that. That time he went too far."

Jo became thoughtful, turned from stacking boxes and said: "You know, that could be his epitaph. 'He always went too far'."

Then she added: "But we mustn't talk about him as if he's gone."

∘ ∘ ∘ ∘ ∘ ∘ ∘

Jess, who had just driven down from Lancashire, was relieved to have arrived at Viv's. She had felt out on the edge of developments. Viv asking her to drive to Norwich to pick the men up when they'd finished the ride had given her a sense of being involved.

She had talked Viv through her route down, the missed turn-off and the hold-ups. Now she was eating croissants, and talking about Sniffer, while thinking mainly about poor Viv.

Jess liked Viv – and slightly enjoyed pitying her.

It would have been easy for her and Terry to side with Sniffer that time when things were really difficult, blood being blood, but Viv had her sympathy.

She had said to Terry only recently: "What must it be like to have to live with Sniffer? I'll tell you this – if ever you play away, Terry, your feet won't touch the ground."

She sipped her coffee contentedly and enjoyed the fact that the journey was over and that she was at the centre of things. She knew that poor old Terry would be having a testing time. Things were never easy with Sniffer.

Jess had always been eager to join any conversation centred on the destruction of Sniffer's character. She had finally written him off last year when she had first begun to put on the weight, and he had patted her belly and asked: "When's it due, Jess?"

The man seemed to thrive on humiliating others. No grace, no manners. How could Terry have ended up with someone like that as a brother?

Of course she was very sad about Sniffer's problems but it would be so false to pretend that he had been anything but a constant worry. With him, you were on permanent alert.

As Viv poured more coffee, Jess said she wondered whether

Sniffer was dyslexic – or was it autistic, or that other one? Anyway, one of those medical conditions that they did TV programmes about.

Terry had once said: "I think you mean he's psychopathic, Jess, and I do sometimes wonder..."

Jess added a sweetener to her coffee and decided to pass on her pet theory to Viv, now she had her on her own.

No-one could say that Sniffer wasn't bright in some ways, Jess ventured, but she truly believed that he was envious of Terry's career path ("you know, degree, teaching qualification, deputy headship").

Viv looked intrigued as Jess recalled an occasion as the drink flowed during a weekend away when Sniffer had called himself a "thicko."

"Remember it, Viv?" Jess asked, picking up flakes of croissant on her plate with a dampened finger. Viv shook her head but Jess described how, revealingly in her view, he said: "When I left school I was still calling a chimney a chimbley and talking about skellingtons. Tel there got what brains were going, didn't you Terry?"

o o o o o o o

They had been talking about Sniffer, only the night before, a few of the old crowd, quenching their urgent Indian Summer thirsts at The Webbed Foot.

They were out at the "smoking tables" but when the sun had begun to go down and the late-season coolness settled round them, they picked up their pints and trooped into the lounge.

Meanwhile, miles away on the fringe of the city, Sniffer snoozed, propped up against the bedhead. He had been reading a book about reincarnation but had found the text so dense he had been forced to re-read each paragraph and had finally surrendered to sleep.

He was dreaming of being in a flat-bottomed boat – of the sort that the old wild-fowling parties used to use. The boat was deep in Wicken Fen.

The water at Wicken was curtained in parts by tall, dense, reeds that teemed with tiny creatures - insects, dabchicks, quicksilver tiddlers.

Sniffer loved this dreamy sensation of gliding unseen, smoothly, slowly - as if on oiled glass - through pale green gloom of the shallow water, with the sun on his back.

Viv was in a cane chair in the corner of their bedroom, poring over a script. Whenever she came to her own lines, picked out in marker pen, she gesticulated and made facial expressions, as if she was signing for a deaf person.

While Viv lost herself in her script and Sniffer floated in his dream through Wicken Fen, the Webbed Foot crowd were growing noisier and drunker.

Billy the landlord was pinning a newspaper cutting on the noticeboard next to the front door. He motioned with his thumb to direct the regulars to it.

"Sniffer," he said. "Bit about some charity ride. Have a gander at that photo. He looks bloody awful."

A clutch of people put down their drinks and gathered round the cutting. One said: "We'll have to give something. Can't believe it, a bloke like him, full of life."

"It's not all he's full of!" said Matt, an elderly wag, camouflaged against the dun-coloured wallpaper.

Billy hauled on the beer pump and then topped up pints with a series of short, sharp jerks.

"We had some bloody good nights with him!" Billy said with emphasis, addressing the room. "The stuff he did! Some of the tricks he pulled!"

A couple of customers told tales about Sniffer that showed the unappealing side of his nature but a serious man playing the fruit machine said, by way of mitigation: "Curiously, he's good as gold at his job, the same Sniffer. Not like these fly boys nowadays who should be wearing spurs and stetsons when they weigh up a job."

Stories of Sniffer's buffoonery climaxed with a tale told in his laboured way by Matt, the gangly, doubled-up old man on a stool at the furthest end of the bar.

"Remember the bloke who used to come wearing a straw hat? With a basket of Cromer crabs and prawns and stuff? Most of you won't. Smart ol' boy dressed like the fellas on those boats...in Italy."

The customers looked at each other, unanimous in agreement and mutual dismay that this would be one of Matt's longer tales. The door to the toilet banged behind an escapee.

"A gondolier?" asked a young man, chomping noisily on crisps, at a table that had a beaten copper top.

"Yes – like one of them. That's it. Straw hat. Apron. White van I think. Very red-faced bloke. As if he'd got some skin problem. Or maybe it was from living on the coast. Because of the weather. Fridays he came in. Friday nights."

"I never saw him," said a serious man playing the fruit machine, "and I've been coming in on Fridays for six years or more."

"God, no, I'm talking about way, way back, maybe ten years. You need to get your knees brown. No, it was when Toddy had the pub, Toddy who had a heart attack watching Posh. Fat as a pig. Once ate a 28-ounce steak, and chips with it. A bet. Forever at the pork scratchings." "Crack on Matt," said Billy, "I want to be locked up by midnight."

"They say he drank the beer slops," Matt continued blithely. "Kept this place for a year or two before the brewery found he was mixing the sugar with the flour... I'd always wondered about those fancy holidays..."

"Get on with it Matt, for... fuck's... sake!" spluttered the young man at the copper-topped table, spitting out crisp crumbs, and turning an alarming shade of red.

Matt continued. Slowly.

He said that when they were all three sheets to the wind one night, after the gondolier bloke had gone off carrying his tray, Sniffer started to cough and splutter.

Everyone was getting worried – they thought he might be

choking, Bill said. They started slapping him on the back.

"Anyway – suddenly he let out this bloody great sneeze. Into his hanky. It was when we all used to have a hanky. Remember? In your top pocket? They ought to bring them back. I much prefer them to paper. Anyway, then he made a big thing of opening it and … there was a horrible pile of wet stuff in it. A sort of mound. Everybody was just about sick."

Matt appeared to have left the story with no ending. He turned his beer glass round, very slowly, several times on the beermat.

"And?" said the crisp-eater, impatiently, his face flushing once more.

"You know what? The stuff was actually a mussel! A mashed-up mussel! Sniffer'd bought a bottle of them and gone off and stuffed one up his bloody nose!"

Matt was, for once, rewarded with raucous laughter but Betty, the landlady, screwed her face up and said: "Eeeugh! The dirty swine! How is it that so many women have found a man like that attractive, I ask you!"

It was Viv she pitied. "A lovely girl and a smashing singer – not that she's got much to sing about with him," Betty said. "It's only two or three years back since she came bursting in here one night with a face like a slapped arse and, little as she is, bundled him home without so much as a good evening. Think she'd found a text."

"But then," ventured Matt querulously, "sometimes with Sniffer it's just a joke. Like the fishing da."

The young man at the copper table exploded – "A joke? Balls! Cheating, that was!"

"Well I'm not so sure about…" Matt protested but the young man shouted him down.

"Right, we get on the boat. We each put a tenner in the kitty. Biggest catch wins. We spread round. Sniffer's at the back of the boat on his ownsome. Now I wonder why that was?" he asked his voice breaking with anger.

"Every so often he's saying 'Come…come. Come aboard,

my silver darling' and, pissed as we are, we actually believe he's catching fish hand over fist. Then...then, after we've weighed in and he's won the money and we're heading home in the minibus, this barefaced bastard says: 'Guess what, boys – I bought those fish when we got there and hid them in my carrier bag.' Then he laughs like a bleeding drain!"

"Actually", said the wise man at the fruit machine, turning to give his considered verdict, "actually, I think you'll find that in law, strictly speaking, that was indeed fraud, something calculated to deceive. But because it was Sniffer doing it, it was all just a laugh. Cracking brickie but a flaming psychopath, well to be accurate, a sociopath really, that's what the trickcyclists would call him."

7

"Just the gents we've been waiting for!" shouted the man in a high visibility jacket, waving to Terry and Sniffer over the gathering crowd as they picked their way through the car park towards the football ground.

"Recognised you from the photo in the Telegraph," the big man said, leading them down a brick-lined corridor, out of the milling fans, away from the noise and relentless late-summer sun and into the cool gloom of an echoing subterranean room.

At a table sat a small, plump, bald boy in blue-and-white football kit. He was shiny with sweat, drinking from a can and clutching a match programme.

He was being teased by an eight-foot white rabbit carrying a large knitted carrot.

"That, matey, was a wonder goal just now!" the rabbit was saying. "Did you hear the crowd? Not every 'ol boy can say that they've actually scored a goal at Posh when the goalie was a giant rabbit!"

The rabbit patted the boy on the head with a paw. "Thanks. It was awesome," said the boy mascot, shrugging his shoulders and smiling as if struggling to come to terms with the thrill of it all.

"Drink up. You'll be walking out with the teams soon. Don't forget, when the captains start talking to the referee, we walk off. We go to the tunnel. Mum and Dad will be waiting."

The boy nodded shyly.

"Wow – you're going to have something to tell them back at the hospital!"

"Hospice," said the boy.

Hospice. Sniffer couldn't bear to look again; it was the little boy's baldness, his unhealthily bulging cheeks and the fact that he was so happy.

Sniffer had become slightly anxious about the rabbit, especially the way it talked. In fact there was something about the entire place that was disturbing.

He felt panic rising. He could hear rousing calls and the sharp clack of football boot studs being stamped on concrete, and, from outside somewhere, the hum of a thousand conversations, wavering canned music, the wail of some kind of trumpet.

The big, square man in the yellow vest answered a call on his radio and then said to Terry and Sniffer: "Mr Posh is just finishing his bit on the pitch. Seems we've got a fair number of Ipswich fans in."

He drew the back of his hand across his damp forehead and flapped the sides of his yellow jacket in an attempt to cool himself.

"All set for the bike ride are you?" he asked. "Anyway, good luck. Worthwhile cause. We'll get you out there in a minute,"

Mr Posh, slim as a pencil, immaculate – tailcoat, white carnation, dangling monocle, spats, and silver-topped cane – his parading duties over, put his head round the door. He tilted his top hat in encouragement to Sniffer, who wore the disbelieving face of a child overcome by the lavishness of a gift.

"Well I'll be…" Sniffer said under his breath. "It's Mr Posh. And I'm actually in here, after all those years."

The announcements had started, and as Sniffer was being led down the players' tunnel into the dazzling sun, and on to the fresh turf, he recoiled in fright from a man hurrying past him, coming from the pitch pulling a rubber mask from his face. He could hear his crazed laugh.

Terry recognised him immediately – "Fred! Fred bloody Barber, Sniff! Used to run on wearing that mask. Used to clown about, and then play a blinder."

Images of sensational goalkeeping and crowd-pleasing antics flowed through his mind. Fred was unforgettable.

Sniffer gave no response. He leaned against the wall at the tunnel entrance, waiting. The brickwork was warm, the sun dazzling. The feeling of panic was easing.

"Now our Fred really is a Posh legend!" said the announcer over the speaker system. "Thank you Fred…"

He continued his monologue as Terry and Sniffer were led onto the grass.

"…Now let's give a rousing Posh welcome to some brave gentlemen who are about to set off on a weeks' charity ride. They'll end up here at London Road when we entertain Tranmere. I'm told one of them is a lifetime Posh fan who hasn't been very well but he's determined to get on that bike! So…let's hear it!"

Terry and Sniffer stepped on to the pitch, and bowed their heads in acknowledgement of a pattering of applause from the stands.

Returning to the gloaming of the room beneath the stands, Terry and Sniffer drank tea from paper cups, and listened to the crowd noise ebbing and flowing, a hum punctuated occasionally by bursts of drumming.

"Well?" said Terry. "What about that, Sniff!"

"Great!" Sniffer said. The shine had come back into his eyes, Terry noticed.

Terry moved to leave and took Sniffer gently by the elbow.

"No need, Tel," Sniff said, looking down at Terry's helping hand. "I'm not a bloody invalid."

"Well, that's a matter of opinion," Terry replied good-naturedly.

They were both surprised by the growing volume of noise welling up from inside the ground.

"Only a friendly but they're full of it," Terry said. "Glad to be back watching, I suppose, after the summer. Gagging for live football."

They could still hear the chanting of the fans as they neared the car, and the discordant singing of last season's club song being revived in the terraces.

Terry stopped, listened then said: "Bloody hell! They need a few lessons from your Viv."

He felt so happy to have been back to London Road. Long-buried memories flooded into his head – memories of great goals, late goals, filthy weather, goalkeeping howlers, unforgivable player transfers, cup-tie sensations, hip flasks, hot pies and cold feet.

That was years ago but players would be still coming and going, as they had always done. Football clubs were ever-changing. Like the Nene, or any river – the water passing was never the same but the river was the same, the name didn't change. It was the same unchanging spirit, something you could never pin down, that was "the club."

Terry steered Sniffer towards the car and as they walked he remembered the insults thrown out like projectiles from the East End stand, opposition players bombarded with obscenities over last-ditch tackles. He'd always found the bias of fans highly amusing, the way reasonable individuals turned rabid, how refs had their eyesight questioned, their sanity doubted, their parentage disputed.

It was because football mattered so much to them. It was a safety valve. Maybe after the ride, when he was back home, he would start to watch Bury or even Accrington.

The sound of the crowd welled up again, accompanied by drumming. Terry cocked an ear and asked: "What's that they keep shouting, Sniff?"

"Blue army."

"No, not that."

"Is it Boro, Boro come on Boro?"

"No – sounds to me as if they're taunting the opposition fans by yelling 'Who are they, who are they?'"

"Could be, Tel," Sniffer replied, suddenly looking vague, then adding: "Actually, good question. Who are they anyway?"

"Ipswich, Sniff. The Tractor Boys. The Posh are playing Ipswich. A friendly. You knew that."

"So the other lot's Ipswich? It foxed me. But then some days now I don't know who I am, never mind who they are. It makes you frit."

8

Nearly two years had passed since Viv had first got wind that the Egg Woman was more than just another satisfied user of Sniffer's building skills.

Things had happened before but this was different. This was not just an alcohol-fuelled grapple, like the one she had once witnessed when, out of kindness, she had gone out late at night to pick Sniffer up. It was more than the silly sexual teasing conducted by text with that barmaid at The Webbed Foot.

This was a slow burner, significant, threatening. And it had all been so cruelly public.

Viv had been appalled to learn that people in the village and her workmates at the veg plant had known for weeks that Sniffer had been calling regularly at the Egg Woman's woebegone roadside house.

Later she had joked, bitterly, that the Egg Women's Rhode Island Reds had been more in the know than her. In a sense it was true. The hens had wandered, pecking contentedly round the visitor's feet, the quail chirruping in their pens as he went past. The Egg Woman's terrier Tonto had stopped barking when Sniffer dropped in, accepting him as family.

The humiliation of knowing she had been duped weighed on her almost as heavily as the infidelity itself.

It was so hard to keep a secret in their part of the Fens; and Viv knew these sightings must have been succulent titbits to be chewed on and just about everyone would have had a taste.

The open countryside and the closed community allowed people to see things that some would prefer to hide. Even items in shopping baskets - an anniversary card, tablets for the flu, or a bottle of whisky - told stories.

Adding to the mortification she endured during the brief separation, that sent Sniffer into self-pitying shock and forced him to doss down at Mad Mick's, was her reluctant acknowledgement of her dependence on Sniffer.

When he came back home, he had pleaded, she had thrown things - in particular the framed picture of him and Mad Mick grinning like idiots after Posh won at Wembley.

She wasn't aware of having consciously selected the picture as a weapon but she had. She had been impressed that as she drew back her arm, Sniffer turned to her and presented himself full on, as if to a firing squad. Perhaps by sustaining an injury, maybe losing an eye or a tooth, he would be taking punishment he knew he deserved.

The photo had hit him in the chest and fallen at his feet. He had picked it up, looked closely at the cracked glass, and carefully put it back where it had been.

When, over days, they reached the end of what proved to be an emotional cul-de-sac, for a moment they stood face-to-face and made pledges to try again.

She couldn't admit it to anyone but she was relieved. Despite everything, she wasn't ready for life without Sniffer.

But this was no brave new dawn, they both knew that. Nothing fundamental had changed. The ramshackle marriage was only fit now for trundling along, hopefully holding together on bumpy patches along the road. It was not long before it was tested.

Sniffer began to see the Egg Woman again. Probably.

One morning, having said she would stay at home to enjoy her day off, as it was raining, she changed her mind. She would go to the shops. She called after Sniffer as he walked across the yard to the van.

Running out with her coat and umbrella, she saw Sniffer taking a plastic-wrapped bale of wood shavings out of the passenger seat of the van. He was hurried, and to her seemed furtive. She knew of no use he might have for wood shavings. When she asked, as they moved off, Sniffer mumbled.

The bale was from the man who made the windows and banister rails, he said, with what to Viv sounded like forced casualness. It would "come in handy."

That night, as she drifted into sleep, a chilling notion came into her head. She sat up suddenly in the dark and yelled: "Sniffer, you devious sod! That bale was for her, for her chicken coops."

Even though Sniffer had been deeply asleep, the alibi he had contrived after the confrontation of the morning tripped off his lips. A believable explanation. One that would make Viv ashamed of her suspicions.

"For God's sake, Viv! That stuff's for the workshop floor," he said huskily. "To catch oil from the lathe, and when I'm servicing the van. It's like a skating rink in there."

And so the creaking framework of their marriage had held again.

"Now, for Christ's sake let's get some bloody sleep," he said.

Viv turned over, plumped up her pillow. She was less agitated now but the gnawing insecurity felt like a physical sickness. She supposed it would always be like that from now on.

Unless they moved house, of course.

Moving house… something she had not thought of. She dwelled on the idea as she fell asleep.

Moving would help her not so much forget what had happened but spare her the daily reminders.

With cruel irony, the Egg Woman's house and empire of pens and coops could be seen from the bedroom, Viv's bedroom, the marital bedroom.

The fens let you see miles when the weather was clear. She could often pick out the Egg Woman's little car, the reflection from the little duck pond. She could even see (but only just) the bright yellow plastic board the police had nailed to a post nearby, with the appeal for witnesses of that hit-and-run accident.

The anger over the Egg Woman was never extinguished but the move meant that the Egg Woman's place was just a memory. The two years since the move had given her a new perspective on past events.

In retrospect she had been pathetically weak when she had phoned the Egg Woman, ostensibly to stop the weekly egg delivery, but really to vent her anger, to speak to the enemy, to warn the woman. But she had only added to her own pain, hearing a cultured, and gentle "I quite understand. And I am so very sorry."

She had never before spoken to the Egg Woman who, most Saturdays, stopped the bouncy French car and left the tray of eggs out of sight, behind the big stone gatepost. It was Sniffer who would chat at the roadside, or would call on her at intervals and pay. That led to the work at her house. And that led to lies and in to heartbreak.

Viv supposed that the Egg Woman must have suffered too, but that didn't stop her regretting not having turned on her when they had found themselves in the queue at the paper shop.

They had both blushed, one with shame perhaps, and the other with anger, before the Egg Woman replaced her newspaper on the rack and walked, in a slow, dignified, manner out of the shop.

She was dignified, Viv had discovered, well brought up. Also, she knew she was called Lydia, a name that lodged in her throat, a name she had never wanted to know. Sniffer had defiantly blurted it out during one of their rows, even though she had dived on him and tried to cover his mouth.

She had not wanted to know anything that turned the Egg Woman into a person and she was outraged when during another particularly furious fall-out, Sniffer switched, in a second, from self-defence to the defence of Lydia.

"Christ Viv, she's a woman! A person," he shouted. "And she has got a name, even if you hate her. She's a nice person and she's not to blame."

Viv felt that she would burst with the injustice of it all.

"And you, Sniffer, are this nice lady's bit of rough," she yelled, her voice cracking.

Sniffer thought about this. It was true - he was rough. And practical, and lacking in education. That's why he had been surprised and flattered that Lydia seemed to value the things he said. She would nod and be encouraging and understanding if he faltered. The stolen hours were filled with conversations that ranged wide, and explored little nooks and crannies of knowledge.

She drew out feelings that he had always kept stowed away, the stuff behind the bluffing and the banter.

He had done wrong by Viv. He'd been caught. Viv was right to be so upset. But he wasn't going to devalue what Lydia and him had found. He responded out of loyalty to Lydia; ridiculous, he knew, when he had shown none to Viv.

"Yeah, true. Maybe just her bit of rough," he said, agreeing mechanically because the argument was going nowhere.

But he knew that it was - had been? - much more than that. And anyway he suspected that they were sharing a secret that would always bind them, no matter how posh she was, or rough he was.

9

The woman at the door had spiky, silver-white hair, a ruddy face and a smile dominated by startlingly white teeth. Viv took her to be a doctor or a nurse.

The visitor said "Morning!" enthusiastically, then: "It's OK, I'm not selling double glazing! I spoke with your husband when he was with us at the hospital and he asked me to drop in one day. For a chat. The chaplain."

"Ah," said Viv, surprised that Sniffer had not told her of the planned visit, but then he was forgetting so much now. They stepped into the hall and the chaplain's voice dropped to a woman-to-woman whisper. "He was a teeny bit shy about people knowing that we were talking. Perhaps he didn't even mention it to you?"

"No. He hadn't but he's in. Tea?"

The chaplain glowed with energy and enthusiasm. Her eyes were a watery blue and seemed to Viv to reveal everything about her in their clarity and sparkle.

"Tea? You must be a mind reader!" She extended a hand to Viv and at the same time inclined her head, in case a kiss on the cheek was offered.

"I'm Ursula by the way. Named after a saint who was a martyred virgin. Actually, the good book says the poor girl was one of thousands of them – so perhaps they were not as scarce back then!"

She rolled back and let out a whooping laugh, and then glanced to see whether the ice-breaker had done its job. It had.

Viv was an instant convert. She led Ursula through the hall, which was cluttered with gear for the ride, and shouted into the living room: "Sniffer! Visitor."

She went into the kitchen as Ursula took Sniffer's hand and smiled her shimmering smile.

"And how are things with you today, Sniffer?" adding, "By the way I'm still so uncomfortable calling you that! Can't I call you Clarence?'"

"Not if you want to live," said Sniffer said without humour, and seeming confused as to the identity of the visitor.

Sniffer said suddenly, pointing at Ursula. "You're a singer. Viv's a singer. You sang Your Cheatin' Heart to me. In hospital."

"Well, I have been known to burst into song before anyone could stop me!" she said coyly. "I always use Cheatin' Heart because it's true – about how things we've done that can make us, well, blue."

Ursula decided that she would leave a period of silence, and then judge whether Sniffer was going to get any benefit today from talking. She took her tea, and as Viv left the room gave her a reassuring nod.

"Dickman's coming for me," Sniffer said, matter-of-factly. "Today. Or tonight,"

After a pause he said: "Dickman. He chases people. They used to say he goes about in the dark up near Clench. A sort of ghost but worse. We were frit shitless as kids."

Ursula had not heard that particular description of terror before, and took a second to file it in her mental glossary of expressions humans resorted to in extremis.

Sniffer craned his neck to locate Viv.

"Viv!" he yelled, shocking Ursula, who had to put her hand over her teacup to steady it.

Viv's head appeared round the door.

"Viv, tell her about Dickman."

She came in, and sat on the carpet at Sniffer's feet, clutching his knees.

"The thing is," she explained, turning to Ursula, "Sniffer's been getting these terrible dreams. Guilt, I think. He sees the ghosts that they used to tell him about. The fens were full of that sort of stuff."

She was ashamed to find herself once more talking to a third party as if Sniffer wasn't present.

"His brother says that Dickman was invented by samphire gatherers round Clench, up near The Wash, to frighten others from getting in on the act. But right now, in his dreams, to Sniff he's the devil. He can actually see him sometimes when he's half asleep, can't you Sniff?"

"Poor, dear man" said Ursula, with pity. "Maybe we could deal with this - and help you, Viv, to find some way of placating him when he's distressed."

"It's guilt Ursula," Viv said decisively. "I'm certain of it. Am I right Sniffer?"

There was no reply. She said he seemed to want to have a load off his shoulders in case "things happened".

"You even mentioned St Peter the other day, didn't you Sniff?"

Sniffer was looking down sadly at his knees. "You don't know half," he said distractedly.

Ursula extended her forefingers upwards and began to sway like a metronome, singing, quietly but tunelessly...

"Who's sorry now, who's sorry now. Remember that one Sniffer? Connie Francis? Well, eventually we're all jolly well sorry when we've done things we shouldn't. I know I am. But we can wipe the slate clean...after we've eaten a bit of humble pie off the plate of course."

She looked searchingly into Sniffer's eyes and said softly: "That's the thing about true repentance, the easy mind that comes from the act of fessing up - is that what we call it now? God isn't chairman of the bench giving you a spell in choky. It's about being sorry. Simple."

She explained that, like in those washing powder adverts on TV where the woman holds up the shirt that's snow white, everything could be washed clean.

"Believe me Sniffer, God can make even the worst stains disappear."

Viv's thoughts turned to her own accumulation of real-life laundry. Caring seemed to take all her time. And she'd hardly looked at the script for the new production. It lay on her dressing table upstairs, waiting accusingly for more attention.

Ursula put down the teacup and waited for some sort of response from Sniffer.

None came, and as Sniffer still looked anxious she ventured: "You see, nowadays God, well, my God, isn't so much about mortal sin, He's about fresh starts, about hope."

"Nowadays?" said Sniffer, puzzled. "I thought God had always been the same."

"True. God has stayed the same; it's just that we constantly change in the way we understand Him."

Ursula felt in her element, savouring this mix of debate and friendly banter. Counselling the terminally ill, and people losing their minds, needn't be dire. Far from it. But sometimes you had to be proactive.

Household props, especially photos, could be a boon.

She looked first at the silver-framed picture of Viv, wearing garlands with the cast of what she was sure would have been South Pacific, and a fading colour print of a youthful Viv dressed in gingham and a straw hat.

Her eyes rested longest on the biggest picture, of three deliriously happy football fans holding their blue-and-white scarves aloft. Ursula knew nothing about football but she did know that these were Peterborough United's colours. She easily picked out the youthful Sniffer.

There was a crack in the glass that passed over a man in a bobble hat that had The Posh across the front.

"Now that must have been a happy day!" Ursula said, pointing to the photograph.

"It was," said Sniffer. Viv feared he had forgotten the occasion.

"It was the play-offs wasn't it Sniffer? Wembley. Who was the hero for Posh, Charlie somebody?"

"Charlery not Charlie. Ken Charlery. Got two."

So, she thought optimistically, another perfectly fitting piece in the jumbled jigsaw of Sniffer's mind. He was so unerringly accurate in remembering that she suspected that sometimes Sniffer was deliberately appearing to forget when it suited him.

As Ursula and Sniffer chatted, Viv watched and listened to try to decide whether any part of Sniffer's confusion seemed to be self-induced.

Eventually Sniffer said: "Tell me - is it all cock, or is there one? A devil."

Ursula began to roll her head from side to side, smiling in disagreement. But before she could speak Sniffer demanded that she give a yes-or-no answer - "And I want the answer in talk, not singing."

"Why, does the Devil come into your mind a lot?" Ursula asked gently.

"It's not only the Devil, it's ghosts. Up near Clench, the fens were snided with ghosts. At night you daren't go down the garden for fear of having your collar felt by somebody invisible. I think they've followed me here. I only felt really safe at Granny Pud's." He looked sorry for himself.

Viv interjected: "They called her Granny Pud because in winter, when she used to pick them up from school, if their mum was still at work, she'd always have the fire banked up and a rice pudding in the oven. That or a pie."

Sniffer seemed to be looking into the distance now.

"Nothing scared Granny Pud. She was..." he said and then faltered.

Viv prepared herself for the stock anecdotes about going out to the fields bird-scaring, about frozen inkwells at school, about the old village lady always asking for three pounds of potatoes insisting on small ones because, she said, you got more for your money that way.

Or – yet again – the tale of the slow-witted "'ol boy" in Frognall who used to stand at the front door posing with his dad's shotgun. Showing off with the barrel resting on his foot. And how the gun went off and took away his big toenail. And how, weeks later, standing at the door again with the gun, a passing girl asked how he had come to hurt himself and he said "Like this" and demonstrated, shooting off the end of his other boot.

They were like favourite song tracks, selected and grouped and then played from time to time, nearly always in the same order but sometimes shuffled.

The tales were true, in essence. But all of them were second hand. Not one was from Sniffer's childhood experience. These things happened in Great Aunt Nancy's vanished land. Sniffer had begun splicing it into his own reminiscence.

Ursula put down her cup and said: "Ironic, isn't it Viv? All those historic Fenland churches – Ramsey, Crowland, Thorney, not to mention the cathedrals – and the locals end up full of mumbo jumbo about ghosts and ghouls!"

Realising that she was sounding rather too intense, she let out another hoot of laughter and then asked Sniffer, teasingly: "Tell me Sniffer, was anybody devout in Clenchwarton?"

"Maybe the vicar. We had St. Margaret's in Clench," Sniffer offered. "Not that I went in it."

Ursula was determined to leave Sniffer reassured. It must be ghastly to feel terrified, fritless or whatever Sniffer called it, like being hunted down.

"Dear Sniffer," she said reassuringly, "I really want you to know that you are quite safe. Viv is here. There are no ghosts. You may not believe it but I know God is also watching over you…"

"OK. But you still haven't answered me. Is there a devil?"

"N.O. No. No character with horns and a long tail carrying a trident. It used to be like that."

"You mean the Devil took early retirement?" Sniffer said

mockingly.

"No, I mean, we in the church used to think of evil taking the form of a fallen angel, a satanic figure we could picture. We know better now, most of us. Of course, some people still believe that people can become possessed."

"That's me," said Sniffer.

No, said Ursula, possession by an evil spirit was an outdated idea. It was still espoused by some over-excitable fundamentalists she said, Bible-bashers and rednecks.

Sniffer looked unconvinced. Viv felt the urge to help Sniffer to become secure in some comforting belief.

"But you've got to admit, Ursula, the church does seem to chop and change," she said. "I know it's a lot to ask but it would be great to know, to actually know, about… well, afterwards. Sniffer needs something to be sure of but even the Church doesn't seem to be united in what it believes."

Ursula replied earnestly: "Correct! We don't all sing from the same hymn sheet. But basic faith is still at the root of it all. Unchanging faith."

Viv replied: "Faith means believing, but even the cleverest people in the world can't give you any proof. I suspect Sniffer just wants to settle things, to know someone's listening."

She raised an eyebrow and looked at Sniffer, to check that she was representing his views.

"So there isn't a hell?" Sniffer demanded to know. Ursula was choosing her words when Sniffer asked, with sudden aggression: "So did the fire go out? And what about the brimstone they used to talk about? And anyway, who exactly decided it was brimstone coming down and not endless buckets of dog muck?"

Sniffer had become ashen.

"Even in this day and age, and me a grown man, I've still got this idea that there could be a hell you can't get out of, even if I know that's daft. But it's your lot that planted the idea, Ursula."

Ursula leaned back, holding her palms up as if to push away the very notion.

"Not me. I'm not of the hellfire persuasion, Sniffer. Yes, I'm a sky pilot but I'm strictly freelance. I fly under no flag. Not now. My offering is simple: Love, and the things that spring from it – compassion, care. And as much hope as I can find to give, of course."

Sniffer was not placated.

"But bloody brimstone, Ursula! Come on - who dreamed that bugger up?" Sniffer snorted. "You know, your lot put the fear of God up millions of kids. My Great Aunt was always talking about Hell, threatening us with it."

"Look," said Ursula, taking a conversational diversion, "I'm very happy to be a sounding board. I want you to know that anything you say here stays with me. It's me, thee and nob'dy else as my granddad used to say."

"So what can we do for him?" Viv said, frustrated. "I hate it when he thinks he's damned. You can actually see the fear."

"Fear?" Sniffer protested. "Believe me, it's more than fear. Sometimes it feels like I'm in an asylum. Like when we went to the football there was that masked man and a bloody enormous rabbit. My eyes stood out like racing dogs' balls. It's beyond words."

Viv hated the racing dog analogy, one Sniffer used frequently, whatever the company.

Ursula tried to move things along. There were others who needed her ministering.

"If it helps, Sniffer, let's talk through past events. I could even hear your, quote, confession, unquote. You'd feel relief, and your secrets would be safe with me. Even Viv here needn't know, if that's what you wanted, need you Viv?"

Viv thought hard and then nodded. She noticed that tears had welled up in Sniffer's eyes.

"I'm all of a mizzy-mozzy," he muttered to himself, childishly.

Viv had never heard him use this phrase; maybe it was something the old aunt or Granny Pud used to say when he was small. But he was saying "frit" a lot now too, as if reverting to the odd word he could have in childhood, or excavating from his mind the things Great Aunt Nancy used to say.

Very occasionally, before he was ill, he used to say "chelp" for cheeky talk – he would tell Viv that she was giving him "too much chelp" – but now it had slipped into his day-to-day usage.

At one level she despised this pretence of being steeped in rural talk that had almost died out more than fifty years ago – before Sniffer was born. It seemed bogus, to be appropriating fragments of "the old ways," parading his fen heritage.

After much thought she had come up with a theory. As Sniffer's grip on reality was lapsing, and as he seemed to be wrestling with some inner torment, perhaps he was consciously tracking back, trying to find refuge in a long-ago world that was unchanging, uncomplicated, slow, safe.

Ursula leaned forward and said earnestly: "Sniffer...remember when the teacher used to keep us all from going home until somebody owned up to a little transgression? Then some nipper came clean and everyone went away feeling better, even the culprit?"

Sniffer slowly rubbed his eyes with the back of his square, worn hands and said: "That only works if you get a confession. What happens if it's so evil that the person can't say?"

"It has to be said," Ursula said. "And confronted. But God takes some shocking. He's seen the lot."

Ursula reached over and put a hand tenderly Sniffer's shoulder.

"Sniffer," she began. "There's a song ..."

"Don't sing it..." said Sniffer, suddenly becoming alert.

Ursula obeyed, speaking the words...

"...it goes 'Boy you're going to carry that weight, carry that weight a long time.' Remember? Well, now it's time you passed that weight over to someone else, Sniffer, someone with broad shoulders. Then, like that naughty child, you could go home feeling totally free of guilt. Absolutely spotless, like one of those shirts they hold up on the telly."

10

"You're not a bit like what I expected," said Sniffer, with relief, to the man in the recliner chair. "No robes. No big book."

He ran his eyes over the relaxed, avuncular figure.

"Well, look at you! Sweater, jeans. Jeans. And this place! I thought there'd be thunder and steam and people down below wailing and that you'd be carrying a dirty great key."

"A key?" asked the smooth-faced man in the salmon jumper.

"To let in people who pass the test – or lock out those who don't. Sinners like me."

The man pressed the control button of the chair and the back slipped back gently with a purring noise.

"No key. That's an old-fashioned idea. We're much more informal now. For a start you can call me Peter."

He added, with a pinched smile: "You know, we don't have to be floating on fluffy cotton wool and wearing bed sheets to mean business." The hardening look that accompanied the word "business" sent a slight chill through Sniffer but the informality of the man was such a relief.

He had confessed to Viv that it was the very idea of eternity that scared him; endless time. It was that making him, in the colourful language of his forefathers, "frit shitless."

In fact, maybe because of the medication, he'd actually said he was "shit fritless" but Viv, who had noticed, did not correct him. There was so much to correct lately, she had begun to let things go.

But now, to Sniffer, the fear seemed groundless. Here instead was a man who could have been his Uncle Clarrie; easy, mild, approachable.

Or was he? Peter's face seemed to have become less cordial.

Sniffer looked around for a chair but there was none.

"We think it's best if penitents stand," Peter said. "Shows respect and good intentions. But we must press on – so many people, so very many sins, so little time. Even eternity doesn't seem long enough."

Eternity.

Peter shuffled his shoulders in a search for the most comfortable position and brought the spread fingers of one hand to the fingers of the other.

"Now, tell us about yourself, Sniffer – as if we hadn't had you on the radar for, what is it, the last 47 years and 56 days…"

Sniffer was aghast at the thought of that all-seeing eye, watching, watching. But it couldn't have seen everything, not the most private things. Surely not?

Peter grew intense.

"Just one thing. What is being judged is not your actions (Sniffer sighed audibly in relief) but your open-hearted willingness to recall what you have done, confront it, then to confess and show abject remorse."

Sniffer's shoulders slumped. It was settle-up time, just like it had been at the bank and at the bookies, at Johnsons the building suppliers, with mistresses and pub landlords. Settle-up time with jealous husbands, with Viv.

He was ready. Ready to own up to everything. Well, near enough.

"First off, I'll tell you straight up, Peter – I'm worse than most people," he began. "It's worried me, the idea of hell. I met a chaplain who filled me with trust but I still couldn't tell her everything. But she did explain that sometimes we make our own hell. I know I did, and I started early…."

"Is this going to be about the coin?" Peter said, interrupting.

"Yes," Sniffer replied. "How did you know?"

"We know it all, Sniffer."

"So, I don't need to say it?"

"Yes you do. Saying it is the important bit."

"Well," Sniffer began, "as you know I was just a kid and we were living in Clench. There was a drain outside the house and I was messing about with my two-bob bit while mum came out to take me and sis into Chatteris. I dropped the money and it rolled into the drain.

"To blame someone, and get another two bob, I said that the sluice man's lad next door had pinched it from me. Didn't foresee consequences. Not looking ahead has been my problem all my life."

Peter was nodding as if to approve of the accuracy of the story so far.

"Of course, being mum, she went round and raised hell. I heard the sluice man's wife yelling: 'Stolen? Stolen? Two bob? I tell you my boy has not left this house!'

"I never owned up. I made it a policy never to own up, not unless it paid to. You see - that's the sort of bloke I am. The sort of bloke I've been..."

The man in the salmon sweater interrupted gently.

"We know Sniffer. Nothing is hidden from us. Nothing."

"Dear God," Sniffer said to himself, wringing his hands. He felt perspiration tickling his forehead. "You really have seen it all? Oh, dear God" said Sniffer, appalled at the thought.

"And what we take special note of includes profanity..." Peter said tersely.

Sniffer took a moment to gather himself then said: "I remember one summer and one of my sins. A sin showing how I have always hurt people....'

"Pam? The schoolgirl. The innocent girl of just, was it, fourteen?"

"Yes. You don't have to rub it in about her age."

"Go on," said Peter.

"It was when I was so full of it I thought I'd got too much life about me. I used to think I'd burst."

Sniffer described that summer in his youth. The hunger and thirst for it all. Being agile, light. Having brown arms from working outside and enjoying how his tan showed up against his white shirt with the collar spread out onto his lapels.

"I've washed off my work muck and I'm on a motorbike tear-arsing along a dead straight fen road. The sun is blinding and the wind trying to rip the jacket off my back. No helmets then. Young gods didn't need helmets. Just Silvikrin.

"It was on one of those hot nights, a Friday, bombing along on the Triumph, headed for The Plough at Pigwash Fen, and a nice, cold shandy. There was me on the Triumph, Rob on his Dad's old bike and Dave pootling along behind us on his farting little hair-dryer."

He said that he loved the roar that him and Rob left behind – "It was like fog rolling over the fens," Sniffer said, smiling at the recollection of that noise.

"We always gave the bikes two or three final twists of the grip as we stopped. It was *Brrrrm* We *Brrrrm* have *Brrrrm* arrived."

"And what did all this lead to Sniffer...?" said Peter, coldly, looking at his watch.

"We could hear music coming from the community hall. The records always made me..."

"Expectant?"

"Yes. But not as much as the sight of all those girls. They were flushed and hot from dancing. Fiddling about with their clothes as if their bodies were just getting used to going-out dresses. They were in that giddy phase where they're awkward and just getting sexy.'

He said that he remembered exactly how this Pam had seen him, and how she whispered to her school friend with the bubbly, blonde, almost-white, hair. He had been sure she was saying: "He's here."

The girls moved to where there were empty seats, ensuring he had no reason not to sit near her.

"We didn't touch each other until the band dropped the rock 'n roll and the youth leader announced the last dance. She felt good and firm. She was shy but her hips weren't."

He said that before the music stopped it was agreed, without a word being said, that instead of the car ride home with a friend's dad, she'd come on the Triumph.

Sniffer described how her arms encircled his chest and how he could hear her laughing behind him. He stopped short of her house, so that her parents didn't hear the bike.

Somehow, he said, automatically, they walked in the moonlight to the grassy bank of the fen, over a ridge and to a spot just on the top of the slope going down to the water, hidden from the road.

"There was Pam leaning back on her hands pretending to be fascinated by the water. The moon made everything silver.

"We had a kiss or two and she said that she thought we were meant to meet. She was all romantic and said maybe we were in love and I said that I thought we were.

"She said I could do anything I wanted, so I did. And then I did it again. Then we had a smoke which made her feel sick. She started rushing to the house because she was late and she'd get into trouble, but she stopped and she turned round and blew me a kiss and said 'I didn't think anybody would ever want me.'"

She was just about crying with happiness, Sniffer said.

" 'Night, night,'" she said, this poor little lass, this bit of a kid. 'Don't let the bugs bite.' She said she couldn't wait for next week and asked me to promise that I'd be there at the dance, and, bastard that I am, I said 'Course I'll be there...'"

He added, grimly: "But, surprise, surprise, I wasn't. As you well know. And I never went dancing again that summer, never asked after the kid, never saw her again."

Peter left a pause and picked a trace of fluff from his sweater.

"We do callous things when we're young and wrapped up in ourselves," Peter said matter-of-factly.

"Yes, but some people grow out of it. Get better. I got worse," said Sniffer.

Peter nodded, then gestured with his hand to show that Sniffer should continue.

Sniffer paused and seemed to be delving deeply into his memory.

Then he began to talk about a morning when he spotted some fledglings that had fallen out of a nest somewhere up in the guttering. It was when they lived in Clench. He thought it would be humane to drown them so he had brought a bucket of water and kept poking them down with a brush. But they kept bobbing up and cheeping.

"When I thought I'd finally finished the deed and I went inside I heard just one tiny cheep as if to say: 'I'm still here.'" Lately, every so often, he said, he could hear in his mind a little sort of cheep but in a schoolgirl's voice.

"Yes, Sniffer. It's the little voice of guilt. Every single frailty, every failing, every hurt to others registers somewhere. Here."

And so they will have seen me up in Cowbit that day, Sniffer said to himself. Oh dear.

Seen me joking with the woman, telling her I could do the job for £100 but she'd have to mix the cement. Looking at where she wanted the alcove knocking out, having coffee, going in the bedroom to check where the chimney led, and on the Monday morning seen me get into a bed that was still warm from the husband leaving.

And they will have seen the husband come home the following evening and shake my dirty hand and say thank you for a lovely job, and pay me cash, and add a tenner for a drink.

"Shameless, Sniffer. But what I want now is to hear what have you got to say about that time, the thing that troubles you so… you know…"

"I can't. Ever."

"You only have to say – and feel truly, deeply sorry."

"I do feel deeply sorry. It never lets me rest."

"Then just come clean, say what happened."

"I can't, not ever."

"Well then Sniffer, you'd better go downstairs."

"No, Peter, please. Not downstairs!"

○ ○ ○ ○ ○ ○ ○

"Downstairs love? Shush! You are downstairs!" Viv said as Sniffer began to come round.

"Look at you, all scrunched up. Lean forward and let me get a cushion behind you so you can hold your tray."

She returned with hot food, a mug of tea and pleasantries but seeing his brooding look, put the tray to one side so she could clasp his cheeks in her hands.

"Now then my baby, what's got to you?"

"Dreaming" he replied.

"A nightmare, love?"

He was going to say that it was about a bloke who looked like Terry Wogan sending him to hell forever and a day but instead switched to another image that came into his head: "It was a dream about that bloody horrible rabbit that could talk, at the football, and the man with the mask. He had a real scary laugh."

Viv made a mental note to jot down a line about this episode. She'd be ready next time they asked her at the hospital to describe how Sniffer had been. Childlike, scared like a kid would sum it up.

She wrapped her arm round Sniffer's neck, kissed his bald patch and said: "Now eat your sausages. There's absolutely nothing to be scared of."

Sniffer's eyes showed that he didn't believe her.

11

Next morning Sniffer was tranquil. Showered and shaved. Back in the real world.

Talkative, inquisitive. He lowered his knife and fork on to his plate, sighed, pushed back his stool, got up and announced: "The condemned man ate a hearty breakfast."

Viv's eyes followed him as he left the kitchen, and to her disappointment saw that despite his brightness today his movements were leaden.

She listened to his trudging step on the stairs. Six months ago he would have gone up two steps at a time.

Sheryl and Terry had been up and about early, and were loafing in front of the TV. Malcolm had woken even earlier, having set the alarm on what was a chronometer rather than simply a watch. He was outside now, restlessly sorting gear, calling in to hint that Terry ought to be stirring himself and helping to prepare for the ride.

Viv busied herself with the shopping list for the trip - bacon, sausages, coffee and dried milk, bread rolls. At the bottom of the list she wrote, in underlined capitals, WATER.

It was supposed to be nearly autumn but it was hotter today than midsummer, even hotter than Lanzarote, the forecaster had said. How ironic, she thought, if the boys ran out of drink in the Fens of all places. What was that poem? "Water, water everywhere and not a drop to drink"?

Malcolm, Dusty and Terry were now busy at the front of the

house sorting all the gear for the ride. Suddenly she felt moved by the whole enterprise, and wanted them to know it. So she added "Steak" to her list, a treat. Terry loved steak sandwiches.

She imagined them in a circle round a bit of a fire beneath a huge black fen sky, beside an unlit road, with the moon catching the long straight lines of the drains and ditches. This, she was sure, was how Sniffer had imagined it. It was a crying shame he couldn't go.

The three riders were in and out of the house, fetching and carrying, checking that they had all they needed. Sniffer looked on, betraying no sense of disappointment.

Viv was amazed at the stuff they would have to carry – two tents, food, the blow-up plastic beds and all Malcolm's stuff. His box was in the hall last night and she'd peeped in. It was a mobile field hospital.

Terry had told her that Malcolm was fastidious. At work, he said, his technology lessons were programmed to the last detail, and his social life was so meticulously structured that there was little scope for relaxation. Although they were friends as well as colleagues, he sometimes found himself driven to distraction by Malcolm's pursuit of perfection.

Viv was struck by the comical contrast, seeing Malcolm and Dusty together – Malcolm so lean and serious, with a fixed expression of intense focus: Dusty, a foot or more shorter, round-faced, cheery, looking for things to laugh about, prodding, teasing.

She noted that he had allowed his much-hated curls to grow back and now once more resembled a pie-loving cherub.

He had been delighted to lose the curls when the trend for shaved heads came in. But when Sheryl, in what she thought was a loving moment, had compared his head to a partly-deflated pink balloon, the post-party kind that puckered at a touch, he had taken umbrage and put away his electric shears.

What Terry's presence said was: Strength. He had broad shoulders, thick arms, tree trunk neck. He was what Sniffer had been until lately but the charcoal chins and the bald bronze crowns still marked them out as brothers who might have been identical twins but for Sniffer's bent nose, a souvenir picked up years ago outside a fish and chip shop in Wisbech.

Both men loved the sun, and she could see that Terry had thrown off the shackles of the classroom and spent the school holidays outdoors.

He was like Sniffer, who stayed brown all year, as if a life of all-weather bricklaying and roofing had cured him, like sun-dried leather.

She could hear Sniffer running water upstairs, and then a sound that made her shiver slightly with pleasure – he was singing in the shower. It was a discordant attempt at I'm Into Something Good.

Viv stepped out into the dazzling day, and found Malcolm spraying the gears of the tandem. It all looked so organised, professional, even down to the plastic plate mounted beneath the crossbar bearing the words

Sponsored by
POSH PUSHBIKES

Malcolm had the contents of his plastic chest lying out along the edge of the concrete path and was ticking a list. She could see bandages, sprays, an eye bath, packets of tablets, scissors, finger splint, mouthwash, cotton wool. There were tubes of cream. Plastic bags contained a Wildness Trek Flannel and a Trek Towel. Wet wipes, ultra soft toilet tissue. An ex-army trenching trowel.

In another line, equidistant from each other, were shiny new spanners, tyre levers, packaged inner tubes, a torch, and matches. Four sets of camping cutlery lay, like museum exhibits, on a soft, white cloth. Alongside was some sort of knife, a big one, the sort baddies in cowboy films picked their teeth with. She knew Malcolm was new to the Fens but what on earth was he expecting – a bear attack?

On the front lawn, spread out in the sun, she could see three bright orange tee shirts, and a fourth, Sniffer's, poignantly still in its wrapper. The slogan on the front said "SNIFFER'S FEN

CHALLENGE" and beneath it the logo of a cancer charity and "Johnson's trade supplies. Let US help YOU build."

As Viv got into the car, Dusty was absorbed by the problem of connecting a trailer to the tandem, while Terry held it upright and gave advice.

Sheryl had arrived to keep an eye on Sniffer while Viv went shopping. As she reversed into the road she chanced to look at the bay window.

There was Sniffer, looking out, watching the preparations. She couldn't read his expression but she felt trepidation, a worry that Sniffer might be preparing to defend his right to ride.

o o o o o o o

Malcolm had his own shopping to do. Last-minute stuff. He was happy enough to bike into town but being short of things at this stage – the first day of the ride – showed a lack of planning, and that really irritated him.

He'd shaken a gas bottle and there was little gas left. It was fiercely hot, and "they" had not even thought of sun-cream – and Dusty hadn't brought a hat.

Malcolm was not blameless, he would readily admit: during this morning's check he'd noticed that the box of diarrhoea tablets was not in the box. Silly - he hadn't thought to replace them after the spoiled holiday in Egypt when he missed most of the tombs, finding himself almost permanently entombed himself, in the cruise ship's deeper recesses.

He'd slipped into his new Italian-style riding gear so he'd be ready once everything was packed into panniers and the final checks had been done.

As Malcolm came out of the house, carrying his list and his cycle helmet, and encased in lightweight, shiny sky-blue top and drainpipe bottoms, Terry looked up from his packing duties and exclaimed: "Hell's teeth, Malcolm! You look like a six-foot condom!" He tweaked the fabric, and said sensuously: "Mmmm – ribbed for added pleasure…"

Malcolm looked mystified. Some humour was not so much lost on him as belonging to another world he had yet to visit.

Dusty, holding up a tee shirt and trying to work out the chance of it fitting, glanced anxiously as Malcolm lifted his featherweight bike by a gloved hand, actually merely two fingers, towards the front gate. He then looked hard at his heavy, fat-tyred, slightly rusty borrowed bike.

He was comforted by what Terry had told him about the terrain – "Ride a mile and you might have climbed an inch, but not much more" … "When God made the Fens he got his rolling pin out."

When he'd moved north and they'd got to know each other, Terry had been tormenting about the hills. He used to yodel and make cracks to Dusty, a local, about buying a ski chalet in the Pennines.

So he was prepared for Dusty, ever provocative, to give him some stick in the next few days about the Fens which Dusty had already mentally characterised as the most tedious landscape in Britain.

For bike-riding, tedious was OK, flat was fine. But windy wasn't. Dusty feared the famed "fen blows." Malcolm, on the other hand, had come for a challenge, to do a job, not drink in the scenery. His fear was that it was all going to be so easy.

Dusty watched Malcolm slip his feet into the pedal clips, arch his sinuous back like a bow, and accelerate down the road. He stood at the gate and watched him disappear.

"Terry. Did you see that? He goes like shit off a shovel!"

"It'll be right," said Terry, guardedly, as if he, too, was having misgivings about relative abilities.

"No, I mean are we going to be compatible?" Dusty asked nervously. "I'm not at full fitness you know." He said this seriously but his faced cracked into a smile when he realised that the comment was superfluous; it was obvious to anyone who wasn't blind. He had worked up a sweat just standing still.

Terry looked evasive and, turning his eyes very deliberately to the front window, and said quietly: "We've got bigger problems than that. By the look of Sniffer, he still thinks he's coming with us. And I don't want to be the one who tells him he's not."

Sniffer was watching every move with mild curiosity.

They gathered the rest of the gear to be packed and when it was stowed they were pleased to see that there was still enough room for anything they had forgotten, and for the food. Malcolm would do the final check.

Dusty leaned back on the garden wall and asked: "Tell me, Terry, what makes him tick? Malcolm. For a teacher he doesn't communicate much. Bit anal, is he?"

Terry replied: "Gets very little backchat at school. I think they're scared of the zombie side of him. Anyway you don't have to be human to teach technology."

Dusty wanted more. He prodded. "Seems a bit, well, remote."

"No, just guarded. He's been so unlucky so many times in so many ways I think he likes to lie low and get prepared for the worst because he knows the worst will happen."

They laughed and gradually unwound, sitting side by side on the garden wall, beside the concrete drive, enjoying the sun and the prospect of adventure, starting in an hour or two.

Dusty was still trying to weigh Malcolm up.

"He looks a bit odd doesn't he?" he asked at last. "I mean, the bowie knife. And he's a bit funny round the eyes. And what happened with that weird crooked finger. Birth defect, or is it arthritis?"

"Poor bugger lost his eyebrows. Using some highly flammable glue to resurface a table top. Being Malcolm, he read the warning extra carefully but then he forgetfully went to turn the gas on to warm a tin of soup – and bang! No eyebrows, no eyelashes. Table on fire."

"Of dear..." said Dusty, feeling much more charitable towards his ill-fated co-rider.

"Somebody once said in the staffroom after one of his disasters – 'You know, if Malcolm fell into a barrel full of nipples, he'd come out sucking his thumb.'"

Terry took a certain pleasure in relating relationships that had left Malcolm perplexed and alone. By contrast, he was so lucky: being married to Jess was comfortable, unchallenging. He would miss her while he was on the ride and would look forward to her coming to Norwich to pick them up at the end.

He sounded genuinely empathetic saying: "You know, when poor old Malcolm's love life goes pear-shaped he takes up another hobby to compensate. It's biking this summer and it was aero-modelling last back-end. He volunteered for this ride because the challenge will stop him confronting his loneliness."

"Poor lad. Sad job," said Dusty. He felt like giving Malcolm some uplifting words, even a hug, when he returned.

"But what happened with the finger? It looks like one of those nail things sloths have for winkling out grubs from rotting trees."

"Bit of a corkscrew look, hasn't it? Well, first off, he dislocated it when he started archery. The doctors sorted it and then he got it shut in a car door," Terry said tonelessly.

Dusty winced. "Ooch!"

"Yeah. He'd got a new girl friend. A real looker but she was stone deaf. Anyway, evidently she got out of the car one night, and he reached over and shouted to her to leave it open because there was more room for him to get out at the passenger side. She didn't hear him and she slammed it and walked off."

"The poor bugger..." said Dusty, vowing to be as nice as possible to Malcolm during the ride.

"There she was, at the house door, happily opening up, while he was squirming about in the car, screaming blue murder. She looked back and thought he was just waving in a loving way so she waved back and went back inside."

When he had finally been taken to A & E, Terry said, Malcolm immediately blacked out with the pain but of course the girl couldn't tell them what had happened with the finger.

"Swore he'd never go back to hospital."

Sniffer had approached silently. He was smiling benignly. He was in shorts and his sponsors' tee shirt; his sunglasses were pushed back on his Posh bobble hat. Under his arms were clothes, and in his hands a selection of boxed medicines.

"Where do you want this lot?" Sniffer said.

Terry looked transfixed, mute.

Sniffer seemed to have got his old spirit back, and the twinkle in his eye.

"Actually, the bum feels tip top this morning," he said. "But that tandem saddle will be like perching on a bloody razor blade. I need one of those wide springy ones. And one of those jelly covers. It's a bloody long way to Clench."

"Norwich. You mean Norwich, Sniff. Norwich Cathedral."

"Same difference."

12

Terry judged it best not to reply. As he enticed Sniffer away towards the house, he was relieved to see Viv pull onto the drive.

"Come on Sniff, let's have a brew and talk it over with Viv," he said.

"Don't baby me, brother. Nothing to talk about. The marbles are all in the right place today."

Viv called Sniffer and he went into the house.

Malcolm had arrived back and was unpacking the front panniers of his bike while Dusty added another few strands of nylon rope to the fitting where the trailer joined the tandem.

We're going to look like a bloody wagon train, Dusty said to himself. He pictured them heading towards the sun, over the limitless plains, under a big blue vault of a sky with some background track from a cowboy movie playing in the background.

Malcolm interrupted his reverie, loping past, heading for the house to get his tick list.

Dusty called after him: "Not now Malcolm. Think there's a family pow-wow going on. Listen!"

They stood still and could hear strangled cries and gruff shouts coming from the kitchen.

"Sniffer seems determined to come," said Dusty, shaking his head in despair.

Malcolm thought deeply for a moment and then said: "And why shouldn't he?"

Dusty looked up, surprised.

"It's his idea. It's him who wants to re-live something now he's ill. We can't re-live it for him. I think we could manage him."

"Well…" blustered Dusty, overcome by shame. "We'd be having to watch him like a hawk. Come on, he's not up to tenting, Malcolm, surely?"

There was a crash. It was the front door slamming behind Sniffer who stood, legs apart in a posture of defiance.

"I need to say something!" he shouted. Terry and Dusty followed him into the house. Malcolm hovered at the door and then joined the rest. In the kitchen, Viv had her face to the wall; Sheryl was on a stool, bolt upright, alert, white faced.

They all waited. Sniffer looked self-absorbed for a moment, as if he was trying to pick up mental threads.

Then he said: "They've told me I'm probably dying. Saying 'probably' is being kind. OK, I've said it. Now, I think it's pretty reasonable for a bloke who's about to fall off his perch to be allowed to do what he wants with what time he's got left. Within reason.

"So all I want to do is to go on a bike ride, and I want to sleep in a tent again and get up to sunshine and a nice fry-up. If I don't wake up one morning, so be it. Terry'll eat my bacon, won't you, buh?" he said. He switched off his smile and added: "Or more likely Dusty."

He said that Viv and Sheryl feared that riding a bike would kill him and so they'd offered a nice day out in the car, so he could see his old haunts.

He turned to his wife and said: "But going by car's not the same, is it Viv? It's the ride that's the whole point." Viv sniffled and gulped.

Sniffer continued: "Anyway, we've got mobiles and there's paramedics and we'll never be more than a hour or two away from home but it'll be feel like being in the wilds, like it used to feel."

Sheryl had relaxed on to her elbows, but was shaking her head to show that she had not been won round. Terry, Dusty and Malcolm stood, heads down, side by side along the breakfast bar.

Viv noticed that Terry and Dusty were now in shorts. The upset she was feeling was lightened by the thought that some men shouldn't ever be allowed to wear them, by law. Terry and Dusty could feature on the warning poster. Dusty, especially.

With his short, thick little legs, and his skin-tight sponsorship tee shirt, he looked as if he might deflate noisily at any time.

"I've lived in a few places in the Fens," Sniffer continued. "I want to ride near a couple of them and I want go to sleep thinking about those places I've seen, and the things that happened."

He stopped to gather his emotions, swallowing hard.

"I know you're all trying to be protective but I want to take mum's book and know it's safe for the future, where kids can learn what it was like. Daft as it seems, I want to light some candles."

There was not a countering word, and Sniffer pre-empted any by looking at each face in turn and saying coldly: "Wouldn't it look bad in the Telegraph if it said 'Family foil dying man's charity ride'?"

He turned to Viv and said: "Now, can you find that hard hat – and do you mind popping out for a flat saddle and one of those jelly bags to go on top?" Before she could answer, Malcolm said: "Leave it to me Sniffer. I know just what's needed."

By the time they returned to the front of the house to start packing Sniffer's essentials – his medicines, his mum's book – Malcolm was standing high on his pedals, a blue arc disappearing round the corner and along the road to town.

13

Barely had the last of the kit been checked, and the cycle helmets donned, the farewell kisses exchanged, than Malcolm's medical box was opened for wound dressings.

This did not augur well. The party was not even off the house drive and it was already early afternoon. They'd be lucky to get past Ramsey today, Terry concluded with a tinge of rancour.

Sniffer was to blame for the bungled start but in the prevailing ambience of empathy no one let him know.

He had claimed to have ridden a tandem before ("fore and aft") and so hadn't listened to Terry's careful briefing about the back man having to pedal as they moved off, so that the front man (i.e. Terry) could find his feet in the pedal clips, and look up to steer.

It had not gone like that.

After a final wave, with Dusty wobbling along on his mini-bike, Malcolm poised like a tensioned longbow, and Sniffer – wearing his woolly Posh bobble hat, despite warnings of getting overheated –

seated woodenly at the back, Terry steadied the tandem and gave the 1-2-3 for the off.

This first leg of the ride took approximately two seconds, just enough time for Sniffer to remember (too late) that he had to pedal, and for the tandem to slam into a gatepost.

Viv stopped waving and put her hands to her mouth in horror.

The tandem was lifted off Sniffer, and Terry and Sheryl began rummaging in the trailer for plasters. Malcolm sprang off his bike and ushered her away saying he had a place for everything.

Terry noticed that the nylon rope attaching the trailer had shredded under the strain of the crash; the trailer had stayed put when the bike gone down.

With knees dressed and fresh rope secured, Terry repeated his instructions to Sniffer who, plainly, was not listening. "When I shout, you pedal, Sniff. And don't forget, buh, we'll be taking corners wide because of the trailer."

He walked the tandem to the road, and, with Malcolm and Dusty looking on anxiously, primed Sniffer yet again and with a push they launched into a swaying forward movement.

"Yes, Sniff!" Terry shouted as they picked up speed. The little borrowed trailer that had once been used for delivering newspapers bounced and rattled behind them.

There was a cry from Malcolm who, standing high on his pedals as if ready for a velodrome finish, a plastic coated map dangling from his neck, was acting as a protective outrider.

"She's fish-tailing!" he yelled, as the trailer began to waggle from side to side.

"What's fish-tailing?" shouted Sniffer, who was now pedalling wildly.

"She's swinging from side to side. Look!"

Sniffer swivelled round and, as he did, upset the weight distribution on the tandem forcing Terry to brake fiercely and, in turn, for Sniffer to topple very gently, almost elegantly, from his rear seat into a ball on the road.

"Frame yourself Terry, for Christ's sake!" Sniffer said as he brushed pellets of tarmac off his blood-spattered knees and picked up his Posh bobble hat, replacing on his head. "If we carry on like this I'll look like a Sunday joint by the time we get to Clench."

"Norwich. Once again Sniff – we're only going to Clenchwarton if we have time to call – and at this rate we won't. We're going to sodding Norwich", Terry said through gritted teeth. "Hopefully some time this year."

Sniffer was sucking blood from grazed knuckles as Malcolm methodically refilled the trolley which this time had tilted over in a slow-motion surrender to gravity.

Dusty was fifty yards ahead as the tandem teetered away again, with Malcolm moving alongside, a sleek jet fighter escorting a lumbering transporter.

The undersize bike and unyielding mini-saddle was making it painfully hard work for Dusty, so he was pushing on while the going was good. Except that the going was far from good.

He didn't know much about bikes but he knew enough to understand that his pedals were going round very fast and he was going forward quite slowly.

Each time he made a gentle movement of the gear-change to ease the ache in his calves there was a worrying rattle and his feet seemed to be circulating in fresh air.

He wondered how many more miles it would be to Holme, where the interesting Victorian post was, showing how the Fens had shrunk over the generations.

Dusty was seeing that now as more of a restful interlude than a visit to an historically fascinating artefact, and wondered hopefully whether the place was touristy enough to have a kiosk selling cold drinks. Or better still, ice lollies.

He was gagging for cold liquid now he had emptied his water bottle. The sun was unbearable and he was sure that all that sweat had begun to shrink his already drum-tight tee shirt.

He stopped to look back at the tandem party. Malcolm seemed to be turning and heading away. He could barely make out what Terry was shouting but it seemed to be "Candles!" He really begrudged going back even ten or twenty hard-won yards to hear properly.

"Candles! We've forgotten the bloody candles!" Terry yelled. "Got to hang on till Malcolm's back."

There is a God, Dusty said to himself. We can rest. Please take your time Malcolm. Waiting is heaven.

Seeing Malcolm streaking away brought a different analogy into his over-heated brain. He decided that Malcolm was an Afghan hound, no, a Saluki – sleek, tensioned, aerodynamic. And they (him, and Terry and Sniffer) were comical, assorted mongrels – stumpy, raggy-arsed and decidedly unathletic.

Through eyes stinging from the rivulets of sweat pouring into them, he chose a spot on the grass verge, threw down the bike he had begun to hate, and with a self-pitying groan lay on his back.

He had managed not to think about work so far but now worries about the Aardvark account began to surface – again. The Aardvark thing was like stuff reappearing in a toilet you thought you'd unblocked.

Dusty had hoped that the ride would give him the chance to come up with a clear solution, a strategy that might save his job. But if anything, matters looked worse viewed through half-closed eyes, from his resting place on the roadside verge.

He fell into a light doze overlaid with troubled thoughts about fat-laden internal organs and mortality figures for men of his age and had just descended into rapid eye movement slumber when Terry tugged at his tee shirt and shouted: "OK, y'all! Wagons roll!"

Dusty felt leaden as he got back on the little bike and was irritated to see that Malcolm, who had cycled all that way back to the house for the candles, hadn't shed a droplet of sweat and, by the look of him, was up for still more action.

There was hardly any traffic and so Dusty allowed the tandem to go two abreast with him.

His own discomfort made him want to annoy someone else,

and Terry – panting rhythmically to each turn of the pedals – was nearest.

"So when does the famous scenery start, Terry?"

"Look around you, man. Some of the best soil in the world. Look at the cabbages. Look at the…" He ran out of words because in this part of the Fens there were only cabbages, some red, some green but still only cabbages. Black soil, drainage ditches, cabbages, sky.

"I told you, what's best out here are the skies. You'll see," he said gasping now, even though the incline amounted to centimetres.

"Funny. I thought the sky was everywhere. Myself, I like a nice old soot-blackened mill set against the sort of crimson skies you get with a bit of nice pollution. Yes, a dingy mill against a filthy sky at the top of a slag heap, post-industrial blight. And there'd be a brass band playing…"

"Piss off," Terry hissed, gasping for breath, and then with a sideways glance mouthed the words: "Is he pedalling?"

Dusty took a glimpse at Sniffer and replied grandly: "Shall we just say that the master is resting?"

The sound of a car horn forced Dusty to pull in behind the tandem. Dusty recognised the car and the women in it: Viv (disguised in headscarf and big sunglasses) and Sheryl.

Sniffer would have been furious if he'd spotted them doing a check but Terry knew that he would be too busy at the moment concentrating on staying upright.

Malcolm had gone off trail-blazing again and when he came back was smiling.

"I think we've got visitors…" he said enigmatically before tearing away again.

At a bend in the road, beside a clump of bushes, sitting on the grass beneath a banner reading "Go Sniffer!" were Brian and Jo. Nearby, propped up on a shooting stick in the shade, was Old Man Johnson smiling inanely.

"Well, bloody…Look who's here!" said Sniffer.

Boxed drinks and chocolate bars were passed round and Sniffer, who had been quiet today throughout the ride, took on the role of modest hero. Jo looked at him admiringly as he described the trip so far.

"That was really tough going," he said in all seriousness, as Dusty and Terry looked at each other in astonishment. It was harder still for those who'd had to pedal, Terry said to himself.

Although the sky appeared cloudless there was a deep roll of thunder somewhere in the distance and Jo said: "You'd better get going. They said we might get some rain later."

She kissed Sniffer but no one else.

After handshakes and backslapping the riders set off again and soon reached Holme where Terry rejoiced in showing Dusty the cast iron post which, since the 1850s, had shown the degree of shrinkage following the draining of the Fens.

"You, Dusty, are now standing at the lowest point in Britain. Look, the ground has sunk nearly four metres. Nothing to do with your weight, mind. We came here as school kids, and it's gone down loads since then."

Dusty had glorified the place in his imagination. It was a post and lots of trees. There was no ice cream stall, no freezer full of ice lollies.

While Sniffer just sat and stared, and Malcolm pretended he needed the rest, his bike propped against a tree, Terry fell into teacher mode.

He proudly regaled Dusty with facts about the 500 fungi that lived in this special place, the biggest area of birch woodland in England, the wildlife.

"There's Hairy Dragonflies, and there's reed warblers...

"Oh."

"... and chiffchaffs, and red kites..." he proclaimed to Dusty who, out of weariness, could not muster enthusiasm.

"There's even raptors...oh and... great tits."

"Thanks for noticing," said Dusty, looking to break the monologue.

Terry took umbrage.

"OK, if you want to be bloody stupid…!" he said, flouncing off to the tandem.

14

There was another deep roll of thunder and the upper half of the sky was now a deep blue-grey and the lower half the palest blue with a golden band along the horizon. Three massive vegetable processing vehicles were moving in convoy along a distant road, like a family of mammoths heading off to hide from the weather.

Sniffer looked anxious as a crack of lightning sent up fingers of energy into the darker area of sky. Malcolm urged the party to get moving so that if there was a storm they could sit it out at Ramsey.

He then rode off, presumably to check that the ancient town, founded more than a thousand years ago, on the site of a Benedictine abbey, had not disappeared or relocated since his map had been printed.

"Yes, Ramsey. Straight ahead," he reported, returning from a high-speed recce.

They were bombarded by splattering rain as they arrived for a break, and had locked the bikes in the pub yard and had settled snugly inside before the heavens opened.

They sat with their drinks contentedly listening to rain and hail pinging against the pub window, waiting for the toasted cheese sandwiches they had ordered.

Sniffer seemed distant again. He had pulled the old exercise book of his mother's jottings from the front of his shorts and was mulling over it, in his own world.

Dusty was reading the product description from a tatty, discoloured box that bore the legend Lambert's World Famous Loosener. He took from it a flattened tube of ointment.

As Sniffer read to himself from his mother's memories, Terry took the little cardboard box from Dusty.

"God – how old is this stuff?" he asked.

Dusty said: "Well put it this way, this tube was my old dad's and he died 20 years ago. He swore by it. Used it when he got a twinge from working in the pit. Haven't seen it on sale for years. It'll be banned by the EU now as being too effective."

Terry was fascinated by the box. It bore a drawing of a badly knocked-about rugby player (Albert Haig, Hunslet RLFC), in an early example of sponsorship. He imagined the company boss saying: "Advertise for us, Albert lad, and you'll have Loosener for life."

The face reminded Terry of old etched illustrations showing physiognomy bumps, with labels such as Propensity for Violence, and Excitability, and Bladder Control.

There was only an inch of the lead tube that had not been flattened so he took only the smallest sample and rubbed it on the back of his hand where the bones ached from gripping the handlebars of the tandem.

As the sandwiches arrived, he felt a hot glow.

"Wow, Dusty. It's like being branded. Strong stuff."

While Terry, Dusty and Malcolm began to eat, Sniffer showed no interest in his food, nor, surprisingly, his beer. But he was devouring his mother's writings.

"Well I'll be…!" he said at last.

"Ramsey's mentioned, buh," he said, turning to Terry. "In the bits about those toffs who came to sail the mere."

Terry felt the need to explain for the benefit of Dusty and Malcolm.

"This aristocrat thought it'd be fun to sail through the Fens, so he got a posh mate from the Hellfire Club and some lackeys and a fleet of boats with fancy names and they drifted round all over this area, fishing and looking down on the inhabitants. Late seventeen hundreds I think it was."

Sniffer said: "There was water just about everywhere then."

"Hence the boats," said Dusty flippantly, drawing a steely stare from Sniffer.

Terry leaned towards Sniffer to read an extract and began to laugh.

"Get this." Terry said. "One of them wrote this: 'Ramsey people are famous for their long teeth and hair.'"

The pub landlord, who was as bald as a billiard ball, overheard and gave them a piqued look but decided not to engage with this rather strange-looking bunch.

They decided to have another round, having shared Sniffer's unwanted beer. Malcolm went to order, as Terry was now in full flight. He was pleased to see that Dusty, now revived by food and drink, appeared quite interested.

"They had the locals dismantling the top of bridges for them and they sailed around looking at people as if they were in a zoo."

Sniffer passed the book to Terry saying: "Where's that bit about the warty man, Terry?"

Terry soon located some of the diary entries his mother had taken from an old book put together after the voyage.

"Ah yes. That's it. Lord Orford's Voyage Round The Fens, 1774. Mum's picked this one out...

'I observed going into Deeping a man in a one-horse chase with large warts round his eyelids much resembling a carrier pigeon.' And this: 'Outwell' – which we'll be going near, by the way – 'is equally remarkable for the ugliness of the inhabitants as for the handsomeness of its church.'"

Sniffer seemed outraged anew. "Nothing's changed. They're still taking the piss. No wonder our old mum used to get so vexed when she talked about toffs."

The room was suddenly lit up as if someone had pressed a switch. The storm had gone, the sun was here again.

The plates and glasses were empty. They decided to press on but as soon as they got up, and walked, realised that the beer had been a mistake. They had over-relaxed and stiffened up. But at least the air was clear and cooler now, and they knew the next leg of the ride would be the last of the day.

Terry flexed his hands, marvellously revived by the Loosener. Sniffer trudged unwillingly to the tandem. Malcolm announced that he was going ahead to find a camping spot, a clear patch of ground that would be dry by the time they set up the tents.

Terry was now having to make much less effort. He could feel that Sniffer was pedalling.

Dusty had set off in front of the tandem. Terry noticed that he had now adopted a semi-standing pedalling technique and had maintained it for a couple of miles.

He shouted ahead: "Dusty. You've got a saddle you know."

"Yes," he gasped, "and I've… also got… something amiss down there. Think it… might be boils starting. Prone to them."

The last miles of the day were covered in silence, broken only by Terry's heavy breathing and the occasional obscenity that accompanied each clank of Dusty's dodgy gear system.

Eventually they were relieved and happy to see Malcolm standing at the roadside, arm extended, ushering them into the camping site he had selected after an extensive search, and having taken all elements into consideration.

15

The site was a flat patch, covered by short-cropped grass and shielded from the road, a small thicket that enclosed the site on three sides. Malcolm had already been foraging and had well-rotted logs and kindling wood drying in the sun.

The tandem and bikes were chained together out of sight of the road. Sniffer volunteered to get the fire going and set about the job slowly and purposefully. With Malcolm directing operations, the trailer was unpacked, the tents unrolled, provisions stowed in the shade, toiletries allocated.

Dusty took the two six-packs of lager – thoughtfully bought by Viv – and lowered them into a water-filled hollow on the bank of the drain that cut through the wood and flowed under a channel beneath the road.

Half an hour later they had all changed into trousers and fleeces. The huge sun was edging towards a featureless horizon, giving a glow to the camp and to sun-blushed faces.

Malcolm used his special inflator to pump up the plastic airbeds and had placed a torch in each tent. "Better now than in the dark," he said with satisfaction.

The logs on the fire were becoming chunky ash and, with the lagers retrieved from the water hole, the biking party formed a circle to watch Terry cook supper.

"She's a gem, our Viv," said Terry. "Look at that. Thin-sliced sirloin. And she's even given us a tube of mustard, and sliced the bread buns open to make it easier."

"Bread buns? Barm cakes, not bread buns, I hope Terry," Dusty said. "If not barm cakes, it has to be oven bottom muffins."

"It's bleeding bread buns or baps... or...bugger all!" Terry insisted, snappily.

"Just a nice barm cake then," Dusty countered. "You only move into bap territory when you're on the outer edge of civilisation. Like here."

"Button it," said Terry menacingly and Dusty retreated.

Malcolm had put the kettle at the side of the fire, having declined the offer of steak sandwiches. He had a mountaineer's powdered meal, thank you very much. It was in a silver bag, with the word Endure printed on it and came with a plastic spoon, and when the kettle whistle blew, and he added hot water, it gave off what to Terry was a smell like you got from a hiker's sock.

Terry's pan was hot now and, shielding his face from the fire, he dropped a couple of slices of meat on to it.

"Well done, everybody," he said above the sizzling.

"And well done to you," Dusty said. Terry glanced to check whether he was being sincere.

"You'll have to have the steak as it comes," Terry said. He sounded weary.

"Fine," Dusty said. "But as I don't like bread buns, so can you make mine a barm or a bap."

"Give it a rest!" snapped Terry, too tired to come up with anything witty or wounding. Dusty would start a squabble with his own shadow.

"Actually," Dusty said, gently leaning back onto a pannier. "I think you did especially well, Sniffer."

Dusty patted Sniffer's back, a little nervously, as if he were a dog that was OK but had been known to bite.

Terry said, "Yes, Sniff, you really stuck at it."

"We all did OK, buh," said Sniffer who tottered to his feet, and slipped away, returning a minute later with forked twigs he had

91

stripped of leaves.

He strung a steak slice from each of the prongs and, as Terry cooked with the pan, suspended the branch over the glowing ashes. Terry was struck by his resemblance to a garden gnome dangling a fishing rod.

"Always wanted to do this. Cowboy stuff," Sniffer said.

It was dark now and Sniffer's eyes picked up the firelight. He was smiling like an excited boy.

"You know what, Tel?"

"What?" said Terry.

"I've forgot…"

Darkness fell, and the only sound after the meal was the occasional crackle from the fire and the pop of cans being opened.

The tents were side by side, and the occupants settled in twos at the entrances, Sniffer next to Terry, Malcolm with Dusty, all looking out over the fire embers to where the sunset had been, a sky turned now into one vast, black expanse, like a giant, dead TV screen.

Somehow the meandering conversation had moved on from the number of pumping stations working night and day to keep the Fens from being submerged ("Just imagine, three hundred!" said Terry; "Why do they bother?" said Dusty), to the topic of Malcolm's finger. Then on to space, ailments, and to childhood cruelty, prompting tales of frogs being inflated using stems of corn, butterflies being gassed, and the Indian Burn being used as an instrument of torture.

"Sometimes I feel regret, profound regret, about inflicting pain on nippers when I was at school," Dusty making it clear by his delivery that he felt no such thing.

"But we in the red rose county used the Chinese Burn, rather than the inferior Indian one …"

"You lot would," said Sniffer. "Just to be bloody contrary, like calling your bread rolls barms and muffins."

"Anyway, even worse than le feu Chinoise, a la Oswaldtwistle was the heartless art of arse-flicking. You know, as the small fry left the pool, getting your wet towel to crack like a whip on a wet young bum. Cruel. The shame of it! I repent! Forgive me Lord, for I have flicked..."

For a moment they all enjoyed the silence, the blackness and the glow of the fire.

Then Sniffer started to talk about real wickedness and about forgiveness.

He recalled that his mother had described how when she was young, lads in cheap suits and shirts and ties, with their hair slicked back, would go past her house on Sundays.

"Casuals from Ireland. Came every year to the Fens to make a few bob on picking. They were walking to mass. Three miles there, three miles back."

The fire spluttered and there was a brief and faint rumble of thunder somewhere, miles away.

"Lately I've been thinking how lucky those 'ol boys were. To be able to get rid of their sins for the price of a bit of shoe leather and two or three hours of their Sunday."

No one spoke, perhaps out of a recognition that something deeply troubling was going on inside Sniffer's mind.

Dusty had something vexing on his mind too - the Aardvark business, back at the office. He'd have loved to chat about it here, round the fire.

Surely, someone would have had something encouraging, something hopeful, to say, a few objective words to put it in proportion.

"Well," said Dusty, locking away his problem for yet another day, "I suppose it's time to hit the hay."

"Goodness!" Malcolm said, looking at his chunky outdoor man watch with its luminous numerals, "It's only 8 37!"

Early, but their bodies told them it was bedtime. After much awkward undressing, grunting, and sighing, silence fell over the tents. It was broken by Sniffer saying "I don't know whether to go again before I go to sleep" then, "No, I think I'll risk it."

Sniffer and Terry lay top to toe but as soon as Terry had begun to drift into sleep, he was roused with a start by Sniffer clumsily backing out of the tent, rear-end first, saying: "No. I think I will try to go."

A few moments later he could hear Sniffer mumbling, somewhere in the thicket. He fought off sleep until Sniffer came back.

"You've been phoning, haven't you Sniff?" he said.

"No, buh'

"You have Sniff. After you told Viv you weren't taking your phone, you've gone and brought it. God knows who you've been ringing but I know it won't have been Viv."

Sniffer didn't reply. But after a lengthy silence he said: "Difficult to explain, Tel. What's in my head. If I could tell anybody it'd be you. Or Ursula."

"Ursula. Bloody hell Sniff! Viv's only just over the Egg Woman."

"It's not like that. She's a chaplain, somebody I talk with."

"Heard that one before."

"No. She's the chaplain who came to the house."

"Oh, yes. Tell her then. Whatever helps. Or tell me, Sniff. You can tell me. Is it about what might happen over your health? Is it about a kid you've fathered? It's about the future isn't it?"

"Not the future. The past, Tel"

"Is it because you've been forgetting things?"

"No, it's because I remember."

"Tell me!"

"Can't."

They lay there, top to toe, at an impasse in the conversation. An owl hooted and the sound echoed round them. Fatigue and the blackness combined to lull them to sleep.

Next morning, Terry woke to see the back of Sniffer's head in front of him, resting on a rolled-up towel.

He was sleeping peacefully, his breath coming and going in little rhythmic whistles, and as Terry raised himself on an elbow, he could make out, under the disarray of hair, traces of Sniffer as a child.

Despite the passing of the years, the black bristles, the toll the drink had taken, the deep criss-cross lines of his lived-in face, and now the illness, miraculously the essence of Sniff the boy was still discernable.

Terry watched his brother for a while. He knew why Sniffer had moved up to sleep with him, side by side. He had been scared in the night, just as he had been as a kid, especially when he was in trouble.

For some reason, just as Viv had said, big as he had been, bold as he had been, in the night now he was sometimes frit shitless.

16

Viv paused at the top of the stairs. She was relieved that they had remembered the candles before they'd gone too far. They seemed so important to Sniffer. Of course, she was hurt that he did not tell her who they were in memory of, or whose future wellbeing they were dedicated to but it was not the first time she had felt excluded.

She looked out of the landing window and could see only other houses, bungalows mainly, lines of them, each with a measured patch of space, front and back.

The surroundings here at the new house were nothing like what she had been brought up with, or had moved from. Space was plentiful in the Fens, in fact when she thought about it, the Fens were mostly that – just space with weather happening in it. Here there was a shop within a few hundred yards, a regular bus service but you never noticed the sky or saw a totally flat horizon.

That said, there were times, before the move, when looking out of the landing window on to the wide-screen picture you got from viewing the Fens from even two floors up, would have given her heartache.

Viv remembered particularly brilliant cloudless dawns when she could see perhaps fifteen miles to geographical infinity. But her focus always fell on the Egg Woman's house. When the weather was clear, cruelly it appeared so much nearer than it was, as if overlapping her life.

There was one particular day when she had imagined that if she opened the window, she would have heard the Egg Woman's cockerels crowing. It would have been too triumphant a sound to bear. And it was on that day that she decided they should move to be near the city.

Some manipulation had been needed. Sniffer had been reluctant but she had aggravated his guilt over the affair and made it seem that agreeing to a move would go quite a way in wiping the slate clean.

It wouldn't, of course. Nothing would. But lately Viv had felt less vindictive towards the Egg Woman. Maybe the physical distancing had helped.

She walked downstairs, made herself coffee and sat at the breakfast bar. The local paper was open in front of her, and her script was to hand but she hadn't been able to concentrate on reading either.

Then her eye caught a news item about the young doctor who had been mowed down on the road not far from them. It turned out that there had been a lapse in security at some place for people with mental problems, and that the mother had finally received an apology, and that the official report – that took an age to come out – was saying how things must be improved.

It was easy to think that you were the only one with troubles.

That poor woman had a son who had gone mad and then been run over. The thought did little to put Viv's own tribulations into perspective.

It was so easy to begin to believe that there was no way forward. But she remembered that by sheer strength of will she had managed to put aside her anger and see things objectively. She had even accepted, for brief spells at least, that there was absolutely no logical reason to hate the Egg Woman.

It was true that in her moments of jealousy she had characterised her rival as a siren, a calculating bitch. But, like lava instantly cooling as it gushed into the air, the scalding rage subsided as quickly as it erupted and she was left with an uncomfortable feeling that her more vicious sentiments had been unworthy of her.

She had known that the Egg Woman had lived alone for years, always seemed to be struggling, and was probably very lonely. She had also faced the fact that Sniffer was an opportunist.

But her fair-mindedness could evaporate within moments.

What helped Viv to channel her anger, unhindered, towards Sniffer, and make some sort of allowance for the Egg Woman, was that she knew so little about her – and that was still the case.

If she searched her memory, she would see a wiry, fit-looking woman of middle age, fine facial features, crumpled wax jacket. Occasionally she had glimpsed her on her market stall with the stacks of egg trays laid out in front of her. She was a little weatherbeaten, her femininity lit up by a flash of lipstick and some bright shiny ornament in her hair that fell over her face as she stooped to gather eggs for customers.

Viv also seemed to remember having seen her once in the rain in a bright yellow plastic cape, and there was a fleeting image in her mind of a delivery in summer when the Egg Woman wore a broad, red cotton band to hold her hair in place and tatty jeans that had been bleached by years of wear rather than in some designer factory.

She had picked up on some indefinable indicator of class but also of down-at-heel stylishness. But beyond that she had to rely on gossip to learn more.

Viv recalled having felt disappointed that the feedback had been so positive. The Egg Woman would be a difficult person to hate. Evidently she was "very nice". Bright. Nicely spoken. And "strong" – she had to be, someone had said, having been left in the lurch, bringing up two children and keeping that egg business going in this day and age.

She was the absolute opposite, then (Viv thought at the time), of the sort of woman she expected Sniffer to be attracted to.

If she had been challenged to describe the Egg Woman, from the little she knew or had seen of her, she would have said "middle class but broke," though she would have been hard-pressed to explain what she meant by middle class.

Strangely, Viv's mind had preserved a better description of the car than the woman; the bouncy old Citroen 2CV, cream and brown, with that funny rippled bonnet and tatty canvas top, the trays of eggs stacked on the back seat. It was cute.

To Viv, the car – obviously ancient – said "economy," but also "eccentricity." She had an idea it was the car French farmers used to use; there was a scene in some film from years ago where one was shown tootling through a village with a pig sitting upright in the passenger seat.

She remembered that there were numerous dents over the bodywork that told of mishaps accumulated over years. Viv guessed that the Egg Woman was an erratic driver, like some other clever people she had known, a bit dotty at the wheel.

Viv decided that she'd have a sandwich before she set off to check on the boys' progress. She would have to be stealthy. Sniffer had told her that if she hovered around mollycoddling him it would spoil the whole thing, that he'd weaken. She would never forgive herself if she spoiled things for him, even if it was out of love.

She gave the kitchen surfaces a quick wipe. This place was so easy to keep clean, so modern, she thought with satisfaction. What a contrast to the Egg Woman's place – dilapidated, the fascia boards rotting, the guttering undulating and the timber window frames hollowed out by rot.

That said, Viv suspected that inside would be a very interesting home – proper paintings, bulging bookshelves, furniture with history, well-used ethnic cookbooks.

When this imagined picture came to her again, her anger rose to block it out.

She saw Sniffer there, living his secret part-time second life, unwinding with the Egg Woman and then, bold as brass, coming home as if everything was normal.

That thought made her swallow hard and try not to cry as she picked up her car keys to go in search of the riders.

º º º º º º º

It will be today that the ride starts, Lydia guessed. The report in the newspaper had given an idea of the route, and said it would take a week. So...yes, they'd be setting off today.

The feeling of separateness gnawed at her. It had been so hard and lonely not being able to communicate with Sniffer and not knowing how he was, what the doctors were saying about his health. It was unbearable.

She would have to find a way of seeing him. He would need her, she knew that.

Everyone saw Sniffer as super-confident, certain of his opinions, and that's how he seemed to her at the start of it all. At the time all she needed was some practical support, some sex, and to be appreciated for a while as a person with ideas, appetites, dreams of something different.

Sex apart, another woman could have fulfilled her needs. But instead she got Sniffer, or Clarrie, as she would call him when they were larking about (he would call her Posh Tart).

But what Sniffer had brought into her life turned out to be extra special, as she found when they began to talk, spanning their yawning differences with relaxed exchanges, confessions, a feeling of freedom from commitment.

They both felt torn each time Sniffer had to leave to keep up pretences, and protect Lydia's children from knowing the depth of the relationship. Both remarked on how incompatible they would have appeared to be, if they'd gone public.

Lydia was sure that neither her crib friends at the pub, nor the girls at the market, would have linked her and Sniffer in a million years. Chalk and cheese.

She herself was struck by the contrast between Sniffer (opinionated, strong, irreverent) and the long-absent Bruce (vacillating, mealy-mouthed, spineless).

None of this mattered. They both knew that what they had was as wholly good as it was wholly wrong, as unlikely as it felt right.

Lydia had been amused when Sniffer had claimed not to know what romance was but he said things and did things that left her glowing, and smiling, at their kind intent.

He couldn't get away from home to spend time with her on her birthday but on the day had left a small space heater at the back door, and rolls of draught excluder, and some timber offcuts that might be useful for patching up the hen houses. No card. No message.

The heater was for what she grandly called "the new office." She wanted to tackle something, a course, to research something, initiate something for the future. Sniffer had been encouraging and told her when he'd moved the desk back in and installed a light: "Right, girl. No excuse now."

Of course she wondered about Viv, and how he was with her. She was curious about how the marriage worked, or failed to – but Sniffer was reticent.

She didn't know Viv but would have recognised her in the street – slim, girlish face, glasses that enhanced her looks, curls tumbling onto her face (tumbling unfashionably, she imagined, although she was not up with trends in hairstyles).

She'd glimpsed Viv a few times when she had dropped the eggs off each week but it was always Sniffer who was out and about and who called in to pay.

Lydia had heard someone say that Viv was an outstanding singer – musicals, light classics. From what she had seen of her she would have put her down as moderately pretty, conventional maybe, but guessed that beneath the almost meek, bookish appearance bestowed by the glasses, she could be formidable.

That strong streak, and her power, was confirmed beyond doubt when Viv first found out about their friendship; "affair" was more accurate but it was a term Lydia judged too racy for the circumstances.

Viv's anger had been monumental and Sniffer had been made to suffer. He had been clearly nervous whenever he managed to phone, and suddenly seemed shy of saying anything intimate.

Frankly, he had looked like a whipped dog when he came to her unexpectedly on that November night to explain Viv's terms and say that it all had to end. She didn't like to see him so humbled.

Two years on and she could still not get over this transformation. He was often confused. His certainty had gone. She knew that the ultimatum had forced him to acknowledge that he needed Viv.

She had no reason to begrudge Viv having Sniffer entirely to herself- she was his wife after all. Nor was there any reason to hate her. In fact, Lydia sometimes saw herself and Viv as adjuncts to Sniffer, actors in a play in which he was director and star.

But there was one aspect of him she knew she could claim exclusively: Sniffer had spoken more openly with her than with Viv, or anyone else, in his life.

He owed her nothing, and she owed him nothing, and because they both knew that they would lose each other just as serendipitously as they had found each other, hearts could be emptied without recrimination.

When she last saw him he was perfectly well or, rather, he was unaware of what sinister changes were happening inside him.

Viv was at work. They'd arranged to meet in the café of the town museum, as safe a haven as he could think of.

He had been low, pessimistic. He left half his coffee, and as they stepped into the street to take different roads out of town she had touched his hand and asked: "Are you all right?"

"It never goes away," he had said in a distracted voice. She did not ask what "it" was but had said, "I know," and simply squeezed his hand.

They had been so close at that moment. She knew that Sniffer was keeping something close to his chest. Some instinct told him that she, too, had something to tell him but couldn't, or had chosen not to.

Lydia was feeling that sense of intimacy now, thinking of Sniffer, possibly facing death, cut off from the comfort she wanted to give him, setting off on that silly bloody ride. She didn't want to disrupt what Viv and Sniffer were rebuilding but she knew he would want some sign that she had not forgotten him.

She decided that she would try to get a rough itinerary of the ride, from the sponsors. She would say that she wanted to support them and cheer them on.

She would then get a message to Sniffer, and then see him – even if it was only for seconds as she drove past in the old 2CV.

Even seeing the car go by would show that she had not abandoned him.

17

Viv had slept deeply, selfishly. It was good to be able to think of herself, not to have to worry about Sniffer and his needs.

The sun was up, the toast was on, the radio was playing, the tea was poured.

She almost had a holiday feeling. Until the phone call.

"Viv. All OK. No worries, but got to be quick. Just need to know. Has the hospital asked Sniff to save his wee?"

"Sorry Terry. Has the hospital what?"

"Have the nurses asked Sniff to keep his wee. For testing or anything?"

"Wee? No! Wee? Not that I know of. Why do you ask? Is he OK?"

"He's doing fine. Memory's much, much better and he's having fewer panicky moments. Actually he's just wolfed down four sausages..."

"But what's this about wee?"

"Well, I'd heard sloshing from the trailer yesterday and when we unpacked the breakfast stuff today there was a big sealed jar. Wrapped in a tea towel. And it's two thirds full of you know what."

Viv thought hard. The tests had all been done. Surely they wouldn't give instructions about urine samples to a man who was losing his memory, and not tell the person caring for him?

Terry explained hurriedly: "Malcolm thought at first it might be some medicinal potion so we daren't chuck it but we can't get any sense out of Sniffer. He just grabbed it and shouted to Dusty to leave it alone, that it was his. Think he was embarrassed."

"I'll get straight on to the hospital."

"Maybe they have to analyse it over time, do a sort of average? It's just that it weighs a ton and what with Sniffer only pedalling when he remembers that he's on a bike, I could do with lightening the load."

"Sure you're managing OK?

"I'm OK but sometimes he just sits back as if he's in a rickshaw and I'm the bloody coolie."

Actually, said Terry, pausing, no one had actually witnessed Sniffer using the bottle.

"He just wanders off saying 'Just going to strain the greens' or 'Off to splash the boots.' From now on we'll be looking out for him carrying the bottle from now on."

After the call, Terry felt bad about troubling Viv. She should be resting up. But if Sniffer had been told to keep samples over the entire week, there would be a weight problem… More jars would be needed and they'd maybe have to organise for Viv to do a pick-up.

"It'll be like a bloody milk-round by the time we get to Norwich," he said to himself.

Terry knew he was becoming short-tempered, because of tiredness and concern over Sniffer.

He would have to watch what he said, especially when needled by Dusty who loved to poke and prod, rattle his cage. It was not for nothing that a pub landlord had once presented him with a wooden spoon after a vote among regulars to name the Stirrer of The Year.

There was an example this morning. Over breakfast, when he had mentioned a possible camping spot beyond Ely, Sniffer had asked when the party was likely to reach Clenchwarton.

Terry had said: "Look Sniff, we're going to try to divert to Clench for a bit if there's time but Norwich is the big one. The target."

"Clench! Oh to be in Clench now autumn's here…" Dusty had said, dreamily, holding a rubbery flap of fried egg aloft on his fork, as if the name was redolent of a distant land of myth and romance.

"What's wrong with Clench?" Terry had snapped.

"Nothing. Nothing. Just struck me as the sort of thing you hear in hospital. You know, nurse comes in with a whacking great syringe, and says: 'Right - clench for me.'"

Terry had nailed him with a stare: "This, from a man who was born in Ramsbottom and went to school in Oswaldtwistle."

Terry had stood up and looked down threateningly at Dusty, who was even smaller than normal in what was a new stance. He was in pain, and Terry took pleasure in his discomfort.

"Back and boils," he had said when Sniffer, with uncharacteristic concern, had asked about the stoop.

Dusty had explained that since waking he had been forced to keep bent forward with his hands near his hands on his knees because of the ache in his back, but when he went forward the pain from the encroaching crop of boils increased. Terry thought he resembled one of those silhouettes on tee shirts showing man evolving from the ape, a middle one, when man was homo almost erectus.

Yet Dusty's smile was undimmed. But it was clear he was suffering. His plan was to encase his bike saddle in surgical wadding from Malcolm's medical kit.

There was compensation in all this - Dusty had woken feeling that he had lost some weight.

He was sure of it. He was back in his sponsor tee shirt and although it was tightish he could now nearly raise his arms. He was also wearing the clean, oversize shorts he had thrown into his pannier "just in case." It was blissful not to have the added agony of the painful squeeze the other pair exerted.

o o o o o o o

The settled weather was back, so breakfast was cooked outside and, with Malcolm in charge, there was an orderly advance. Ely beckoned.

However, for Terry there remained the wee problem, not really cleared up by a call from Viv that brought the party to a halt five miles into the day's ride.

"Terry," she said, sounding stressed, "I spoke to someone on the ward but they were run off their feet. Couldn't reach the consultant or find the papers. They said people starting with dementia sometimes hoard things so that might explain it. The wee thing."

"So can we get rid?" Terry asked.

"No, they said keep storing it until we hear. Just in case."

Keep storing it. Just in case! Terry left Sniffer straddling the tandem and stomped furiously up and down the road. By supreme effort he kept the lid on his anger, venting it as he clicked the phone shut and took up the strain once more.

"Wagons roll!" he shouted. "Or, rather, piss wagons roll!" he said, acidly.

He turned to look over his shoulder and said: "You'll understand that, Sniff. And don't think I don't know."

Sniffer looked mystified. The bobble on his Posh hat shook from side to side in denial. He was sure that Terry was losing it.

Dusty, still riding upright, standing on his pedals, a style that made him rock from side to side, slowly drew alongside and cocked his curly head inquisitively.

"Terry, did you just say piss wagons?"

"Forget it," said Terry, who was heartened to see ahead a road sign for Ely.

They biked in silence. The steady progress eased Terry's mood. Sniffer had not whistled today, and it felt as if he was pedalling. Not only that, Ely Cathedral - The Ship of the Fens - had come into view. It was good to have a visible destination to aim for.

But moments after passing the Ely sign, Sniffer said: "Stop, buh."

"What is it?" Terry asked anxiously.

"I want to see the cathedral."

"But you can see it as we go. It'll be there till we get there. Anyway, you've seen it loads of times. Sniff, you lived at Ely for a bit."

"You're wrong on one point, buh. I've looked at it before. Yes. But I've never actually seen it."

"OK, but we need to push on… We want to make sure we keep up with the schedule."

"Course Tel. But think about this. I probably won't be around here again. What's a couple of minutes when you're facing eternity?"

Terry had never heard Sniff talk like this. Deflated and suddenly sad, he lay down the tandem and they both stood and looked over the hazy flatlands and drank in the beauty of the distant towers.

He was on the verge of putting his arm round Sniffer's shoulders, as the enormity of Sniffer's illness struck home once more, when Dusty caught up with them and stopped his bike with a stuttering bent leg.

"What have you spotted?" he said, panting. "A red kite? Batman? A gradient?"

"No, just looking at the cathedral."

"I saw it ages ago, miles back."

"No," Sniffer said earnestly, "you looked at it but did you really see it, Dusty."

"Actually, I can see it when I look at it," Dusty replied, making a goonish face that suggested he wasn't quite all there.

"It's a miracle," Sniffer said in a portentous voice.

"No, a mere building. But, granted, a wonderful building," Dusty said, through his little smile. "But still a mere building."

Sniffer kept his eyes of the great edifice lording it over the landscape and said: "You sit in an office, all year round, Dusty, occasionally scratching your arse. I lay bricks. I build. My work lasts. Take it from me that is a miracle."

Dusty felt that he didn't deserve the look of abject hatred that Sniffer then directed at him. The man had no idea of the strain involved in his job, how you could lose sleep, even crack up. The simple act of laying bricks seemed very appealing.

Dusty looked crestfallen behind the rictus smile. He had begun to worry again about the Aardvark debacle.

Watching his face, Terry was concerned that Dusty was suffering in the stifling heat, especially with that standing pedal-action that really must be taking it out of him.

He was constantly trailing and drenched in sweat and there was much huffing and puffing, and occasional childlike cries of pain, indicating that the saddle upholstered with taped-on lint and bandages was not a complete success.

Terry found the beginnings of sympathy rising in him but quickly curbed it. From the start, the bloke had been so scathing about the Fens, riling Sniff with his sly jibes.

But there had been a pleasing incident involving Dusty just as they were about to roll up the tents and move off. Terry found himself laughing vengefully as he replayed the scene in his head.

After breakfast, Dusty, still tilted forward like a Neanderthal, had picked up the kettle and polished the chrome top with the tee shirt he was carrying. Strangely, he had then taken the kettle away.

When, a bit later, Malcolm took hold of one corner of the tent and Terry the other, and lifted it off the ground, there was Dusty, shorts in hand, straddled bare-arsed across the kettle that lay on the floor.

Everyone had stopped, speechless.

It occurred to Terry that a future archaeologist, seeing some record of the incident, might have concluded that it was an auspicious ritual, this stooping, pants-off, bow-legged dance, involving worship of a precious source of refreshment.

Malcolm immediately apologised for the intrusion; Sniffer merely looked on then shook his head in despair, sidled up to Terry and said in a voice he knew would carry to Dusty: "I knew there was something about him…"

Malcolm then had a short consultation with Dusty then walked away saying: "I've just the thing for them…"

It turned out Dusty had been trying to look at his boils in the reflection of the kettle lid.

Malcolm delved into his medical kit for antiseptic salve and more padding. "Look," he was saying quietly to Dusty, "don't ever suffer in silence. And if you want to see yourself, I've got a mirror in here.

I use it for signalling, using the sun."

What, in Cheadle Hulme? Dusty thought but did not say, as he went off to apply the cream behind a tree.

Malcolm called after him: "It'll sting a bit but it's what we used to use when I was in Wilmslow Wheelers. Most of us had a tub. But if you had to share there was a strict rule: No double-dipping. Hygiene, you see."

"Thanks," said Dusty in a slightly self-pitying voice.

"OK. I don't want it back," he said firmly, making Dusty feel that he saw him as a carrier of something unpleasantly contagious.

It bothered Terry that though the ride today was going better than he had dared hope, Malcolm - who had now shot off ahead after a few miles - had not returned.

But at a point when Sniffer had started grumbling behind him, and Dusty had fallen a hundred yards behind, a thin, blue, vertical smudge far ahead gradually mutated into Malcolm.

"There's a nice pull-in just down the road," he said, braking, then arching his back and heading off again like a cowboy turning his steed in a new direction.

By the time Terry and Sniffer, and, later, Dusty, had settled under scrubby trees on a bank of mossy grass out of the sun, Malcolm had unpacked a pannier laden with goodies.

The sausage rolls ("for the meat-eaters" Malcolm said with only a tinge of disapproval) were still warm, as were the doughnuts. Malcolm had also somehow managed to transport coffee in polystyrene mugs.

He himself gnawed on a nut bar and sipped from a bottle of purple, mineral-rich drink and bathed in the glow of appreciation coming from the rest of the party.

Dusty brushed pastry crumbs from his tee shirt and, feeling the throb of his phone that was wedged somewhere deep in his clothing, he stood up and walked to find a private spot.

It would be Sheryl. Last night when they had spoken she had been fretting about him.

Terry looked over to Dusty and couldn't help quietly chortling at the figure he cut; round, red face, encircled by curls, skin-tight tee shirt, army-style shorts that with a few judicious snips of scissors would have been a voluminous skirt. The stance of a gorilla. Terry was sure he'd seen a little comic actor in shorts like that, singing Whispering Grass.

Dusty was unaware that he was still within earshot and the three picnickers tried to keep talking to cover the marital sweet talk… "of course babes"… "And you, sweetpea"…. "I will, darling, I will."

"Ely's nice," said Malcolm. "And I found your pub, Sniffer."

"What pub?" said Terry, feeling left out.

"The Happy Monk," said Malcolm.

"Smashing little place," Sniffer said. "Used to be in there every night when I was stopping over doing up some houses."

Malcolm took another bite from his chaste snack.

"There's a nice spot we could camp at just before the city. At the edge of a paddock. I'll check with the owner. As you suggested, we could set camp, do the candle business and have a meal at the pub, then bed down."

"Done!" said Sniffer with an eagerness that made Terry uneasy.

18

When the convoy reached the cobbled frontage of the Fenland World museum, on the fringe of Ely, Sniffer gathered together the gifts he had brought. He refused help, asserting ownership, so that no one would be in any doubt about the identity of the donor.

He carefully placed them on the reception desk. Dusty diverted himself by selecting tourist leaflets from a rack while Terry looked round and found a seat, grateful for the chance to rest his legs.

There was no one behind the counter. Posters pinned up on one wall announced sessions for children who could learn about eel nets and water fowl, alongside a flyer about a book on the Great Flood of 1912.

Dusty mischievously pointed to a poster announcing a forthcoming lecture on Fenland fauna, under the title Sedge From Edge to Edge. He pushed Terry's shoulder and clicked a thumb and finger saying: "Damn, we'll miss it. Sounds riveting. Obviously they're born to be wild in these parts."

Terry glared but decided not to rise to the bait. He turned instead to watch Sniffer whose arms encircled his hoard – the skates, the reed-cutting tool, a sheaf of old photos, and the carrier bag containing the underwear that had been passed down via Aunt Nancy.

He had tucked his mother's dog-eared red exercise book about life in the Fens down his shirt to present with a flourish.

A slight, modish young woman with glasses of a 1950s design

and a crisp bob emerged and settled at the cash desk. She was flushed and short of breath.

"Sorry about that. Panic. Leaflets to unload. Bit short of staff. The cuts."

Terry started to say "This is my brother and..." when Sniffer asked: "Are you the top banana, love?"

"Well," the girl replied pleasantly: "I suppose I am today as there are no other bananas about. We used to be a bunch," she said with a hysterical giggle. "How can I help?"

"Well, I've got a right treat for you!"

Sniffer looked down at his booty, eager for her to be amazed by the treasure he had brought to her door.

"Ah! Sorry!" she said, much too loudly. "You're the gentleman with the book, the cycling gentleman! So sorry!" You will be sorry, Terry thought to himself. Sniffer looked settled for a long session.

"How exciting!" said the museum lady. "I understand you have an old diary...?"

"I have. It's crammed full of bits you'll love. Old sayings, history, everything. Precious. And you need to look after it for future generations."

"We will! Wonderful. The man from the Eastern News is coming so we can capture this moment. What a thoroughly lovely acquisition."

"You'll remember some of the stuff from way back," Sniffer promised, seemingly oblivious of her age. He wasn't to know that she came from Dorset, that her degree was in oceanography and had not heard of the Fens until a couple of years before but clearly he didn't notice that she was barely thirty.

Sniffer spoke to her as a contemporary who, like him, was fen-bred.

"Stuff like...well, remember when we were kids we used to call ladybirds bishy barnabees? We all said it round Clench way... And if you were bad tempered you'd be told not to be so damn well runty...well it's all in there."

"Wonderful!"

"There's bits about those toffs who came up and sailed round in their fancy boats laughing at us locals. All the names of the boats are there...the Whale that had the cooks in, and the Dolphin and the Shark, and the Cocoa Nut that was for the horses that pulled them when there was no wind."

He's away, said Terry to himself.

"You know, love, the only compliment the buggers paid us was that when one of the cooks went off to buy a cabbage and it weighed 15 pounds. Oh, and that there was the odd handsome Peterborough woman, not beautiful, mind, and there was only a few."

It struck the museum lady that this gentleman was personally aggrieved about the aristocratic pleasure cruise; still angry, as if it had happened last year rather than in 1774.

Two more potential customers had now arrived and the flustered museum lady was trying to speed things up in a way that Sniffer did not detect. She picked up a skate to steer him towards the handover moment.

"Fascinating now to read it," Sniffer said enthusiastically. "Things like what people like my dad used to eat for his dockey break, and how from September onwards my uncle wore his chummie. You know what a chummie is...?"

"Well..." There was an uneasy pause.

"Come on, you must know what a chummie is! Bloody hell. A woolly hat! So that he wouldn't get brown titus. They used to call bronchitis brown titus didn't they, in our grandparents' day?"

"Em... This all sounds superb."

"If granddad got a dose he'd be dudderin', especially if everything was watter-jowled, wouldn't he?"

"Well, yes, I suppose..."

Terry intervened. "Sniff, show the lady what else you've brought for their collection."

Sniffer drew breath and launched another marathon of reminiscence, explaining that the ice skates ("ice patterns to you and me") had been made by a local blacksmith.

The museum lady was obviously straining to maintain her engrossed expression. Dusty caught Terry's attention, pointed at his watch. The waiting customers sighed meaningfully.

The door from the street opened and in bustled a large overdressed and sweaty young man, lugging two cameras and a big equipment bag.

The museum lady and Sniffer posed, Sniffer holding the heel of a skate and the museum lady holding the toe.

As the photographer turned and left the couple of visitors made a show of leaving too, the husband glowering as he left, shutting the door rather too firmly.

The museum lady noticed, and would have given anything to go into the office, take off her Fifties glasses and have a short, controlled cry among the boxes of leaflets. It had always eased the stress a little. Latterly it had all been too much.

But her nightmare continued as Sniffer reached over and took her elbow.

"Now for something that will have you absolutely wetting yourself. Funny I should say that – it's underwear. Look…" He drew out what appeared to be two white cotton windsocks, joined at one end.

"Go on. What are they? Go on…" he said.

"Are they Victorian…?"

"Got it in one! Victorian split-arsed mechanicals. That's what they called them in my Great Aunt Alice's mother's day. That, or ever-readies. She used to say that Victoria herself wore them on the throne so she didn't have a lot of faffing about to do."

Terry decided it really was time to call a halt. They ought to be off and get settled for the night, at a site Malcolm had already ringed on the map hanging from his neck.

He announced firmly over Sniffer's shoulder that it had been a pleasure, that they were so pleased to know that the heirlooms were in good hands.

The museum lady grasped the opportunity of escape, as if it were a relay race baton, and, maintaining the pace while Sniffer droned on she bid them what she knew must have sounded like an over-assertive farewell.

"Oh, and may I give you this?" she said, moving to the door. "This card makes you a Friend of Fenland World. A token of appreciation for your kind gifts."

"A pleasure," said Terry. He and Dusty turned towards the door while Sniffer carefully gathered up the family heirlooms and put them in the carrier bag. They waited for him finally to present the bag, in what they knew would be a ceremonial way, to the museum lady, who held out a hand, ready.

But to their amazement, instead, Sniffer turned and walked to the door, bag in hand.

"But Sniffer, you'd given that stuff to them!" Terry protested as they stepped out onto the cobbles. "Get back in there!"

Sniffer looked affronted.

The museum lady lowered her arm and stood at the door, like a waxwork figure, until it closed. She hurried to the storeroom, taking off her glasses as she went, in readiness for a short, cathartic cry.

When they reached the bikes, Terry was shaking his head in disbelief.

Sniffer said narkily: "Tel – did you expect me to *give* them that stuff? Do you really think that I'd ever *give away* precious historical stuff like this? Give it away?"

"But you promised Sniff…"

"I did no such thing. Honestly Tel, you must be going soft in the head."

19

Terry lay flat out on his back enjoying the cool turf beneath his aching back. Sniffer was asleep, his pillow a plastic water bottle, his Posh hat pulled over his eyes to shut out the sun. They had made it to the site Malcolm had selected.

Terry hoped upon hope that they could pitch the tents here. He felt he couldn't have ridden another yard although it would be light for another hour or so.

Malcolm strode up the long, cinder drive that divided the paddock and was soon at the door explaining that he was with a party of cyclists raising money for cancer research. The owner's wife was sympathetic and came out to the edge of the patio to wave and point out the best place to pitch the tents.

"She's as nice as pie," said Malcolm, returning. "We can even have a bit of fire for Sniffer if we're careful. There's old branches over in that little copse she says," he said.

They were trudging to the paddock gate along the drive when Terry looked around and said: "One of our number is missing." The words were hardly out of his mouth before Malcolm, head down, was retracing the route they had taken.

Meanwhile, Sniffer and Terry set up camp and lounged in the deep, lush grass. Whatever the calendar said, autumn seemed weeks away, and they drank in the sun, enjoying the balm of heat on their tired muscles.

At last, Malcolm appeared with Dusty, both pushing their bikes,

Dusty dragging his feet.

Terry said chirpily: "Ah – as the poet said, 'Home is the hunter, home from the hill…'"

He looked disdainfully at the pitiful figure before him.

"Actually, as you've noted, there are no hills in these parts. Just as well, Dusty, seeing the state of you," he gloated.

He immediately regretted this when he looked more closely. Dusty seemed to be on the verge of melting away before his eyes. His curls were stuck to his forehead and he appeared to have been freshly basted. He was holding his legs apart in a way that suggested that he might have been kicked by a horse.

Whatever the cause he was obviously suffering from disabling pain in the nether regions. The sweat-soaked tee shirt had tightened to turn the fat on his chest into symmetrical rolls. And yet, there was that indelible little smile.

"Drink," he croaked.

Terry stepped forward to hold Dusty's elbow as he lowered himself on to the grass.

When he sat down he let out a blood-curdling cry – "My boils!" Malcolm brought a blow-up bed and they laid Dusty on his back.

"Heatstroke, dehydration," said Malcolm with great authority, after questioning Dusty, who sounded as if he was talking under water.

Malcolm had been checking symptoms with a diagnostic booklet he kept in his first aid kit.

"Got to cool him. Get his pulse down. Hydrate him"

Dusty lay panting. He seemed semi-comatose. But suddenly he looked up in alarm as he saw Malcolm towering over him. He had drawn his bowie knife.

Dusty let out a weak whinny and tried to sit up so he could run for it if necessary. But the pain from his boils, and from his back, and the crushing restriction of the tee shirt, rendered him helpless.

Anyway, frankly he was past caring. Maybe this was how he would go – sweating like a pig, his clack as dry as a dog biscuit, bum scorching, as if someone was busy down there with a blow-lamp.

So, a goner at 36…knifed by an introverted misfit, one of life's losers. Suddenly even the Aardvark disaster seemed a mere frippery.

Malcolm stooped lower and moved the bowie knife towards Dusty's chest.

"Now. Listen. Stay perfectly still," he said. "This is the only way we're going to get that tee shirt off you. It's as tight as a sausage skin."

Dusty felt Malcolm pull up the bottom of the shirt and then heard the knife slice through the cloth. His lungs expanded as the shirt pinged open.

"Thanks Malcolm. What a relief! For a minute I thought you were coming at me to open a vein. Or worse."

Dusty took to the cool of the tent - playing the invalid, Terry thought, uncharitably - his head covered by the trek towel which Malcolm had dampened.

Meanwhile Sniffer changed into his trousers; he wanted to look decent for his visit to the cathedral. Malcolm found the candles he had brought and Sniffer leaned against the gatepost holding one, waiting until Malcolm and Terry got changed.

"Are we leaving Goldilocks?" Sniffer inquired.

"Best for him to rest," Malcolm replied in a tone a nurse might have used.

As they were about to leave the site, they heard Dusty say from within the tent, in a thin and slightly pitiful voice: "Where are you off to, boys?"

"Cathedral, and then the pub. The Happy Monk," Terry replied.

"Not sure I…can join you…" Dusty whined. "So weak…" Then, with hardly a pause: "OK then, I suppose I'll give it a go. Maybe a drink will help…"

o o o o o o o o

Sniffer asked to go into the cathedral alone, taking his candle with him. The rest of the party strolled to an area of cropped grass and rested. He came out after half an hour wearing an expression no one could read, perhaps one that was calculatingly neutral.

Once at the pub he brightened.

"I remember this," he said, pointing to the back wall of the pub. "That eel trap and the old photos of the skating races at Whittlesey. They must have needed a few eel traps here. The monks used to send 3,000 of them a year to Peterborough to pay for quarrying rights."

"So quoth the Old Soke of Peterborough..." Dusty ventured bravely, attracting a puzzled look from Sniffer who wasn't sure whether he was being insulted.

Dusty looked round and came to the table with a chair he was exchanging because it had a deep cushioned seat. He lowered himself on to it like a cautious bather easing into an icy pool.

They ordered the gammon and chips special, all except Malcolm, who chose something made mainly of leaves.

After the first pints of Fen Tigress they felt a warm kinship, a feeling of having overcome something together.

Dusty looked refreshed and rather stirred things up again by asking Sniffer whether his mum had taught him the Jack and Jill rhyme. Sniffer didn't quite know where this was going so he didn't respond.

"I just wondered what happened when you got to the part where they go up the hill. Did you say: 'What's a hill, Mum?'

Terry made a threatening face at Dusty and turned the conversation to football. He said he would enjoy going to Posh at the end of the week, and seeing Sniffer hand over the cheque to the charity people.

The mention of football prompted Dusty to recall a match in the previous season, between Altrincham and Hednesford and, as he wittered on, Terry feigned a long, exaggerated yawn.

Sniffer cut Dusty short. "We're talking about real football, Dusty. Not some kick-around in Lancashire."

Sniffer then recounted the milestones in the glorious march of The Posh, since 1934. For Terry, it was the same old Sniffer record on the turntable...Posh the fabled Cup giant-killers, the fantastic season of 1960-61 when goal-scoring was like podding peas, the time they lost an FA Cup replay at White Hart Lane when a lad of 16 saw his penalty saved at the end of a shoot-out.

Inevitably, there would be a roll call of Posh heroes, Terry knew that. But here the record stopped turning. Sniffer appeared not to be able to remember any of the names that normally tripped off his tongue whenever he reminisced.

Terry intervened.

"Well, there was the great Terry Bly, wasn't there, Sniff? Imagine, you two; this bloke got 52 goals in one season! A record. In a year when Posh got more goals than any League team had done. Ever. A record. And there was Charlery, and Turner the manager, and Mick... was it Halsall, Sniff?"

He waited for Sniffer to respond but he seemed not to recognise the name of a much-lauded Posh captain.

Then, with fear in his eyes, Sniffer said: "All I know is that I didn't like the bloke in the mask. Or that bloody big rabbit."

They ate their food in silence. There was something deeply disturbing about Sniffer's lapses; Terry concluded that it was as if, for a minute or two, he became someone else.

Helpfully, and unusually, Malcolm initiated a conversation. He announced that his first priority when he got home would be to collect his pet dog from the kennels. "He'll go wild," he said. "We've been especially close since his accident."

"Accident? Oh dear, what happened?" asked Dusty.

"Man who came to unblock the drains ran over him. But only the one foot. At the back."

"Lovely dog," said Terry. "I've seen him in action. Manages really well without the leg, doesn't he Malcolm? Seems to use his tail as a rudder."

"Yes, he's a great companion is Lucky."

Malcolm cleared up the last of his salad leaves. He then leaned back with a sigh, as if he was full. Dusty glanced at the flat solar plexus and taut, flesh-free limbs with deep envy.

The next priority, Malcolm said, would be to check that all his preparation for the new term was done. The school holidays absolutely flew by, he said. Terry did not reply but would have bet his mortgage that Malcolm already had every single thing in place for school.

Dusty looked downcast at the mention of the return to work. He speared a leftover chip with his fork but had no interest in eating it. "Not sure I'll have work to go back to," he said, without emotion.

"Bloody hell, Dusty – what do you mean?" Terry asked.

He'd always believed that Dusty was a smooth operator in the world of public relations, swanning around in some swish office in Manchester. That's the way it came over, in the pub back in Lancashire where they met from time to time. He remembered him getting an award for some campaign or other.

"Bit of work that went decidedly pear-shaped. I put it together and it blew up in my face."

He placed an elbow on the table, and put his big, round chin on to a hand. He outlined the scenario, the unburdening done at a slow pace.

"Family firm, Bloods The Butchers. Going 70 years. Customers dying off. Profits plummeting. Grandson of owner has new ideas, none of them reflecting the old brand values. Needs expertise and is willing to pay. But then he decides he knows best..."

Sniffer was clearly listening closely and with sadistic pleasure although his eyes were blank.

"We had heated discussions, presentations where he called my ideas shit. Nitpicked over logo ideas. I gave ground on just about everything, but managed to overrule him on his crap new slogan idea. 'Meating your every need', I ask you!"

"Anyway, my boss takes me on one side later and gently reminds me that Bloods were being charged the equivalent of my annual salary for the re-launch so it had better work."

Dusty shakes his head and pushes away his plate. Terry thinks of Sheryl, and how she will take it if Dusty gets the push.

"And then... and this is what leads to the P45 I am about to receive... I let him flush seventy-odd years of brand-building down the tubes, and actually went along with him changing the firm's name."

"What to?" Terry asked.

"To Aardvark. Aardvark Meats"

Dusty now looked close to tears. Terry thought it wise to organise another round of drinks to let Dusty gather his composure but Malcolm helpfully sprang up and said: "Let me," and Dusty continued.

"Granted, the name's distinctive. Exotic even. Memorable. Yes, it would appear high in telephone listings. Yes, the logo was arresting – a classy line drawing of an aardvark."

He said that the concept even seemed to research reasonably although the budget didn't allow him to delve too deeply. But at the end of the day, he said, what no one, absolutely no one had considered was that aardvarks are animals. They themselves are meat. Snuffly meat on four legs. Badger meat.

"How did I not see that?" he said agonisingly, gently hitting his knuckles against his forehead, making his curls shake.

The aardvark proved not to sit well with the traditional Sunday topside, he said, and that soon became evident when someone in the trade sarcastically asked Justin Blood whether they still dealt in pork and beef, or did they just sell aardvark now.

Customers reacted, he said. When linked mentally with aardvark, lamb chops and braising steak seemed to turn stomachs, send customers scurrying to the supermarket for a tray of something that did not smack of an African zoo exhibit.

"It bombed. Aardvark Meats is as dead as a bit of brisket. Extinct. And now young Blood wants compensation and, I hear, my head – on a meat dish no doubt."

He held out his arms in weary resignation.

"So goodbye career, hello Job Seekers," he said pitifully, his chin trembling.

Sniffer suddenly became alert again: "Have you ever thought of telling them to bollocks?"

He took a draught of the drink Malcolm had placed before him and then smacked his lips and said: "You can keep your cocaine. You cannot beat beer. As Uncle Clarrie used to say, 'I don't care if I'm elbows out, as long as I've got the price of a pint.'"

Dusty could see that he was not going to get any sympathy from Sniffer.

"Telling them to bollocks might not be the best route to job security, Sniffer. Anyway, elbows out – what does that mean, in the curious argot of Little Holland?"

"Used to mean skint," Sniffer said. "And you know what, Dusty?"

"What?"

"There's loads of special fen words. Take water. In that book of my mother's she's written down all the words, tons of them, all the words she ever heard to describe water, and the wet ground, and bogginess, and some of the old words for different sorts of ice."

"How depressing," said Dusty. "Not much call for other adjectives I guess, back then. Not much to describe. Not much has changed, as a matter of fact."

Terry's hand tightened on his pint, his sympathy for Dusty evaporating.

"Just think – a dozen words for wetness," Sniffer said, the sarcasm lost on him.

"Bit like the eskimos," Dusty remarked. "They have loads of words for sorts of snow."

"True. True," said Sniffer. "But you know what?'

"What?"

"Eskimos are OK on snow. But you say "radiator" to them and they'll just stare. They just don't have words like condensing boiler. Don't need them, the poor little frozen buggers."

When Dusty stood up, slowly and cautiously, like a statue coming to life, to get one last round in as darkness was falling, Terry declined, and Malcolm followed suit. Best not leave the tents and bikes unattended too long, said Malcolm, in his customary cautious voice. Dusty agreed.

"Well, I'm staying for one," said Sniffer. "I'll be with you in a bit."

Terry, who was turning towards the door, froze.

"Best come with us Sniff so we can all settle down together," he said as casually as he could.

"Staying, buh."

"But Sniff...let's get a fire going and have a brew, then get some sleep.""

"Staying, buh"

Malcolm intervened. "Sniffer – Terry's just concerned you find the tents OK if the lights are off. Tell you what, Sniffer. Stay on for a bit and I'll bob back in an hour or so, and we'll get back for some shut-eye."

"Done," said Sniffer.

20

Although darkness had already fallen, Terry decided to build a fire. He wouldn't be able to sleep, he was sure, until he knew Sniffer was back safe.

Malcolm led the way across the dark meadow to the copse, wearing his head torch, and he and Terry brought back an armful of wood and, once the fire was crackling, filled the kettle. Terry had fallen asleep at the fireside, on his haunches, before the water boiled.

Dusty and Malcolm brought out the blow-up mattresses and sat in the glow of the fire, and began reviewing the day's events.

They speculated about the chances of Sniffer making it to Norwich. Terry had woken, and out of the blue, Dusty said: "I was wondering, Terry. Was your mum a bit of a leftie?"

Terry thought for a moment.

"Not really. Just somebody who got fired up about injustice. After Dad left she seems to have become more feisty."

The question was a manoeuvre that would enable him to get at an itch that he had been desperate to scratch: Sniffer's tattoo.

"I was just thinking about her anger about those aristocrats sailing round here," he said, "and wondered whether Sniffer turned into a bit of a red when he was young."

"Sniffer? No chance. Socialists care about others. What made you think that?"

"It's just the tattoo. You know. The CHE, he's got on his backside... just wondered whether he'd gone through a revolutionary phase... you know, Guevara."

"Oh, that! The CHE. Other people have wondered about that," said Terry. "A medic had thought that, when Sniffer broke his coccyx falling off an outhouse roof."

"His what?" said Dusty.

"Should have been his cock instead of his coccyx. Would have saved a lot of grief. Anyway, it happened when her husband came back," Terry continued.

"This young doctor was examining Sniff's rear end when he suddenly started talking about brave little Cuba, and put his hand to his heart. Sniff thought he'd got a screw loose."

Terry poked the fire with a stick, sending up a plume of sparks. Malcolm passed round cups of coffee and Dusty sat expectantly, like a child awaiting a treat.

"No, what happened over the tattoo was this..."

Terry described a day when Posh had travelled north for a game and he had taken a train to rendezvous with Sniffer and Mad Mick.

"Big, big mates, for years. Worked together. Mick and Sniff would have fought for each other, and did a couple of times. We met just as the pub opened and by kick-off we were a bit worse for wear. Posh lost, 3-0 I think, so we had a meal and then a few more bevvies in town to cheer ourselves up. When I went for a wee, Sniffer and Mick disappeared."

Dusty's boyish face, lit by the firelight, showed that he was hanging on every word.

"It was getting late so I searched for them and I spotted Mick in a tattoo parlour. Grubby place. The bloke looked as if he'd been a paintball target, all splashes and cobwebs."

Terry had gone in and found his brother face down on the couch being tattooed on his backside. He was snoring.

Terry continued: "I asked this tattoo chap if it was ethical to be tattooing a sleeping person but he said he was only doing what the customer ordered before he'd fallen asleep.

"Mad Mick was off his face, slurring, saying 'And don't forget the thing at the end' and the tattooist was saying 'You want a shouter? A dog's cock on the end?' and when Mad Mick said 'A what?' he said 'An exclamation mark. We call them dog's cocks. That'd be another tenner. Dog's cocks cost a tenner.'

"Mick called him a robbing bastard and said he'd rather biro it in later which would have been funny except that I realised that we were going to miss the last train."

Dusty pulled his sweater more tightly round his shoulders and moved nearer the fire. He was feeling even more outdoorsy now with the wood smoke rising into the blackness, a chill settling round them and a yarn being told over dying embers. He threw another log on the embers and the sparks flew like fireflies.

"But why did he want those letters on his bum, why CHE?" he asked.

Terry sipped his coffee and said: "He didn't. It wasn't finished when we had to leave and leg it to the station."

"But what should it have said, and why there?"

"Well, for some reason that just might have had something to do with the gallon of beer he'd drunk, I think Sniff thought – and Mad Mick agreed, of course – that a bit of reading down there would prove irresistible in the boudoir department. A novelty.

"But they'd just about run out of money so it had to be short. Sniffer was too puddled to think of anything but Mad Mick decided it would be attractive to have CHEEKY! spread across Sniffer's bum. Complete with dog's cock."

"Yes. So sexy!" Dusty said with mock-seriousness.

Can you imagine, Terry asked disdainfully, some Peterborough vamp seductively tracing the lettering with her crimson talons, then finally devouring Sniffer like a late-night kebab.

Dusty's little round face was glowing pink, his highlighted curls giving him an aura. He was wearing a real smile.

Terry said that they had run full pelt for the train, handicapped by Sniffer having to hold his trousers up.

"So in the end, Sniffer got the CHE but not the EKY. Or the dog's cock. What he also got two days later was a nasty infection on site."

Terry said that the allure of the buttock decoration had somehow passed the nurse by. She'd told Sniffer: "You silly, silly man. It looks as if your backside has eaten the last bit of the word, whatever the word was."

Dusty had so enjoyed his bedtime story. He was chuckling as he waddled off into the dark.

Terry got up with a heavy sigh and said finally: "By the way, the tattooist didn't get his money. But then we didn't get the last train home that night."

o o o o o o o

As Terry got up, Malcolm, who had been silent throughout, looked at his chunky, multi-function watch and decided he should be bringing Sniffer back to camp. He donned his head torch for the walk to the road, although the path was clearly visible in the moonlight.

Half an hour later, when the fire had been damped down and

Terry and Dusty were in their sleeping bags, they heard Sniffer talking loudly, at the turn-off from the road.

Terry pulled open the tent flat and saw that he was drunk, and weaving his way back, one shoulder held higher than the other. Whenever he stopped he rocked gently back and forth.

Rolling past the tents he mumbled "Should I strain the greens for the last time? Yes." They could hear him staggering about in the stand of trees.

"All OK?" Terry called to Malcolm, from inside the tent. "You seemed to be away quite a while."

"Took a while to find him. He was out in the dark, in the car park talking to his cousin."

"Cousin?" Terry asked, incredulously.

"Yes, lovely woman. I almost had to prise them apart when they said goodnight."

Terry and Sniffer only had two cousins, one in the navy, and one working in a bank in Minehead. Somebody had misunderstood.

"Were they close as kids, her and Sniffer? She was a bit emotional. Maybe Sniffer's illness."

All became clear when Malcolm, walking to his tent, said: "It's years since I saw one of those 2CVs, Terry. Cracking little cars. Talk about iconic…"

The Egg Woman, Terry remembered, had a 2CV.

21

All four riders had woken before seven, stirred into restlessness by the golden light of the sun hitting the orange nylon of the tents.

Dusty had groaned at every step, farting and yawning as he waded through knee high grass to relieve himself against a tree.

Malcolm was washed, shaved and primed for action. He had the camping stove going and a kettle on. Before him, on his trek towel, laid out like a picnic napkin, were his herbal tea-bags and some granary bars.

Sniffer, his wiry hair sticking out in all directions, was sitting at the tent doorway, arms wrapped round his knees, hands clasped. He had been short-tempered on waking, snapping at Dusty who responded in kind as he crept geriatrically past the entrance to Sniffer's tent.

Now Sniffer was still, silent and had a benign look on his face.

The expression said: "Now this is what I came for." He seemed to be in some mental zone focusing on a line of trees that distance had turned into grey traces against the bluish horizon.

There were a couple of fields covered with green crops but for the rest, the picture was of a vast black patchwork lit by a rising sun of improbable luminescence. The air was a clear as water.

He had enjoyed an untroubled night and for once had enjoyed his dreams, especially the one about Posh.

He'd had this one before, where he was sitting on the bench in the dressing room at London Road, in his work clothes.

It was minutes before kick-off, and the players were all stamping their boots and chewing gum and hugging each other and saying "Come on!"

The boss was talking tactics when he stopped and said: "Dear God! I've only picked ten!"

In the dream, the boss looks at his watch, sees there's two minutes to kick-off and pleads: "Sniffer. Could you give it a go? Come on – I can always pull you off. Midfield OK? Please."

In the dream it was always the same. Sniffer would reply: "Fair enough. That's where I used to slot in for the Webbed Foot. I'll get my boots from the van."

The rest was the best part. The crowd bellowing approval when the late change was announced, then Sniffer coming on just as the ref was reaching for his whistle.

Then that first touch, and the ball doing exactly what his feet demanded, deflecting off him like a bagatelle ball in a flurry of pinpoint passes, finally slicing through panicking defenders into space where Terry was waiting, Terry Bly the legendary Posh goal machine, the predator supreme.

Then the crowd was roaring again as he launched searching, curling balls into the path of the onrushing Terry who did the business with clinical precision, and then gave Sniffer the thumbs-up for the killer pass.

Within a minute, Sniffer had beaten two men, laid it off, got it back and nudged the ball on before putting it away himself, tickling it off the inside of the far post.

In the dream, after the goals, Sniffer always signalled towards the dugout, drawing his finger across his throat to tell the manager to send a sub on. As he ran to the touchline, and a standing ovation, the boss hugged him and said in his ear, "Job done, Sniffer. You've still got it."

The Telegraph headline was always the same: "SNIFFER SNUFFS OUT LEADERS."

Just as he always did, after this final scene, Sniffer went for a seemingly never-ending wee and then curled up and slept blissfully.

It had been so soothing to have pleasant things in his head for a change. Maybe the torment was going away?

22

Terry moved a few more yards from the tents and bikes to make absolutely sure that Sniffer couldn't hear him when he made a phone call.

"Sorry it's so early, Viv," said Terry. "We'll be hitting the road soon so I just wanted to touch base."

He'd found that it was unwise to think of Sniffer as someone who had lost his alertness.

Occasionally he had seemed to become distant but, all in all, there had been few worrying lapses since they set off. Terry planned to mention this improvement to Viv.

That vitamin bombardment might be working. Or maybe some of the memory loss might not have been genuine…

As Viv answered, Terry lowered himself into the deep, dew-laden grass. The wetness was balm to his tight thigh muscles.

This wild living was such a contrast, he said to himself, picturing how it would have been at home, getting ready for work – the clean shirt and nicely pressed trousers, the stress, the traffic.

"No-no-no", he said to Viv to calm her. "No Viv. Promise you. Nothing's happened."

"You'd tell me, wouldn't you Terry?" she was saying.

"God's honour," he replied. "No, he's fine. Still getting the occasional word out of place, like just now when he fell out with Dusty who's tetchy because of having boils. He shouted: 'Dusty – you're like a bloody sore with a bear arse.'"

"A what? Oh, bless him!" Viv giggled.

"But he's OK now. Looking over the fields. Peaceful."

Viv confessed to having made a second trip the day before, to see them go past.

"Sniffer would go mad if he knew. I parked in a side road where I'd spot you all coming round a bend. Malcolm came racing past the road end then must have turned and come back to join you."

"Yes, him Indian scout. Him ride ahead with bowie knife. Him make sure no paleface ambush. Him at moment pacing round like heap big greyhound waiting for trap to open."

He was pleased to hear Viv laughing.

She said: "Sniff really looked to be in the swing of it. I think he was whistling – was he whistling?

"Yea. No tune. Just whistling. Had it at my back all afternoon."

"Poor Terry. You're getting the rough end of the stick."

"No problem" he said, then, before he forgot, said: Oh, Viv. There is some more news. Bad and good. About the wee."

"Oh no. God! What?"

"The bad news is that he's been drinking it."

"Terry! Hang on. Did you say that Sniff's been drinking his own urine?"

"That brings me to the good news."

"What? What?"

"Most of it's gone, and…"

"What?….

"It's not wee!"

Terry heard Viv's intake of breath and her releasing it slowly.

"Last night, in the dark, when I thought Sniff would be well away I could just see that he'd got his pee jar open and that he was holding a flask top. He must have been able to see me watching him

132

and he said: 'A nightcap, buh? Famous Grouse.'"

"Whisky! The crafty bugger!" said Viv, for the first time in her marriage delighted to hear that Sniff was back on the hard stuff.

When Terry had finished the phone call, he returned to the huddle round the tent.

Sniff was still gazing to the far horizon; Malcolm was spraying the moving parts of the bikes – again. Dusty was unpacking food having had a tetchy exchange with Malcolm who had suggested that they forget the bacon and eggs so that they could "get a flier."

It seemed to Dusty that the word "flier" being applied to present company was like mentioning elephants in the context of needlepoint. They were not flying to their destination, he said to himself. They were limping, dragging their sore limbs.

Dusty was now dressed – in what to Terry appeared to be the sort of loose top some large women use to blur the edges sartorially.

The hem covered his shorts. The feminine effect was emphasised by the bubbly curls that he regarded as an affliction suffered since toddler times. The overall look was of a half-hearted cross-dresser.

"Hell's teeth – you'll get us arrested Dusty!" Terry shouted over the noise of the whistling kettle. "You look like an escapee from a hen night."

"I agree, buh," said Sniffer, in an early-morning croak. He looked at Dusty disapprovingly, as if it had been discovered that in the night he had done something unpleasant on the floor of the tent.

"When I first saw him in that just now, my eyes..."

"Yes, we know, Sniffer. Stood out like racing dog's balls." This was said in a sort of mardy, sing-song voice schoolgirls use to irritate each other. "Sorry, loike racing dog's balls."

Dusty explained that he'd asked Malcolm to bob into a charity shop as they'd set off from the pub, and get the biggest tee-shirt he could find.

"This is all there was. All right, it's not fashionable but it'll be cool," Dusty stated defiantly. The slogan on the front – "Fat by nature, proud by choice"– had been a concern. Dusty believed he wasn't fat fat. He took it off and put it back on inside out.

Sniffer gave him another scathing glance and said: "Just make sure you don't get the hem caught in the chain on that kid's bike of yours"

Even Malcolm was moved to speak up.

"To be truthful, Dusty, I think it would help if you pulled your shorts down a shade to show that you've got something underneath. Or the hem up a bit."

Malcolm had shaken, folded and tied up the tents into neat packages, kicked over the traces of last night's fire and, having double-checked the route on the map around his neck, pointing with his corkscrew finger, announced that they really ought to be off.

For the first time, the convoy moved smoothly, harmoniously (except for Sniffer's whistle, which, to Terry's annoyance, had returned) and with common purpose.

Malcolm was out front, the tandem with its bouncing trailer followed, and then came Dusty, his short legs going like pistons and his tee shirt billowing in the breeze which, he noted with relief, was coming side on and not into their faces.

They were moving as one. There was an unstated sense that not talking was good. The spell would not be broken if they just stayed silent and pedalled.

The sun was up and there was just one stop for a slurp of water, then the journey resumed.

As if he didn't believe his map, Malcolm hared off to check that the various ancient villages and centuries-old churches had not been spirited away. Terry's theory was that all the bad luck in his life had made him insecure, even about geography.

Malcolm returned and noted on the map that they had indeed slightly changed direction so that the wind had begun to benefit them. Confirmation came from the way Dusty's tee shirt was ballooning forward like a spinnaker.

Malcolm decided to do another recce. It would be good to ride ahead and then turn back and do battle with this wind. When he did, he resolutely refused to change into an easy gear. Instead he stood on the pedals enjoying being slapped back by the wind.

As he did, the 2CV he'd seen in the pub yard, the one that Sniffer's cousin had, passed him but he didn't have time to wave to the woman. When he was within thirty yards of the tandem and Dusty, he could hear a strange high-pitched noise. It was Terry and Sniffer and Dusty, as excited as children, shouting "Wheee!" in unison and enjoying every second of a kindly, merciful mini-fen blow at their backs.

He pulled ahead and at crossroads and saw a car moving off from a lay-by. He could have sworn it was Viv's but there was a woman at the wheel wearing sunglasses and headscarf. Not Viv's style.

But what a coincidence, he thought. First seeing the cousin in the Citroen, then, a bit later, a car just like Viv's.

23

"What in God's name was that?" Sniffer yelled into the inky darkness, falling off the edge of the blow-up mattress. "Tel! Did you hear it, Tel?"

Before Terry could lift his head and reply, the inside of the tent was lit by a flash, and then an earth-shattering rumble caused them both to sit up and put their hands to their ears.

Was it another of those dreams of hell and damnation he'd been having?

Immediately there was a deafening, sharp crack high up above the tent, and then thunder that shook the ground.

Terry crawled and opened the door flap and Sniffer joined him. Terry and Dusty had done the same, and the four kneeling figures looked out on the big, black backcloth of the sky being torn by jagged slashes of lightning that at one-second intervals illuminated the fields and flashed along the lines of watercourses.

No-one spoke. They watched spellbound as one lighting flash followed another, each sparking a reciprocal clatter of thunder.

Sniffer, wide-eyed, wondered whether it had been like this at the very beginning of time, before the Fens became the preserve of the whale, the walrus, the wolf and the bear, and before the fishermen in their coracles, centuries before those toffs did their pleasure cruise.

Sniffer's mother had held him spellbound when she talked of life evolving, over a span of time that couldn't be imagined, on what she said was like an enormous black sponge.

"Bloody hell fire!" Terry shouted, tilting back in shock, but he was barely heard above a huge, bellowing roll of thunder. Within a second another quiver of lightning shafts stuttered across the black void. At last, the volume of the thunder abated and they could hear huge drops of rain splattering the tent roofs.

The sky was an even darker blue now, although on the horizon was a tentative orangey glow from the rising sun.

"Wow!" said Dusty, with wonder in his voice. "Now that was something!"

Terry pulled back the flap of the tent so he could see round to the entrance to Dusty's tent and shouted above the sound of the cascading rain: "Just a typical fen storm, Dusty. Now you understand what it's like to really see the sky. Wouldn't have been the same in Wythenshawe now would it?"

Dusty, retreating inside, away from the now-torrential rain, shouted back grudgingly: "OK, I'll give it to you. You could have sold tickets to see that."

Dusty and Malcolm, and Terry and Sniffer settled back in the semi-dark of their tents and listened to the rain. They all found sleep impossible even though Malcolm's chronometer showed that it was only 5 50 a.m.

Terry lay back in the darkness, his head finding the rolled-up towel that was his pillow. This seemed to Terry to be a good point to tell Sniffer about Viv's phone call late last night.

"Viv rang, Sniff," Terry began, sliding back into his sleeping bag.

"She's not planning to come is she?" he said, giving Terry an interrogative look. "Better not! She knows I have to do this my way."

"No," Terry said, "she just wanted to pass on news she got in a letter to you from the hospital. Now they're thinking you've not got Korsakoff's after all. Viv says they think your funny turns might have been to do with a blood flow problem. And depression. That can affect your memory."

"But no Corset's Off...?"

"No. No Korsakoff's."

"But no word from them about the other?"

"No word. Different docs, Sniff."

"Thanks, buh," said Sniffer, softly, and they felt a brotherly bond of sadness over the main problem, the killer problem, that remained.

Terry broke the ensuing silence by asking Sniffer about the candles. Sniffer and candles. It still seemed a bizarre linkage.

When Sniffer had come out of Ely Cathedral he had hoped that his brother would have said: "That was for Mum," or "It was for Uncle Clarrie," or at least given some clue as to who the benedictions were for.

Sniffer had sensed Terry's unspoken curiosity and had said: "Look Tel. There's some things I need to say and can't, in some cases because it's too late. Ursula the chaplain gave me the idea. Penitence with certain people in mind."

"So it's stuff you're saying sorry for, Sniff?" Terry said.

Sniffer didn't reply.

Terry persisted: "Well, if it's to do with family, forget me. You never did anything to me that I need to forgive you for. Sheryl's the same, and as for Mum you never did anything nasty enough to be offering candles. You paid the price in backhanders."

"It's not you, buh."

"Granny Pud?"

"No. But she deserved a candle. A thank-you candle."

They sat silent, listening to the rain still pattering on the tent tops.

They were prisoners in the two tents but, surprisingly, suddenly there was the smell of coffee. Malcolm, wrapped in a cocoon of green waterproof, appeared at the tent door with mugs.

"Room for a little one?" he said, limbo-ing his gangly frame into the tent. "I've left Dusty in ours. He wants to make a private call."

They sat in silence, sipping, gratefully breathing in the steam from the coffee, enjoying the percussive pitter-patter three feet above their heads.

They could hear Dusty's whispered call to his wife, every embarrassing word, but couldn't think immediately of things to say to muffle the flow of endearments.

"Sorry babes! I thought you'd be up," he was saying under his breath. "Oh, is it only that time? Oh hell. Sorry, sweetpea."

Sheryl seemed then to be describing a dream ("a nice one I hope") he had just ruined by ringing, an hour before she needed to get up.

Dusty seemed very interested in the dream. He kept saying "Oh…" and then finally: "Cor! Steady girl! Could you see his face? Was it me?"

After a short silence there was another "Oh," a disappointed one. And then, clearly miffed: "Sounds as if he looked a bit like Goldenballs. That new bloke at work you say is a bit Spanish-looking."

If it hadn't been raining, Terry, Sniffer and Malcolm would have taken a walk. It was excruciating to be party to such intimacies.

"Well, you'd better brace yourself when I get back, babes," Dusty was saying. "Bit of a crisis with my chest but it turned out to be my shirt. Malcolm had to cut it off."

They could just hear a squeal of laugher from Sheryl.

"Not that, you saucy cat! My shirt! No, that's still there all right. Actually I'm fit as a lop, and the belly's going. So get yourself ready... for... the... lurve machine!"

He then threw in a line from some old blues song, for good measure: "Yea, mamma, you betta keep dat skillet good and greased..."

The three listeners winced in unison. Then Sniffer opened his mouth wide and waggled a forefinger in his open mouth feigning an attempt to make himself sick.

They would all have agreed, if they'd been free to talk, that Dusty then rather shattered the erotic idyll.

"Yea, babes. Got a whole crop of them just under my you-know-whats. Agony biking, so I stand to ride. Some of them have burst already, so I should be OK."

Terry said under his breath: "The last of the Great Romantics... bath time, baby oil, soft music...and half-healed boils..."

Malcolm maintained discreet non-involvement. Terry allowed himself a chuckle which he suppressed with his hand when Dusty signed off with "And you sweetpea. Yes. Will do. Kiss-kiss."

Moments later Dusty appeared at the tent door with an anorak on his head and the three shuffled to accommodate his chunky little frame.

"Did you get through?" asked Malcolm.

Such decency, Terry noted; Malcolm pretending that Dusty's squishy bedroom talk had not been overheard, something Dusty might have eventually suspected – to his abject horror – once he'd climbed down from his fluffy cloud.

"Hang on – it's stopped!" Malcolm said, throwing open the tent flaps.

They were all glad to ease their aching bodies out of the overcrowded, steamy tent and to breath the clean, fresh air ushered in on the tail of the storm. Already the sun was burning the rain droplets from the grass.

They all trooped off to the copse to relieve themselves and as they returned to the tent Sniffer began bemoaning the fact that this morning there would be no fire, no al fresco breakfast. Then, looking back, he took heart when he turned to see Malcolm following with an armful of sticks and a few logs.

"They'll be sopping wet, matey!" said Sniffer. "It'll be tea and hardtack this morning."

"No - dry as tinder," Malcolm replied. "Old outdoorsman's trick. I smelled rain last night so I put a few under cover."

By the time they were dressed, the fire had subsided into glowing ash and Dusty was tending a frying pan of sausages that were hissing and spitting and smelling inviting. Malcolm had cutlery and a bottle of sauce ready, and, for himself, cereal bars and a yoghurt bought last night on his way to guide Sniffer back from the pub.

No one seemed keen to get on the road - except Malcolm. He expertly de-camped and packed the panniers and trailer while the rest reclined on their elbows like Romans at a feast.

"No rush," Terry said drowsily. "King's Lynn won't take us long. Pint in Downham Market on the way."

Terry was doing something unnecessary with his bike and looking at the big watch from time to time. He was dying to do the last of the packing.

Once the tents were stowed, Dusty, Terry and Sniffer sat on the air beds to enjoy a few more moments of fresh air and warmth. There was an unspoken conspiracy to see how long Malcolm could last before begging them to let him deflate and pack them.

Sniffer was reading his mother's exercise book that he had kept in a plastic bag. It was by him each night for safekeeping. He had extended a similar security measure to what had been thought to be his wee bottle but which was his rapidly depleting reservoir of whisky.

"What about this, boys..." Sniffer said, flicking over a page.

"Mum says here that Great Aunt Nancy told the story of a village lad who'd been caught pinching. The beaks ordered him to go to Kings Lynn jail to get his twelve lashes. They gave him a note saying what the punishment was to be and sent him packing.

"Anyway, she says that when he got to Kings Lynn he started to pretend to rush about, and went up to an ol' boy of about his age and said: 'Do us a favour. Drop this note off at the jail when you pass will you? I'm late. Got to gallop.' You can imagine what happened to the poor messenger..."

Terry said: "The crafty little bugger!"

"I can't talk," said Sniffer, seriously. "Done much worse in my time and dropped people in it."

Malcolm, still restless, had turned his bike upside down and was spinning the back wheel, fiddling with the gears and appearing to marvel at the seamless flipping from cog to cog.

For no reason he understood, but possibly because he'd been looking back on past misdeeds and regretting, Sniffer thought he'd be nice to Dusty.

"How's the boils today, buh?" he asked as warmly as he could manage.

"Bit easier today, thanks Sniffer. Main problem is my calves. It's all that riding standing up. The muscles are like piano wires."

It was then that - again, for reasons he didn't understand - Sniffer thought of his mother, of the smell of the soap on her hands as she stitched the top button on his shirt that he'd already put on for school.

"Did Mum like me, do you think, Tel? She never seemed to have a minute for me, just for me," he said, as Dusty rose with difficulty to seek Malcolm's help in finding the Loosener.

"Course she did, Sniff! She wasn't one to show it. She'd had it hard."

Terry noticed a passing car and recognised it as Viv's. It was creeping along, being driven by Sheryl, who had her jacket collar up. Viv had sunglasses and a headscarf on and she was craning her neck to see Sniffer.

Terry directed his eyes straight at Sniffer in case he began to look round.

"The other thing I wonder about, Tel, was the Yanks."

"Yanks?"

"I wonder if she was a bit too friendly with them. She seemed to know a hell of a lot about Milwaukie, and where all the States were – and do you remember that she used to say 'so long' instead of goodbye."

"What you saying, Sniff?"

"Nothing really."

"Can't remember her bringing any American airman home but I know she used to go to dances sometimes on some Yankee camp, when Granny Pud came to stay, and she used to smoke American cigs," Terry said. "It was a long time ago, Sniff, so best forgotten."

"You start to think about things, Tel. You know..."

"I can imagine, Sniff."

Eventually Sniffer said: "Looking back, perhaps a bit of a cold fish wouldn't you say, buh?"

Terry didn't answer.

He had no complaint, felt no sense that he'd been starved of love, something that Sniffer obviously felt. And he did have faint memories of Sniffer being slapped and of his mother's fury when he first began to get into trouble. He remembered the terrible fuss over the coin that Sniff said the next door's boy had pinched. It was as if that incident had branded Sniff, put him beyond forgiveness.

Dusty returned to the fireside, his tube of Loosener at the ready. Even though he was still walking gingerly, when Malcolm pulled out the plugs to let the airbeds deflate, he trod on them, stiff-legged like a vineyard grape-squasher, to enjoy the escaping air making farting noises.

Malcolm looked disapproving and hurriedly folded the tents neatly and stowed them.

The quartet lined up at the roadside,

"Right, first stop Downham Market for a beer and a bite, and on to Lynn for the evening," Terry said, with a nod to Malcolm, as he hung in the air, poised, as if he was in a slow-bicycle race.

Dusty held up a hand. "One moment, gentlemen. I'll be sorted in a trice," he said taking the tube of Loosener from his pocket.

"Where are you going to put that on?" asked Terry, who was already astride the tandem.

"My nether regions of course," Dusty snorted.

"No," Terry replied, irritated. "Where exactly do you propose to retreat to, so that we're spared the gruesome sight of you self-medicating?"

Dusty sighed, lay down his bike and squeezed the ancient tube until a long bead of off-white ointment lay on his hand.

"I was kidding. I wouldn't get this stuff anywhere sensitive. It's for the legs. The calves have seized up."

He moved the crumpled tube around until he could read the indistinct print on the side and said: "Got the same stuff you get in chilli peppers, and wintergreen, plus a 'secret ingredient'. Intriguing..."

He rubbed his hands together then massaged the back of his calves, reaching them with some difficulty and panting as he did so.

"Look how red it's made my hands! Liquid fire." He slid the tube into the pocket of his copious shorts.

"Now... let us proceed. Allez!" he announced with mock formality and, standing on the pedals of the little bike, riding along in Malcolm's wake, bobbing up and down like a clockwork toy.

Malcolm, silently circling, waved a pack of baby wipes in Dusty's direction but with his calves rejuvenated, his eyes were set unerringly on the distant horizon.

24

The bikers had taken to having what Terry called bladder checks but which Dusty had insisted on calling PPP, or Periodic Pee Polls. At intervals, as they rode, Terry would ask whether anyone wanted a comfort stop. If two hands or more went up, a break was taken.

And so it was that twenty minutes into the ride to Downham Market, Terry announced a vote and all but Malcolm needed relief. They retreated behind a dense hedge, although there was little traffic and so little risk of being seen.

However, immediately a car approached (Terry saw that it was his) as they emerged. At precisely the same moment Dusty let out a long, high-pitched cry and folded in on himself, sinking onto the tarmac.

Malcolm, waiting astride his bike, rushed to where Dusty lay in a foetal position and, with Dusty's wail deafening him, sank to his knees and expertly checked for signs of a heart attack. From the start he'd had Dusty down as a prime candidate – unfit, fat in the wrong place. Stressed. All that Aardvark business.

"Dusty! Can you hear me Dusty? Is it chest pains? Tell me. Pain in your arm?" Malcolm demanded clinically. "Is it like a vice tightening?"

"Nooo!" Dusty squealed and then gasped breathlessly: "Loosener. Nadgers."

"Nadgers?" said Malcolm, calmly, so as not to increase the patient's alarm.

"Family jewels…fruit and two veg," said Terry, translating, and looking on dispassionately, as if he felt Dusty had had this coming. "He's just got some ointment on himself."

Terry noticed that the car had passed them and turned back, and was now creeping past again. Although Sheryl was wearing big sunglasses, he discerned terror in her face as she glimpsed Malcolm debagging Dusty, who was pleading pathetically "Watch my bloody boils!"

While Dusty lay whimpering, the car passed at snail's pace yet again. Viv and Sheryl were treated to the sight of Malcolm holding a wet trek towel to Dusty's lower regions, and Dusty - his red palms raised above his head - lying on his back and wearing what might have been interpreted as religious ecstasy, the whites of his eyes showing more than they should.

Sniffer, meanwhile, had wandered out of earshot. He was lying on a grassy patch beside the road trying to appear as if he was dozing but was clearly whispering into his phone.

Terry wanted to investigate but his own phone throbbed in the pocket of his shorts. He stepped onto the fringe of a field to answer.

"Tel? We've just been past. We saw… it," Sheryl said in a quivery voice.

"I know, I saw you. You know, Sniffer's going to spot you one day…"

"Sod Sniffer," she said sharply. "Look. I know I promised not to fuss but I have to know: What the hell's was going on between Dusty and Malcolm?"

Terry felt too weary to respond. They had some miles to catch up. They all needed that promised pint in Downham Market (it would be Elgoods, or Bateman's, tastes from his past).

They had to reach Lynn before the light went. They all seemed to need something from him, and he had not much more to give.

"Look, Sis. I'll explain later," he said flatly.

"But Tel…" she protested.

"Look, Sheryl," Terry said, firmly now, "all I can say is that it's not what it seemed."

25

Malcolm returned from his sortie and said: "Just over four miles. The Mallard's on the left going into town."

Sniffer knew that, of course. It was the pub he'd picked when they had discussed watering holes. He'd once done a big rendering job in Downham.

Dusty had declared himself unfit to ride, and - soothed by calamine lotion - so as not to delay the party had set off as soon as he had felt comfortable enough. They could see him now, rounding a corner, walking like a frozen-stiff polar explorer in an archive film.

But Terry was troubled about Sniffer whose face had gone a funny colour and who was stretching back from time to time as if he was trying to ease a pain.

About a mile into the journey, Terry began to feel he was travelling uphill but the landscape told him otherwise. He looked down and it was clear that Sniffer's feet had become dead weights. Not only that, his breathing was laboured.

"Sorry, buh. I'm running on empty," he said.

"Want to stop?"

"No, I'll make the Mallard."

Moments later, Sniffer said, very casually, "I'm going buh" and, as if in slow motion, toppled onto the roadside bank. Terry was alarmed at the sound he was making but was relieved to see that his brother was laughing.

Within seconds, Malcolm was demonstrating his best bikeside

manner, offering water and checking that Sniffer had taken his medication that morning.

Suddenly, the peace was shattered by the sound of a klaxon, then the deep harrumph of a powerful engine and the scrape of tyres locked by severe braking.

Sniffer's face lit up with unalloyed pleasure at the sight of the Dodge Ramcharger with its flaking paint, blistering chrome, body raised on huge wheels, its elephantine presence.

"Well, I'll be...!" he exclaimed as Mick tumbled out of the cab, followed by Pat – tight-lipped and anxious – and the two solemn kids, dressed in clothes that were a shade too small for them.

"You old bastard!" Mick shouted, nudging back his sunglasses and resting them on his baseball cap worn trendily with the peak at the back...

His flashing smile seemed to die as he looked more closely at Sniffer.

"Been in the wars me old mate?" he asked, moving within inches of his face, as if Sniffer were deaf or retarded.

"Just a funny turn, buh. I'll pull round when we get to Downham."

"No. Biking's over," Mick instructed. "You're coming in the Dodge for a bit," he said, lifting Sniffer up as if he were a bag of cement, and staggering with him towards the cab.

"Put me down you silly tart!" Sniffer said, protesting and then laughing helplessly.

With Sniffer installed, Mick walked to the back of the Dodge where Terry waited to talk about the future of the ride, and the dilemma over Sniffer. Dusty could not be consulted – he was a small roundish shape in the distance and Malcolm was off somewhere trying to burn off energy.

Pat skulked about and the children walked around sullenly, nudging each other from time to time.

It was decided that Mick would drive to the Mallard, despite Sniffer's protests that having a lift was cheating. They would call for medical help if Sniffer's condition warranted it but since Mick's arrival he seemed over the crisis, looking forward to Kings Lynn and seeing Clench again.

If Sniffer insisted on another night's camping and was unwell during the night, Viv would be summoned to pick him up in the morning. But the sentimental call at Clenchwarton – the only reason for heading to Kings Lynn – was in doubt as they were slipping behind schedule.

As it was, Sniffer's immediate objective was to survive the short run to the Mallard, given Mick's driving style. His technique was to let the Dodge go where it chose, and then correct its path with the palm of one hand on the steering wheel.

Every so often Pat was thrown against Sniffer's shoulder and he noticed that when this happened she recoiled to show that she found him repulsive. She scowled. As he had said to Viv, Pat sometimes looked like a camel trying to digest a roll of barbed wire. Viv had replied that she had good reason to be miserable, that the poor woman was permanently on tablets and that he should be more sympathetic.

Sniffer was sympathetic at this moment – sorry for the children who were being bounced around in the open back. They had climbed in protesting that the dried concrete always scratched them. Their protests did not even merit a glance from Mick or Pat.

Sniffer had noticed that the Dodge was looking more bashed about than ever. The scarred bodywork told tales of Mick's love of speed and carefree steering. But Pat, who was said by Sniffer to drive as if her arse was on fire, had been responsible for some of the deeper scratches. The beast tended to run away with her.

Once, she had just managed to stop within an inch of the back wall of the garage, or rather the crumbling old outhouse they called a garage. She was as relieved at managing to pull up, as Mick was foot-stampingly mad that she'd not opened the garage door first. They had argued bitterly with the splintered wood surrounding them.

Disregarding the road, Mick turned to face Sniffer and shouted above the roar of the engine, and the wind whistling in from the open windows: "Look buh, you've done your bit! If I was you I'd get off home now and rest up!"

"No Mick. I'm doing it."

"It'll kill you matey!"

"Could do."

"Well, you're a stubborn old twot"

Mick swung the Dodge on to the gravel drive alongside the Mallard beer garden that teemed with parents and children revelling in the unseasonal sunshine…

They took the picnic table of a family who were just leaving.

Mick was concerned when Sniffer didn't seem to be able to lift his leg over to sit on the bench; he took the knee and eased him on to the seat. Sniffer slumped forward on his elbows, breathing heavily.

Pat and the children stood impassively beside the table as Mick struck it with his fist and announced: "That decides it Sniffer. You look bloody terrible. You have three choices. We get you home and I finish the ride for you. Or you carry on, hold everybody up and ruin the whole bloody thing, scare Viv and let your sponsors down."

"You said there was another option."

"Option three is that if you don't take option one I beat the living shit out of you. Now, are you having a drink?"

"Just water."

"Water? Never known you go to a pub and ask for water."

"Well just a pint. Bitter."

Mick ran his hands over his pockets and then asked whether Sniffer had any money. Sniffer burrowed in his shorts and passed on a note, and then another, as he knew the kids would want crisps.

While Mick went to the bar Sniffer took the opportunity to make a call on his mobile. As Mick returned, Malcolm arrived, then Terry, and Pat and the children moved off to sit on the grass and make way round the table for the riders.

Mick had gargled down his drink before the riders had settled and gratefully accepted Terry's offer of another "and maybe a bowl or two of chips. And some for the kids I suppose."

Eventually, Sniffer took a sip of beer and then pushed it away with a look of distaste. Mick, whose glass was empty once again, said: "Don't fancy it mate? I might as well finish it."

Terry was studying Sniffer's face. He was not responding to the banter around the table, or even enjoying Mick's tales that took the form of an affectionate revisiting of highlights from a long and incident-filled friendship.

Terry was highly amused and even Malcolm looked entertained.

When, to laughter, Mick described the time his new fancy mobile phone fell from his pocket into the cement mixer, and how weeks later, a couple reported hearing strange noises coming from under their path, Sniffer's face remained a mask.

Mick followed up with the story of a riotous "male only" trip to Spain. He grasped Sniffer's shoulders and said affectionately: "That was when you went round with a tray on the flight home asking people for a few bob for the driver."

Sniffer managed a token smile and then, with difficulty, extricated his legs from the bench and excused himself – "Just going to strain the greens."

As he reached the pub door, he paused for breath. A sousaphone struck up somewhere in the car park and a party of Molly Dancers – faces painted in patterns of black and white, clothes a monochrome riot – made their way into the crowded beer garden stopping children in their tracks.

As Sniffer went into the pub, a tall man, blacked up and dressed like a draughts board, shouted above the din: "We are Hog Mire Morris. And we're proud to be weird!" and, while the audience applauded, the dancers fell into formation and began to weave patterns to the sweet sound of a squeezebox.

The toe-tapping music was punctuated by squeals from children as a huge wooden zebra's head – carried by a dancer swathed in black material - swooped down on them, its jaw snapping together viciously.

Dusty finally made an appearance, trooping through the crowd, looking as if he was about to faint. Space was made at the table and he flopped on to the seat with a gasp of exhaustion. He seemed to be supporting himself on one buttock and then the other as if to try to be at least half comfortable.

Terry fetched him a pint, forcing his way through the crowds watching what the leader had announced as the Broom Dance. Dusty sank half his drink without a pause and then sat sullen and downcast, seemingly oblivious to the melody and merriment.

"Are that lot from the olden days when everything was in black and white?" he asked glumly.

"What is it, Dusty?" Terry said.

"Call from Sheryl. Boss says I was to make sure to keep my diary free for Tuesday. Aadvark meeting. The big one."

Dusty's glass was empty. Malcolm caught Dusty's mood and said kindly: "Manage another?" Mick overheard and said "OK, but this has to be the last. I'm driving."

"Tell you something Dusty," Terry said. "There is life after Aardvark. Sniffer's right. Tell them all to go and take a running jump and start again somewhere. I want this to be your mantra: 'Go bollocks. There is life after Aardvark.'"

"Yeah, right," said Dusty, far from convinced.

"Say it!" Terry commanded, as Malcolm returned with beers.

"Go bollocks. There is life after Aardvark," he said robotically. "...There is life after Aardvark."

Malcolm looked on with curiosity but decided not to ask about what seemed to have turned into a counselling session.

Dusty mustered a brighter expression and said to Terry: "And how's Sniffer?"

Sniffer.

Sniffer!

"You do the outside, I'll look for him inside," said Malcolm, anxious to spare Terry the possible discovery of Sniffer dead in a toilet cubicle, or collapsed in some dark corner.

Terry slid through the clumps of people watching the dancing, scanning faces, searching as systematically as he could in the crowd. As he reached the pub door, Malcolm emerged giving the thumbs up.

"He's in there, back bar. Right as rain.'

"Thank God," said Terry.

"Amazing. That cousin of his has turned up again so they've been having a proper chinwag. She's a bit emotional but so supportive."

A moment later, Sniffer followed sheepishly and as he came out of the pub door, the man with the zebra head stealthily lowered it within inches of Sniffer's ear and made its jaws slam together with a loud crack.

Sniffer could hear the man laughing manically under the black cloth cloaking him. The laugh and the zebra's huge staring eyes frightened him and he moved away as quickly as he could towards Terry.

"Ah, you've decided to join us Sniff. Sorry to cut short your chat with our cousin," Terry said sarcastically.

Sniffer looked nervously around him, fearing that the zebra head might approach again, and replied humbly: "She just happened to be in there."

"You know Sniff, that tale is like the gravy Jess makes," Terry said coldly. "You can see right through it."

∘ ∘ ∘ ∘ ∘ ∘ ∘

As Lydia was driving back, desolate, to the children and the hens, Viv was having a long, hot bath. She planned to get an early night and be ready to drive to pick up Sniffer if he was no better in the morning.

Terry rang when they got to Kings Lynn and said Sniffer was in good form, insisting on having a fire so they could have fried egg sandwiches before bed.

Having had a glass of wine, Viv took the rest of the bottle and sat it between the taps. She had brought up her magazine but couldn't concentrate. She poured more wine, took a recklessly big slurp, and began to sing odd verses from all the musicals she had been in.

She stopped when she recalled the sight of Sniffer sitting at the roadside, stooped, broken, weak, and probably scared.

She told God that if he spared Sniffer she would promise never, ever to sing another note, and meant it.

Meanwhile, Lydia had reached home and was out in the cool night under a canopy of stars settling the hens for the night, staying out of the way of the kids and the television for a few minutes, thinking of the desperate conversation with Sniffer in the pub and wondering whether that was the last time they would see each other.

○ ○ ○ ○ ○ ○ ○

For the first time during the ride the weather had fallen in line with what the met. people deemed "normal for the time of year."

The high pressure that had blessed the riders with days of unseasonal sunshine gave way - quite suddenly in the early evening - to bracing winds and ominous, scudding clouds.

Leaves tumbled across the camping site which was in a dip alongside a minor rural road in the lee of young trees that swayed like dancers in silhouette.

For Terry, rummaging in the half-dark for the sausages, bought as they left Downham, there seemed to be something symbolic in the disappearance of sunshine and the newly arrived chill in the air. Sniffer especially seemed to be feeling the cold.

They settled for what they knew would be their last night camping together. They wore every item of clothes they had brought but Sniffer was still shivering. Terry arrived at the fireside with the frying pan and took off his own fleece slid it round his brother's shoulders.

Malcolm got a fire going but it was wayward in the crosswind, the flames for the most part missing the bottom of the kettle, the dry branches crackling as they were consumed. Ingeniously

Malcolm propped up a blow-up mattress as windbreaks and, just as the last of the light was going, they sat hunched in the firelight, sipping coffee and listening as the eggs dropped hissing into the hot fat in the frying pan.

The ride would soon be over, quite quickly if Sniffer went home tomorrow and they could burn up the miles and take few breaks. And once the ride was over, Terry knew he had to prepare himself for the stark fact of Sniffer's condition, the finality of it.

Sniffer was silent and had been since they left Downham. Terry could not work out whether he was still feeling ill or whether it was a matter of the heart.

If asked to bet, he would have put his money on it being to do with the Egg Woman, or whatever her real name was.

26

At first, Terry thought the sound had been made by an owl and tried to get off to sleep again. But the noise - a rising and falling wail - was clearly not from a bird.

Terry zipped down his sleeping bag and rested on his elbow, and listened. The sound had subsided into a low, continuous keening, the sound a child made when it had cried so much it could cry no more.

He was about to check whether the noise had woken Sniffer when he saw that his sleeping bag was empty and that the inner surfaces were cold.

Terry wrapped his sleeping bag round his shoulders and slid out of the tent. He could hear the sound clearer now and as he went towards it, he could just make out a black shape. It was Sniffer, on his haunches, with his back to a fence, his arms wrapped round his body as if hugging himself.

"Sniff," Terry said. "What is it?"

When Sniffer began to reply his words were juddery, his teeth chattering. Terry wrapped the sleeping bag round him, so that only his face was visible.

"The zebra. It was in the tent. It came for me."

"The zebra, Sniff? What zebra?"

"The one that the dancers had, bloody great head, the one that can bite you. I had to run."

Terry pulled Sniffer to his feet and slowly led him towards the tent.

155

"It was a nightmare, Sniff! There's absolutely nothing in the tent – I'll show you." Terry went inside and felt round for the torch. "Look, all clear! A zebra free zone. Now let's see if we can get a bit more rest," he said, directing the torch beam inside the tent.

Terry zipped Sniffer up in his bag and said: "Sleep! Back in a minute."

He went out with his phone and the torch and texted Viv, asking her to pick Sniffer up early next day but not to worry, there was no emergency. He sent another message asking Mick to come first thing with his bike so that they could finish the ride, and asking Pat whether she would mind taking a candle to Clench church and lighting it, once she had dropped Mick off.

Terry tried to sleep but the noises Sniffer was making kept him alert and anxious. His breathing seemed shallow and occasionally he would fight for air for a few seconds before settling again.

As the first light filtered into the tent, Terry woke to see that Sniffer had propped himself up against a pannier. He was sitting there awake but not moving.

"Breathing Tel," he said.

When Terry sat up he could see Sniffer's chest rising and falling and could hear an asthmatic wheeze. The darkness of his chin was now stubble, black but peppered with grey. He noted that in the twilight his skin appeared to have tightened, on his cheek bones, at his temples. Terry was afraid to look at him a second time.

"It's home time, Sniff."

"Yea, buh."

"Viv'll come for you. We'll finish it. Mick will do your bit."

Terry was up and going out to look for the kettle, and to find Sniffer's medication.

"I'll tell Mick that you like a bit of whistling behind you," Sniffer said breathlessly.

He seemed to be struggling to smile. His voice had changed. It sounded weak but lighter just like it had when he was young.

27

Sniffer began to shiver again and Terry wrapped his own sleeping bag round him, on top of Sniffer's own and gave him hot coffee, then water to help his tablets down.

The cold wind had not relented and the fen sky was now an enormous grey watercolour wash.

Although it was only just fully light, Malcolm was up and about, fully dressed, restless. He looked in on Sniffer, kneeling at the tent opening and said: "Sorry to hear you're no better. But you're doing the right thing. Trust us to finish it for you."

Sniffer liked Malcolm. So dour. Odd, sad man but one you'd want on your side. Lot of time for other people. Sound bloke, a man you could count on, just like Mick.

As if at the mention of his name, there was a huge roar of an accelerator being over-gunned and Sniffer knew that Mick was here. He didn't have the energy to get up but he could hear Mick now rattling away, giving Malcolm the history of the Dodge Ramcharger, how he got it for £400 from a technical sergeant at Lakenheath before he was posted back to the States.

"Real brute," he said, "V8, 5.2. He'd had a lot of stuff done."

Mick was so proud of that dirty great tank, Sniffer mused, and then thought of one of his mother's favourite sayings: "The bigger the car, the skinter they are." That was certainly right in Mick's case.

Dusty appeared at the tent entrance with another mug of tea. He looked concerned, conciliatory.

"Now then, how are you today Sniffer?" he asked.

"About the same. Fair to crap."

"Mick's here, and Viv's on her way."

As he left the tent, Dusty stopped and said: "We'll finish it for you Sniffer, you'll see, and we'll get back in time to take you to Posh."

His obvious sincerity took Sniffer by surprise. He managed a small smile and then gave Dusty the thumbs up because he wasn't sure how to pitch his voice so that it didn't sound too faltering, or too friendly.

When Sniffer finally left the tent, he could see that the ride, his ride, was already starting to move on, leaving him behind. There was an air of urgency, busyness, and he was just a spectator.

Mick - in new lycra shorts and sporting cycle gloves - came up and crushed Sniffer's shoulders painfully in greeting. Malcolm already had the bikes lined up, and had damped down the fire, offering only cereal and milk for breakfast.

If there was one morning when Sniffer had needed something hot it was today. Terry had a fleece on and Malcolm wore an all-weather top so they were feeling the cold too.

"Need a quick getaway today, Sniffer," he said, stepping off briskly to pack the panniers and the trailer.

Pat, meanwhile, was in the driving seat of the Dodge looking out balefully, avoiding eye contact with Sniffer.

Sniffer saw that Dusty was already on his bike and with a wave set off to get ahead of the rest.

Terry approached with water and Sniffer's tablets. He seemed pressured too.

"Viv'll be here in a minute, Sniff, and we'll be getting off. Mick's finally got Pat to agree to take your candle to the church in Clench and light it before heading back." They looked towards the cab and Pat wiped the condensation from the window, gave them a sour look and turned away.

"Viv knows the score. We're going to go all out to do the fifty miles or so to Norwich by tonight, then have a kip, go to the

Cathedral in the morning with the candle, and then Jess will come in the 4X4 to make sure we to get you to Posh tomorrow afternoon."

Sniffer was bewildered by the air of urgency and knew he must have cut a rather pitiful figure standing there wrapped in sleeping bags while all around him was such frantic activity. He could see that they'd piled his clothes and other possessions together for Viv to take with her.

He thought of that message they put on luggage: "Not wanted on voyage."

Terry added the two tents and other gear to the pile. So they were taking the soft option tonight, a b and b. He was glad not to be part of that.

He patted the pile to make a seat for Sniffer but before he could sit down, Viv was swinging the van on to the grassy camping site.

She hurried out and towards Sniffer and pulled his head to her shoulder where he let it rest.

She didn't say he'd been a fool, that he'd overdone it, that it had been a crazy venture but she wanted to. She just said: "Well done Sniff. I'm so proud of you."

Viv eased him into the front of the van where there was a pillow, a bottle of water, and a blanket. She tucked the pillow under his head and went to speak with Terry who was already on the tandem with Mick behind him, laughing like an excited child.

"See you tomorrow, if all goes well. The big charity cheque has come by the way. All we have to do is fill in a rough figure. Sniffer says good luck."

But Sniffer hadn't been able to bring himself to respond, especially as in their rush they'd made him feel redundant. He had to admit to himself that he was ready for home, and his bed, with the radio playing and Viv sitting around, reading bits of stuff from the Telegraph out to him.

Mad Mick, with his muscle and his freshness, was a powerhouse once the riders got into their stride, heading for Fakenham before turning down towards Norwich.

For the first time, the tandem wheels actually whirred, and Terry felt Mick's driving legs carry his own forward.

They passed Dusty about five miles into the ride, near Little Messingham and shouted that they'd wait in Fakenham for him to catch up.

"Malcolm will let you know where we are!" Terry said, over his shoulder, as Mick drove the tandem on. He was like a man possessed; Terry knew that his frantic effort was some sort of tribute to Sniffer, fulfilling a pledge to finish the thing in style.

They had reached Fakenham, enjoyed coffee and doughnuts and, feeling that time was evaporating, had sent Malcolm off to tell Dusty to just do it at his own pace, that they had to push on and that they'd keep monitoring his progress.

It was only when they took a break to enjoy for a minute the beauty of Bawdeswell, and to shop for pasties, and chocolate and other calorific foods, and sat in their fleeces feeling the cold sweat on their backs that they remembered Dusty.

Malcolm calculated that he must be in Fakenham by now, hopefully sparing the time for a coffee. He would head back and keep him, company for a time, urge him on.

But as the others set off to complete the last 15 miles to Norwich, and Malcolm reached the edge of Fakenham, there was no sign of Dusty. And, more worryingly, no sign of him on the main road through. Malcolm decided that despite the time and effort involved he must search the road that had led into town.

Dusty meanwhile, his eyes stinging with sweat and his calves crying for rest, was thrashing his way towards the coast, to Cromer, leaving Little Snoring – and going in entirely the wrong direction. He only grew suspicious when he saw a mention of Sheringham and knew it was coastal, nowhere in the Norwich direction. His first instinct was to sit and cry. His second was to panic. His third was to reach for his phone but discounted this when he could not find it in his pockets; he guessed that he had sent it away with other stuff, with Viv.

The only real option was to head back to Fakenham, after a fear-induced emergency visit to relieve himself in some roadside scrub.

Malcolm stopped to look at his pendant map when he had gone five miles back towards Kings Lynn. Not a sign of Dusty. Mystifying – and concerning, especially considering his lack of fitness. He decided to return to Fakenham and then put a spurt on and catch the others up as they approached Norwich.

"This could be a police job," he said to himself, feeling sorry for Dusty but at the same time enjoying covering all those miles and having a bit of a mystery on his hands.

By late afternoon, Terry and Mick were five miles from Norwich city centre, sitting on a bench at a bus stop in Taverham waiting for news of the two missing riders.

Terry was relieved when Malcolm final came into view and delighted to see that he appeared to be tired, the first sign that he was not bionic man on a bike. Malcolm edged onto the bench, looking frazzled.

"How's he doing?" Terry asked, suddenly concerned that maybe today's leg, the longest of the ride, had been just too much for Dusty.

"Don't know. He's disappeared. Retraced the ride all the way back beyond Fakenham to a few miles before we turned off. Not a sign of him."

"Maybe he was in a hedge somewhere having a...dealing with a call of nature," said Mick, a suggestion Malcolm found a trifle insulting as he had his scouting Observation badge.

Mick volunteered to get on the tandem and go back on another search, for a "proper look," another suggestion that Malcolm did not take well. His head went up with what Terry saw as hurt pride.

Terry asserted himself. "There must be a police station here. Could be serious. Dusty's a missing person. They could cruise around to check he's not in trouble."

It was at this point that the X29 bus from Fakenham to Norwich pulled in and they saw a round face encircled with curls at the window. The bus edged away and then they saw Dusty jump from his seat and hold up his arm to the driver who braked and with ill-disguised irritation opened the bus door to deposit the missing man on the pavement.

There was so much to ask, and Dusty had so much to say but they were all silent as Malcolm pointed to a café and they trooped towards it.

"So..." Terry began.

Dusty spoke as if traumatised, holding his milk shake next to his bottom lip, staring into space.

"Must have overshot at Fakenham. Absolutely ball-achingly knackered. On the way to shitting Cromer. Turned back. Stranded. No phone. Got to Fakenham. Started down the right road, then thought: I am dying."

Dusty sipped the milkshake as if it was nectar and then resumed his tale in an unearthly drone, as if suffering flashbacks while in a trance.

"Walked along the main road for a while until I thought I'd pass out...starving, no water..."

"Sorry Dusty. Walking? Was it bum trouble? Where's the bike?"

"The bike...? Wensum."

"When some...what?

"The river. The sign said it was the River Wensum."

"How did it get in the Wensum?"

"I threw it in."

"Oh."

"It felt so good. Bloody bliss to get rid of the bastard thing."

Malcolm chipped in. "That's when I must have missed you, you'd be down at the river."

The café seemed to serve as a focal point for the community. Posters and business cards were pinned to a notice board and Terry was encouraged to ask the owner if she knew of a bed and breakfast near the city centre.

She did, she rang ahead, and summoned a taxi for Dusty who,

half an hour later was luxuriating in a foam bath. By the time he dressed and came down to the lounge, the riders had arrived and were planning a celebration curry.

"And a bit of a drink," Mick had added when the idea of a meal was suggested, having checked that someone could "help him out money-wise."

At breakfast next day, Terry was to remember these phrases and file them in his mind as joint understatements of the year.

Mick, who had set heroic standards at the bar the previous night and kept the restaurant waiters busy topping his glass up, showed no signs of having a hangover. But Terry noticed that suddenly he looked downcast once he'd finished his Full English.

"OK, Mick?" Dusty asked.

Terry was concerned to see this acute change of mood.

"It's Sniffer. Can't get him off my mind. You know I'd happily lose a leg if they could pull him round."

"We know, " said Terry. "You two go back a long way."

Mick swallowed hard and nodded and then said: "Look. Would you lads mind if I did the Norwich candle, lit it for him? I don't know who it was supposed to be for, but sod it, but I'm making it for him."

They all nodded their heads.

"Not at all, Mick," said Terry. "You light it."

28

There was an air of despondency during the drive back to Peterborough. The dismal weather seemed to match the melancholic mood, a feeling of anti-climax, within the car. But the glumness was mainly over Sniffer's health crisis.

"He's OK. He's stronger, rested up," said Jess. "Looking forward to his moment of glory at Posh. Viv suggested having a wheelchair just in case but he won't hear of it."

Mick had been silent throughout the journey but as they were approaching Sniffer's home he said: "Would anybody mind if I came this afto?"

"Not at all," Terry said. "You were part of it all."

Sniffer looked far fitter than everyone had expected. Viv had taken him to Peterborough Cathedral that morning and he had asked to go in alone, and had walked back to the car without support.

After Viv had given everyone lunch, she fetched Sniffer's Posh scarf and bobble hat and put the giant cheque in the back of the 4X4.

The crowd was buzzing and Sniffer, wrapped in many layers, looked frail as Mick and Terry, lightly holding an arm each, steered him towards the stadium door and the man in the high-vis jacket who was waving to them.

He patted Sniffer's blue-and-white bobble hat and said: "Well done young man!" and led the party to the echoing room somewhere near the players' tunnel.

Mick was impressed. This was how celebrities must feel. The noise out there was growing with every passing minute.

"They're ready for you now," said the security man. "Off you go."

He led them into the brightness and hubbub, and over to the man from the cancer charity who shook hands warmly while the announcer talked of a tough ride to Norwich, all for a good cause, and all the idea of a brave Posh fan.

Sniffer and the charity man stood behind the cheque, with Terry and Mick flanking and wearing wide smiles.

"One more," said the photographer, and Mr Posh was pulled into the group.

When it was all over, and the cheering had subsided and spasmodic booing had begun while the Tranmere line-up was read out, the security man came over and said to Sniffer: "Are you staying for the match this time?"

Not waiting for their answer he led them at Sniffer's snail's pace around the pitch perimeter to the dug-out and finally to a set of seats behind the staff and substitutes.

As Sniffer told Viv late that night, when everyone had left and they were sitting talking, feeling the sort of contentment that they had never experienced before during the turbulent years, the occasion had been wonderful.

"But what about the match, Sniff? Was it good?"

"Good? It was highway bloody robbery. Their second goal was scandalous. Their bloke was so offside he was chatting to our goalkeeper when he got that pass. That ref should get his bloody cataracts seen to."

Viv listened and thought: There's all this fear around, this invading illness, prospects of death. And yet some things don't change.

29

It was that time of year again. Time again to trudge, day by day, through another grey, uneventful winter that always felt to Lydia as if it would never end.

She could still not see any real prospect of initiating the major life-change she craved, a life that wasn't dominated by near-feral children, coughing hens and encroaching debt.

But there was comfort to be had in the small, instant decision she took – to stay deep in the nest she had formed by tucking round her every inch of the duvet edge.

There was not much to get out of bed for.

No eggs, no luxuries, no helping hand, no nice surprises, no money, no man...No...vember, she thought, ruefully but taking a little pleasure from the phrasing that had fallen into place in her mind. Her brain tended to work like that. Spinning words sometimes tumbled around and then settled in satisfying ways.

Inspired teaching had been a blessing, that and every encouragement at home to enable every inner urge to have expression. She believed that this creative resource had kept her sane; it had even taken the edge off her loneliness, allowing her to retreat into a world she conjured up for herself.

But she still missed Sniffer. Badly. It must have been two years ago now, she calculated with surprise, since the night he came to say that Viv had issued an ultimatum.

Of course she'd always known that the affair was something

impermanent, like a holiday. Holidays always ended, and although the enjoyment of them was heightened by the time limitation it also intensified the sense of regret that there had to be an end.

The little mantra in the Indian picture frame, saying that when all was dark and loneliness encroached she should remember the shining wonder of herself, seemed trite. But how moved she had been when Tara had given it to her on Mother's Day. It was the first intimation that Tara, on the verge of womanhood now, understood her plight.

She retreated even more deeply into the duvet, pulling it round her ears, and tried to fall into sleep but she could hear the kids downstairs arguing, and then Tara's voice breaking into a pained cry. They were fighting.

"Pox-ridden whore!" Theo was yelling. Lydia wondered where on earth he'd heard the words – and whether he had any idea what they meant. Shakespeare, probably. Like her, he was going to excel at English.

"OK, miss the bloody bus then, you spoilt little tosser!" screamed Tara, for whom the periodic table had more allure than literary niceties.

Theo was spoiled, Lydia acknowledged, and he was small for his age, something that made her spoil him even more. She saw in his puny, brave confrontation of the world something of her own spirit in the face of adversity.

There was a thud, the back door slamming, Lydia presumed. She could imagine the scene being played out. Tara would be striding out in the parts of her uniform that – with sparkly tights, barely discernable ear-stud, and experimental hair streaks – combined to keep her appearance just on the right side of "school policy."

She would be hoping that by the time the school bus came, the redness had gone from her eyes. It would have been so gross if they suspected she'd been made to cry by her little brother.

In her mind's eye, Lydia could imagine Theo, small and bony, trailing behind her, bent under the weight of his rucksack, to the school bus pull-in at the small copse, near the Flood End junction.

Lately, Lydia had, in her own words, "let the little buggers get on with it." She had come to the conclusion that having done her bit valiantly for years, she was now entitled to salvage a bit of herself for herself.

To say it had all been a struggle would be grossly understating things. Bruce had left her without a bean and – with the kids at the toddler stage – slunk off back to London in that rather spineless hippie way that she was sure he had never quite lost.

They had moved here to find an independent life on the edge of society, a life of questioning, aspiring to self-provision, of not conforming. The enterprise called for teamwork and unity of purpose.

Bruce turned out to be a dreamy passenger. So, instead of the good life, she had found debt, insecurity, loneliness, and unrelieved worries about a damp house that was decaying in front of her eyes.

The soil was superb, black and friable, like powdered charcoal. So each year there had been enough leeks and potatoes to feed an army, baskets of fruit from three productive apple trees, and year-round salad stuff under the now-tattered polythene tunnel.

But what came with it was the cold, the bone-shaking winds, chicken shit by the barrow load and the occasional, dreaded vet's bill. All this, to produce the eggs that kept a leaky roof over their heads.

Was it any wonder that she had little civility to spare with penny-pinching customers who had no idea of the true cost – financial and human – of producing a tray of perfect, tough-shelled, carefully scrubbed, fresh eggs.

The market stall usually just paid for itself, plus a little bonus at the end of what was usually a long, wet, miserable day. Lately, the quail and the duck eggs had saved her bacon (she liked that phrase). A big hotel and a few restaurants out towards Norfolk, places that were trumpeting their use of local produce, ordered both from time to time, but the menus were ever-changing so there were weeks when they ordered neither.

But she had survived, without Bruce's help.

Lydia would happily concede that for a girl who had been brought up nicely in the London suburbs, she had shown steely resolve and independence that constantly surprised her.

The first time she had used an electric drill she had squealed each time she squeezed the trigger and it burst into life but over the years she had grown confident with saws, and hammer and nails and roofing felt, so that the chicken coops at least were always watertight.

She was especially proud of the sign she had made - complete with the frame it swung from, and had painted quite expertly - to attract passing drivers. She had even come up with a bit of witty wordplay but had agonised over it thinking it might be counter-productive.

"Tara," she had asked one day, "do you think that I should paint in 'Clucking Good!' on the bottom, to make it a bit more eye-catching."

Tara had been dismissive. "Oh my God, no mother! People might think you mean Fucking Good." "Well I do, in a way," Lydia had said, not wanting to let go of the idea, and making allowances for the fact that Tara liked things strictly factual.

"But Tara, isn't the witty thing not saying it, but saying something like it, so people make their own connection?"

"Yes, Mum - I get it", said Theo chipping in. "It's, like, you're mixing up looking good, clucking good and fucking good. I think it's awesome."

She had noted that Tara had directed a sneering look at Theo before calling him "Brown-noser," and then stomping off.

The incident had highlighted another absence in her life - grown-up opinions. Adult feedback, advice. The sort of clear direction Sniffer used to give. Straight John Bull was a phrase he tended to use.

Before she had called Sniffer in for the estimate, she had toyed with the idea of tackling the stud wall herself to save money. With a few words of reassurance from someone, she would have got stuck in. After all, surely an internal wall was just a wooden frame and plasterboard?

Then she lost confidence and balked at the challenge, worried about the electrical wiring.

In the end, she had talked to Sniffer when he brought the egg money and it had worked out perfectly. In every sense.

He made a perfect little creative pod, just a bit wider than her desk, from an unneeded bit of her bedroom. A hideaway where she could plan and set her ideas free.

There was much more to thank him for, of course – the fun and the talks and bed in the afternoons. He had reminded her that she was a woman.

And thanks to him, at this moment, she clung (by her fingertips) to the belief that although cold reality would be waiting for her as soon as she ventured out from under the duvet, it wouldn't always be winter.

30

The cancer nurse had just left when Viv came home from town heavily laden with carrier bags full of shopping. She didn't shout as she opened up, in case Sniffer was sleeping.

She noticed that he had slopped tea on to the table that slid on wheels over his bed and that the photo on the bedside cabinet – of all of them, taken in Ely during the ride – had been knocked over.

He was out of things much of the time now. She thought this a blessing. When the time eventually came, she wanted it to be while he was sleeping.

Oddly, his memory had improved and they were now enjoying long, tranquil talks together, especially whenever Sniffer was scared by fearful half-dreaming and needed to be calmed.

Talking was easier, gentler, now. The combative element was behind them; listening had become as important as talking.

Viv would get out the photo albums and they'd re-live trips abroad, the parties. She censored the memories to ensure that none triggered associations with bad times.

She also kept Sniffer abreast of the local news. He listened to the Posh match on local radio but now without apparent passion or even enjoyment.

Mad Mick was a frequent caller, sometimes with Pat and the kids. Viv had noticed that Mick had never really acknowledged Sniffer's illness, never once spoken seriously about it.

She tolerated the "friendship" for Sniffer's sake, feeling no affection or regard. Sniffer and Mick went back years before she was on the scene. She had hoped that Sniffer would outgrow the friendship but it was still rock-steady.

Mick's support for his ailing friend took the form of slightly hysterical taunts and quips aimed at keeping Sniffer's chin up but which seemed to leave Sniffer weary and irritated. Viv felt sorry to see such a strong man so ill equipped to deal with what would be a devastating loss. It was something he could not counter by using his fists.

Mick would happily have dived on a grenade to save Sniffer, or plunged into a stormy sea to save him. She suspected that when he left the house, said his jokey goodbye to Sniffer, and got back into that motor of his, he would cry like a baby.

Sniffer and Mick had worked together for years, covered for each other and, so far, survived scrapes together. But there was something desperate about Mick, Viv always thought. He would come to a sticky end, or finish up in jail. He courted trouble.

Viv went to put the kettle on and had begun to stow tins and packages in the kitchen units when she heard Sniffer call out.

She strode through to the dining room, now his sleeping place, and found he had managed to prop a pillow behind himself so that he could sit up. The hollow of his cheeks seemed deeper than they had when she left, and the pallor beneath his stubborn tan, lit by the soft autumn light falling on him, gave him an unworldly look.

Viv pulled up a chair and settled at his bedside after bringing coffee and the local paper, and more of the acid drops Sniffer had taken to.

" 'Posh in crisis' it says here," she said, glancing at the back page.

"Nothing new there," said Sniffer grumpily. "What do they expect when they sell the only two players who recognise a ball when it's kicked to them."

Viv leafed through the pages looking for titbits that might interest Sniffer, resisting for a moment the pull of the front page and its strident headline "Hit-and-run mum's heartbreak plea."

"Ah, there it is!" she said.

She told Sniffer how she had just bumped into Pat, Mad Mick's wife, who had told her that the city was going to be mentioned on TV. It was in the paper, she said.

Pat had seemed even more cowed than usual. It was a struggle to hear her sometimes. To Viv, her demeanour suggested that she'd really like to be invisible. The apologetic tone evoked one word: Victim.

Sniffer had his eyes shut but opened them slowly as Viv related how the Close This Case programme would be putting out a new appeal for witnesses on the second anniversary of the death of the young man, a couple of miles from where they had lived.

"That poor mother, the torture she must have been through," Viv said. "She has to live with the knowledge that poor lad lay there behind that river bank for ages before he was found."

Sniffer was unresponsive.

"Remember it Sniffer? The young doctor being killed?"

She was tempted to say: "It was when I found out that you were still playing around with Lydia and told you that I would leave you unless you ended it." That was what had made that time memorable for them both – the blackest time.

"What doctor?" Sniffer said gruffly.

"A poor young man with mental problems. Killed. It was November a couple of years back. Surely you remember the police coming, Sniff? Fat one and a thin one. Little and Large you said. Wanted to know if we'd seen anything, or if we'd been out and about. No one knew his body was there. They said they thought he'd died just before bonfire night."

"And had we seen anything?" said Sniffer.

"No, but it didn't stop them having a crafty look at the front of the van after I'd shown them out. Spotted them at it, devious sods."

She reminded Sniffer that Mad Mick had said at the time that the police also took him out to look over his car, and the big Dodge, even though he'd been given a lift to darts, so both vehicles had been off the road when the accident happened.

"I can understand how they rub people up the wrong way," she said. "But I suppose it's their job." She fell silent as she read the report.

Two years! Time passed so quickly; she couldn't believe so much time had flown by, but the memories were still fresh, and still painful, about that late autumn, when she had gone through hell, when she had found out about Sniffer getting back with the Egg Woman.

"Actually, I remember telling them, the police, what we'd been doing and the thin one wrote it all down, so seriously. I'd been in the bath with my wine, my joss sticks and candles so he wrote it down carefully and when they said 'And you sir?' You said 'I was too busy making a gun.'"

"A gun? Did I say that? I bet his eyes stood out like racing dog's balls!" said Sniffer.

Viv laughed as the scene re-played in her head.

"'Sorry, sir?" he'd said, and you had to explain that you were in the shed making a gun for the last Annie rehearsal, and listening to the Posh match on the radio. And, by the way, making a hell of a racket. Good job we didn't have neighbours."

"Do you know, I've no memory of any of it..." Sniffer said, bewildered.

"I mentioned that I remembered it all because of letting fly at you. The little sod read it out and asked me to confirm it all," said Viv.

"I said it was as clear as day for me, I remember having to go down in my dressing gown and give you a bollocking because your saw thing and the radio were ruining my precious soak."

"Can't remember a bit of that, not for the life of me," said Sniffer, losing interest.

So he would not remember the terrible stuff going on between them, over the Egg Woman. The threat she'd made, and her fear that she would have to carry it out and lose him.

She even remembered being in bed and him coming up, smelling vaguely of turps and saying he'd finished the gun, hoping to sweeten her up, and her being ice cold with him because she was still so hurt and angry at him.

Viv was amused as she speculated how the po-faced young policeman would have described the fall-out in his notebook. She wondered whether he might have written ... "at which point the lady, furious at the noise, ceased her exfoliation, exited the bathroom, descended the stairs and administered a sharp rebuke to her husband...?"

She smiled wryly when she remembered that the podgy policeman had asked, as he got to the door: "And you slept together that night?" and Sniffer had said sarcastically that no, that he'd had to doss down under the lathe.

She recalled that the bloke had actually seemed to wonder whether to write this down when Sniffer had stopped him and said: "A joke, officer! A joke. Of course I slept with her, though it didn't do me much good evidently."

Sniffer hated the police. He felt that he was a marked man, just as Mick was. On the rare occasion he saw the uniform he thought about the points on his licence, trouble over what he regarded as minor bits and pieces, and the odd skirmish over the years.

Out of the blue he remembered the time with Mad Mick in the Indian in Spalding, and that bit of fun with the chapattis. All right, they'd been drinking but they didn't mean any harm, and some of the customers were actually laughing. Of course it had to go down in the notebook as, what was it, a public order offence, instead of just a bit of a lark on a Friday night out.

As Viv went off to wash up, Sniffer shouted something over the sound of the TV.

"It'd be a veg lorry, Viv."

"What would?"

"That killed the bloke. It was near us, so you could bet it'd be a veg lorry. They go like the clappers, even at night. The driver might not even have known, not if it was a really big truck."

"Could be, love. Be interesting if anything comes out of it when they put the appeal out. But two years is a long time and they did a massive local thing first time round."

Mad Mick and Pat, the young couple up towards West Fen, people at work – they'd all had a police visit or a leaflet when it happened, said Viv.

"You can't say that the police haven't tried," she said. Sniffer wasn't going to agree, on principle.

He was tired now. A few months ago he could have worked ten hours, doing heavy stuff, with a half-hour break. Now just listening, never mind talking, sometimes tired him.

He shut his eyes and said dozily: "You watch, it'll turn out to be a lorry driver. Or one of those harvesting machines, the ones they use for cauliflowers.

How can a driver see anything from the top of one of them?"

"Good job you were tucked up with me or they might have had you for it, what with your dodgy record with the local constabulary!" Viv said, laughing, as she turned towards the kitchen to start preparing a meal.

Half an hour later she went in to check on Sniffer. To her surprise he was propped up, wide awake and was writing notes very slowly and deliberately in his writing pad. He had a look of great concentration on his face.

"So I finished that gun for you."

"You did, love. And you made that rustic bench for Annie to sit on. It was a great show."

o o o o o o o

She had tried for the Annie role but Sandra had got it in the end. The part called for someone who could belt out songs, singing that was rough round the edges. Not my style anyway, Viv had decided.

She began recalling some of her lines as Dolly Tate, and launched into a favourite she sometimes sang around the house, *Anything You Can Do*. When it came to the line "I can hold any note longer than you" she loved to see how long she could keep going before gasping for breath.

There was a time when Sniffer could be provoked into trying to sing the male bits. He would do his best, in his deep monotone, and they would collapse into laughter when the lyric got to the point where Viv sang over him, clear and high, "Yes I can... yes I can... yes I CAN!"

Today he showed no response. Even when he was well, he had no real interest in music, was unmoved by it, and Viv accepted that he had no idea how well she sang.

"They clapped a lot, so they must have liked you," he said once, after she took a bow after a Treasury of Song evening. It was as if he was observing, dispassionately, some obscure skill being exercised, something just beyond his ken.

She rearranged Sniffer's bed, fluffing up his duvet. She found herself humming *Doin' What Comes Natur'lly*, very quietly. Once she started singing songs, she couldn't stop but a dour look from Sniffer showed that it was irritating.

He nipped the end of the pen between his teeth, crunching the plastic barrel, and appeared to be thinking hard.

"Do you remember whether they won? Posh. That night you were talking about," Sniffer asked.

He paused, then said with relief at having retrieved an elusive fact: "No – they lost! And I think they were away. Bascot Stadium. Unless I'm mistaken."

"Oh, I see," said Viv astonished yet again by the pin-sharp recollection of a single, particular match coming out of the fog of his memory.

"Walsall's ground," Sniffer said. "It's Banks's Stadium now. Not many people know that."

"Or want to," said Viv.

She was repaid by a weak smile, then Sniffer's brow knitted again.

"No. I tell a lie, Viv. It was Walsall at home."

"God – what a relief that we've cleared that up," Viv said with deadly seriousness.

"Yes. That's it. The Saddlers."

"The Saddlers?"

"That's what they call them. Walsall."

"I suppose no bit of knowledge is a waste…" Viv said with a sigh.

Sniffer gave Viv a glance that was almost aggressive, then began to write again.

Viv looked on, thinking: typical Sniffer.

You talk to him of a tragic death on his doorstep, a poor man run down and lying undiscovered for days, and it's reduced to a mere memory-jogger for a mundane football match, forgotten by everybody. Except Sniffer.

31

On yet another sunless, grey November afternoon, Kath was nursing her grief. Each morning she tried to resume life as it had been but with each passing hour, the loss – like a block of granite within her – dragged her down into despair. Today was like the other days.

All that talk of time being the great healer was rubbish. It was all as raw now with the two-year anniversary approaching, as it had been the moment she had heard the news.

Reminders of Robert were everywhere. A phrase overheard on the bus might make her recall something he used to say; a young man walking by might be wearing a jacket like Robert had; a pop song on the radio could generate such a flood of grief that she would have to hold on to the table to stop herself keeling over.

Bits of stray mail for Robert still arrived, even now, two years on. Last week there was the jolly letter from a fellow medic now in Africa – poor man, he had no idea that Robert had died.

Yesterday it was football news on the radio that caused the tears to come. Yeovil Town had got through a round of some cup or other. How happy Robert would have been! He was touchingly boyish in his love for Town.

She smiled to herself at her memory of friends teasing him about being a Glovers fan, and him challenging them to find a club that was older, joking that, like wine, they were still improving with age. Anyway, what alternative was there in Somerset, he'd say.

Eric had taken Robert to see The Glovers for the first time on his eleventh birthday, and from that moment he was smitten. Now she could not stop herself looking at the Yeovil result each weekend, and at the same time seeing how Peterborough had done in their game.

After a few months in Peterborough, Robert had adopted United as a substitute for Yeovil but worked far too hard to be able to see more than half a dozen games.

Kath was intrigued by the fact that they were called "The Posh," especially as football was supposed to be a classless game, and that Peterborough had not seemed to her a posh sort of place. But she had absolutely no interest in football; she was merely the curator of Robert's passion.

She welcomed all these reminders of Robert, held them to her, stored them securely like jewels in a box. Those who told her - always gently, and with the best of intentions - that she should be trying to "move on" had misjudged her.

That's why she had gone along with the idea from the TV people to put out a new appeal about the night Robert had died.

The nice young researcher lady had assured her they were sensitive to the fact that the programme would "open an old wound." The girl was not to know that the wound was actually a comfort, and that the last thing she wanted was "closure" which to Kath had connotations of a coffin lid being lowered.

So she had said "Yes, please do it" when they rang to talk about the new initiative on Close This Case, to go out around the second anniversary of Robert's death. The appeal and renewed police activity would quite possibly flush out her son's killer, they said.

Strangely, she felt it really didn't matter to her who had done it. What could never be relieved by justice, or even by her faith, was the ache, that permanent feeling of what she could only describe as an absence.

They could lock up some driver and throw away the key but that ache, which she had likened to a permanent feeling of acute hunger, would always be there. And poor Robert wouldn't.

32

The news Viv had been waiting to hear since she was sixteen came at the worst possible moment. The offer of a lead role had simply shown itself too late. And of all things it was as Eliza. Viv loved My Fair Lady, had seen the film, had the DVD.

Her life had been swamped by Sniffer's needs since she got the call. The demands were growing and she knew that even more would be asked of her as Sniffer declined.

Today, soon after the evening meal, Sniffer had gone to bed absorbing that afternoon's news from the hospital. It confirmed what they already knew, but to Viv's relief Sniffer showed no outward sign of distress.

This might have been stoicism but she believed it was more likely to be forgetfulness about the day's events – or was it the guilt thing again, his belief that because of what he'd done in the past he had it coming?

The precise diagnosis of Sniffer's memory problems was still to be made. There was a strong suspicion hinted at, with a smile, by a doctor, that Sniffer had some selective amnesia as well as a medical problem.

After the hospital visit, Viv had stayed up long enough to cry and rage, into a cushion, out of sight, out of Sniffer's hearing.

"Months", the specialist had said – "Certainly weeks but perhaps months now. Sorry that it's all so bleak."

Sniffer simply gave a nod and said (or so she thought) "Fair enough." Fair enough?

The crying had come after Viv had been staring mindlessly at the TV screen for an hour or more. Even after a third glass of wine, she could still feel the knot in her shoulders, and the ache in her forehead from the intensity of her crowding thoughts. Most were about Sniffer but the message from the operatic society had been unsettling.

The call came from Frankie who, self-absorbed and blithely disregarding of Viv's real-life drama, was in a state of hysteria over his own impending problem. He barely managed a "hello" before unburdening himself.

"S.O.S, Viv! Read all about it – Centenary show deep in the dodos!"

Viv had witnessed dozens of these theatrical meltdowns. Off-stage hysteria was the very stuff of amateur theatre; behind-the-curtain shenanigans, petty jealousies, temper tantrums, political intrigue often proved more riveting than the production.

After the hospital visit, the vagaries of amateur operatics were as nothing. But to Frankie a casting calamity that threatened his production was a life-or-death matter. He was breathless with stress.

"Frankie. Can it wait?" Viv said, kindly. "I'm sorry but I can't talk now."

"Oh dear," he said, sounding hurt.

"It's OK – just that I've had some very bad news."

He reacted with customary shrillness.

"Oh, no darling! A bereavement?"

"No. But bad news. Sniffer."

"Not…"

"No, but it's not going well."

He knew of Sniffer's failing health but preferred not to delve. He excused the demands he made on Viv by professing that the company could offer distraction, if not catharsis for her, "if anything happened in the future."

He blurted out his news hurriedly: "All I want to say is that Julie's gone and got a throat nodule, the selfish bitch. She's having to drop out."

"Poor Julie."

"And we can't go back cap-in-hand to Gwen after we turned her down."

He re-envisaged Gwen, holding an edge of the piano top.

"OK, she's got the voice for Eliza but she's simply not built for it. Too many McDonalds for her to pass as starving flower girl." Viv started a blustering defence but Frankie brushed it away.

"Come on, Viv, admit it – she's all arse. Also, her Cockney was execrable. Worse than Audrey Hepburn's, worse than Dick Van bleeding Dyke's…"

Viv silently acknowledged that he was right but this was overridden by her empathy for Gwen. She had been an audition failure, had known what it was like to miss out.

"Anyway," Frankie said, "we tried the new girl but she warbles like one of those whistles we used to have at bath time. And we got Debbie in but her acting is as flat as a fart. The committee agreed that you'd be the best bet. You as Eliza, with Poppy doing your Mrs Eynsford-Hill."

So, at last, a lead role – and in what had once been called the most perfect musical, and for a centenary show.

Frankie was ready for the objections already forming in Viv's mind: there was Sniffer, and how things might play out. There was also the fear that she might look ridiculous.

"Yes, I know," said Frankie, "there's the age thing. The script puts Eliza at between 18 and 30. But you're slim, you're a natural with accents – and we can do wonders with a bit of slap. You'll be fabulous."

Viv knew to trust Frankie's instincts. He had unerring skill at casting. He also knew how to get hold of an audience and lay them low. She had witnessed his genius for showering productions with his own brand of fairy dust. These embellishments sometimes registered as an audible exhalation, out there in the dark, as if a puppy in a basket had been brought on stage.

Frankie also valued her voice that sometimes surprised even her with its sweetness and range. She remembered – and always followed – the advice of her first singing coach: "The notes are in there waiting, like roosting birds. Set them flying!"

Viv loved theatre and hated it when famous actors said things like "I pretend for a living," or "Me? I'm just a professional show-off." They were belittling something magical.

Before she married Sniffer, and moved to be with him, friends would find it amusing that the society she belonged to performed under an acronym SADOS - Spalding Amateur Dramatic and Operatic Society. But the real "sados" Viv always reminded herself, were those who lounged in front of the TV criticising people who were giving of themselves.

They had no idea of the almost ecstatic feeling you got when your voice pierced the silence of a packed auditorium. That was why, although her head and her heart told her that she should turn down the lead role, she could not bring herself to.

In her head, she heard the music; she could see herself in the line-up bowing with the others; hear the cheers and the whistles.

Frankie seemed relieved that Viv had not refused his offer outright but he pressed for an answer.

"We're quite behind now, obviously. It's going to be a bit of a race against time," he said.

Viv begged for time to think about it.

It was simply a question of whether accepting was fair to Sniffer. Whether it would be therapy for her during what would be a terrible time, or whether taking the role would lead to a lifetime of guilt.

It was thrilling to be asked. Whatever she decided, they couldn't take that away.

33

The chief didn't look like a policeman. Everyone said that. More like a company secretary, or an ageing but well-preserved actor.

He was slim thanks to a doting wife's fervent vigilance over diet in which broccoli and blueberries – and lately some trendy grain called quinoa – figured strongly.

The chief was cultivated (member National Trust, and National Gallery) but also ruthless. Pitiless in pursuit of greater rank, influence and pension.

What Kevin wasn't, was the "chief" at Three Counties Police HQ; not really.

He projected himself so as to appear to be the chief, carried himself like the chief, and liked to be called the chief. But if pressed, he'd reluctantly admit to being divisional No 2 at HQ, beneath Helen, who had just months to go before retirement.

The deputy chief didn't correct those who referred to him as the boss; they were just anticipating the inevitable. He had already tried Helen's nice, modern ergonomic chair. She had stayed on much too long, could have retired two years ago.

He felt well equipped for a step up, here at Three Counties, or elsewhere. Kevin liked to think that even in the run-up to fifty he was still pretty cool – and as sharp as a scalpel.

Joining the force with a good degree, some life experience and bags of confidence had served him well. His superiors had been astute enough to spot his potential. He hadn't had to spend absolute years poking drunks in the ribs, being abused late at night by cowardly young loudmouths.

All that was just societal housekeeping as far as he was concerned. He wanted to pit his wits against the big boys.

He sensed that Helen was galled over the reputation he'd been building. All right, she was fair-minded, intuitive and could be surprisingly hard – once he would have said "for a woman" but had learned to watch his tongue. Lately, though, she seemed to be easing down, maybe dreaming of the paddock, and the horse.

When everyone had gathered, the chief looked down at his watch, saw that he was dead on time, lifted a thigh and, after checking that there was no dust on the desk, lowered a buttock to perch on it.

The shuffling and quiet chatting subsided and the chief's cold grey, eyes scanned the room. He was wearing his new glasses with sparkly, clear frames. His wife said they made his face appear lean and clean-cut. He had jokingly ventured the word "aquiline" but his daughter said he looked like a welder. The general view among junior ranks at the briefing was that they added to his reptilian menace.

"Boys and girls – let's do it!" he said, in an inappropriately rallying tone for this audience, a dozen officers of various shapes and sizes.

First, the chief reminded the officers that there would be a national focus on the force over the next few days. The Close This Case team were putting out a TV appeal over the Dr Robert fatality.

He wanted to ensure that the nation saw them at their best. There were national PR gains to made from a job well done.

A superintendent would be doing the on-screen appeal, he said, but he had agreed to do a little bit to camera with the victim's mother in which she would implore him to find whoever wiped out the son she so loved.

"So let's think what we've got here," he said, hitching himself off the desk and walking round the room as he had seen them do on TV in those American police dramas.

"November two years ago. A nice young doctor following orders in his head. He leaves the secure unit and walks into the night. A nurse believes she had heard him shout something about Norwich.

"He is seven miles from the city and bang! – he's bounced to kingdom come by some vehicle, type unknown."

The chief paused at the desk and spread his arms out, resting on his knuckles.

"The nice young doctor is hurled away from the road and comes to rest near the bottom of the sloping bank of a drain. The impact turns him into the shape of a hairgrip. He lies there unseen while we scuttle round like blue-arsed flies looking for him."

The chief puts the palms of his hands together and looks up, like a supplicant. He says that the pathologist puts the time of death around three days at the most before the body is spotted by a farmer in a high-seat tractor.

"Three days takes us back to within hours of him going walkabout."

The chief says that one thing puzzled him: "Absolutely no-one saw this lad striding out, marching to the orders coming into his head. He'd already walked to his flat near the unit and collected a coat. So – a bloke wearing a jacket edged with fluorescent strip. A bloke who must have been noticeable, out on a lonely unlit road. But not a single sighting. Now that – and the ladies will forgive my French – is patent cobblers."

This incident, said the chief, was on a night when Posh were playing. Not a big match, hardly Juventus versus Real Madrid, he said with a self-congratulatory smile. Just Walsall. The nervy chuckles at the back died within seconds.

So… surely some fans coming into the city from the north, or returning home, must have seen something? But none had reported spotting the marching man.

There were no locals from the immediate area known to have been on the relevant roads around the relevant time, he said. No telltale dents on car-fronts. No cracked windscreens, no nasties smeared on bumpers.

Records of lorry movements had not led anywhere. Yet some vehicle hit this man – kapow! – as if he was a sack of King Edwards, the chief said.

"And...and...there was evidence at the scene of concealment. Soil. And, ergo, proof that the driver knew he'd done it and was running scared."

To round up the briefing, the chief said: "We'll be filtering out loads of the nuttier fruitcakes at source on the night of the show but you have to expect a flow of time-wasters in the following days. The trick will be to tease out the people who are worth a proper chat."

The chief covered his mouth as a small, strongly flavoured burp surfaced. The box of alfalfa salad had been welcome but Tess had been a bit heavy handed with the red onion. He would clean his teeth and use his spray once he got back to the office. Then he would brief Helen.

"So... let's find this driver. Let's bang him up. Let's imagine how good this force will look if, in the follow-up show, we have that grieving mother telling me on camera that we're the bees knees, and that she can now move on."

34

On the night the Close This Case programme went out, Wayne Duckitt had managed to get the children to sleep early.

He was quite pleased with his growing skill at manipulating the kids. He had developed a strategy.

When Gemma was out, and he was in charge, he would let them go wild for half an hour – cushion fights, wrestling, racing up and down the hall – then slowly de-energise them.

At bath time he ran a sponsored silence with the promise of a treat for the child who stayed quiet the longest. Then he would then sit beside their bunk beds telling them a story, in a soft, stupefying voice that he fancied had hypnotic powers.

The early fall of darkness now, in November, supported his whispered claim to them that it was very, very late, when in fact it was half an hour earlier than their usual bedtime.

But he had been disappointed that the extra peace and quiet he had won couldn't be frittered on watching TV.

With Gemma at yoga, Wayne had the chance to tackle one of the many jobs that a young husband confronts to avoid the cost of having to seek professional help. Tonight it was the over-heating vacuum. It was soon in bits ready to be fitted with a new part bought on the internet.

They didn't seem to have a spare penny nowadays, and so they dreaded unexpected domestic costs. Wayne looked forward to a time when they were on an even keel and could make inroads into the overdraft and the mortgage.

He had welcomed the move to north London but the weighting allowance that came with the transfer from the fens near Peterborough had proved disappointingly inadequate.

Maybe one day they would be able to take the cleaner for someone else to service. Meanwhile there was nothing for it but to sit on the carpet in front of the set and, with a pair of scissors, prise dog hair and thread from the roller.

Wayne would not normally watch Close This Case. Seeing those staged recreations showing villains clubbing old ladies or hard-working Mr Patels in corner shops infuriated him. Those who knew him as a mild and gentle man would have been surprised at his intolerance of law-breakers.

He had half heard the presenter describing some would-be bank robber who had been injured in his hurry to escape the scene, and who might now be wearing a bandage, and had felt a frisson of anger over the mention of some mindless late-night attack outside a Tube station but had not bothered to look at the screen.

But when he bent down to the electrical socket behind the TV set to plug and test the cleaner he heard the presenter say: "And now to Cambridgeshire, where a fatal hit-and-run incident remains unsolved after two years. Could you have seen this man, a young doctor, on the road one November night…?"

Cambridgeshire. Out of a vague curiosity about an incident in an area he had recently left, he stood up to watch and to his amazement saw a photo of someone he believed he recognised.

There was no doubting it. How could it not be? You only had to look at that crescent of black hair falling to the centre of his forehead, and the intense dark eyes.

Wayne felt his knees buckle slightly and a strange sensation in his chest as the image of the man on the screen sent his mind back to the day he had moved the family to the Fens.

He hurriedly found the remote control and turned up the volume then backed on to the settee, riveted.

The date read out had been the day they moved to the fen house near Watersend. The road and the area the presenter was describing was within three miles of the house they had rented.

So this was the man he'd given a lift to. It must have been early November. A young doctor with medical problems of his own. Killed just after the poor sod had waved goodbye and stepped into the dark.

Wayne thought hard. He could just recall the very serious face, topped by the black scimitar of hair, and see the silvery fluorescent strips on his waterproof jacket.

As soon as the victim's mother had been interviewed on camera chatting to a senior police officer, he felt ashamed that on that night he had turned off on the road towards the new house and not driven straight on and dropped the young man where he needed to be.

In a way he was culpable. But he remembered his tiredness that night and being aware of all he had to do before they could sleep.

He'd been happy, and stupid as it turned out, to believe this chap's assurance that he had only a couple of hundred yards more to walk up the road from the turn-off Wayne had had to take.

Now they were saying that it was believed that the doctor was intent on getting to Norwich. Norwich!

He thought of the stoical face of the mother, her dignity as she spoke to the policeman, and he thought of how it all could have been avoided. How he could have ensured it didn't happen.

He needed Gemma to put all this into place, to stop his inner panic. When she came home he would ring the incident number. Of course, he had to come forward but he was anxious about being at the centre of something that was important enough to be on national TV.

He texted Gemma saying: "Please come home straight away. Kids OK."

As the presenter turned to a report about a jewellery heist in Manchester, he switched the TV off and sat holding the scrap of paper on which he'd written down the police number.

He wondered how he and Gemma had not known about all this at the time about the death, this tragedy virtually on their doorstep. Then he remembered that for a few days they had been without TV, and, anyway, they were absorbed installing themselves in the new home.

He had no reason to feel guilty, he knew, but he did; he knew he would have acted differently if he hadn't been so tired that night.

He'd spent all day moving furniture, four trips – and this had been the last one. Being new to the firm, he hadn't known anyone at work well enough to ask for help and so he'd had to do the lot and it had been so very, very tiring.

Actually, tired wasn't the word. He had been exhausted. He wanted to spread the move but the works van was only available for the day.

He remembered how heavy he felt when Gemma helped him carry in the toy chest and the garden tools and the last cardboard boxes of odds and ends. It had been too much.

Wayne made himself a coffee as the worry inside him began to build. Then a long-forgotten conversation came back to him...

He had picked up the man just outside Peterborough where the countryside opened up. The man had seemed reluctant to talk and Wayne had been pleased not to have to make an effort.

He remembered that the man had been having an intense conversation on a hands-free phone of some sort – Wayne could not see quite what in the half-dark – and as he was interested in getting a new phone, when he pulled in to drop the man off he'd asked: "Are these hands-free phones any good, mate? Doesn't the earpiece get a bit annoying?"

The man had replied almost inaudibly: "I haven't got a phone. I don't use phones. I don't trust them."

So this man had been talking to himself.

In retrospect, he'd not really puzzled over why someone should pretend that he was on the phone. Fatigue, he supposed.

He had put the episode to one side late that night and, having slept soundly, had set about plumbing in the washer, rigging up temporary curtains, re-assembling beds.

Wayne looked at his watch. He estimated that Gemma should be home within twenty minutes.

Ironically, right now she'd be winding down, flat on her back, drifting.

Gemma positively surrendered to yoga. She always came home wide-eyed and floppy as if she had been outside smoking a spliff. He was tired of being told: "I was actually asleep when Jasmine rang the bell to bring us back. You have to try it Wayne. It's so relaxing!"

It struck him as ironic that as she was lying there, floating on some astral plane, her palms open to the heavens, smelling of something exotic and totally wound down, he was being wound up, his hands clenched round his mobile phone.

Wayne passed the time by once more going through the events of that day, and that night.

He saw again the marching figure out there on the road, the silvery fluorescent strip. He could just remember some clumsy exchange they'd had before the passenger had started talking into the underside of his lapel.

When Gemma came in she was pink and radiant. But her beaming smile dropped as she noted Wayne's grave look. She had not read the message to come home quickly.

"Is one of the kids ill?" she asked anxiously. "What is it Wayne?"

He asked her to sit, then told her slowly and in great detail about the programme, the appeal and explained that there was no doubt that the chap who died had been the man he had given a lift to.

"Simple," said Gemma. "You ring the number and you tell them what happened and that you hadn't come forward before because you had not known about the accident."

"Yes. That's it," said Wayne without enthusiasm.

Gemma brought them a hot drink and they sat together on the settee. Wayne dialled the number for the appeal and a woman with the over-sweet voice of someone trying to sell something answered.

Wayne gave a brief account what had happened and the young woman asked him to hold on.

He gave details of personal identity, phone numbers and location, and he was asked to confirm for a second time much of what he had said. At first he had a sense that he was regarded as doing a public service and that it was greatly appreciated.

But he felt a shiver of disquiet go through him when a male voice came on the line and said: "Thank you so much for the information sir. Of course, we will have to send someone to interview you properly. You'll hear from us soon."

Just as he was saying it was no trouble, and that he was anxious to help, the man on the phone interrupted saying, "So you were driving a van that night, sir. I just wondered: Do you still have the van by any chance."

He explained that it had gone back the day after the move, into the vehicle pool at work and would probably have been replaced under the fleet hire agreement.

"No worries," said the man.

Of course it had to be his imagination, his silly groundless fear but he wondered why, unless they suspected him of knocking the man down, the police wanted to look at the van.

He was holding hands with Gemma as the Close This Case Late Night Update came on after the news.

The woman presenting the programme gave a convincing impression of someone excited as she reported that there had been progress in the case of the bandaged thief but, more dramatically, that a man had come forward in connection with the Cambridgeshire fatal hit and run.

"Someone around the area at the time of the death has finally broken silence," she said joyously.

Wayne did not care for the terminology. He was not "around the area." He had gone home and slept the sleep of the dead. And he had not broken silence; he simply had not known about the death.

That night, his troubled sleep was filled with dreams of questions he could not answer, justifications he had no reason to come up with, misunderstandings that clouded imagined conversations with his questioners.

Each time he rose through sleep to consciousness he had a terrifying feeling that because of what seemed to be a pressing need to find the hit and-run driver, he might be a victim of suspicion that would shatter the peace and contentment he had found with his wife and family.

Meanwhile, a senior police officer was drinking coffee with the Close This Case presenter in a room behind the London studio.

"Went well. Very well. But wouldn't it be neat if we can tie this van driver in with the death?" the officer said.

"Mmm…" said the presenter thoughtfully. "Nice. Mum's reaction would absolutely make the show."

She looked up and found herself admiring Kevin's classy specs. They went so well with the grey round the temples and the uniform. Lady viewers, especially the fifty-somethings, would have liked him tonight, she thought.

"I've a gut feeling we're on to something," he continued. "Could be that a guilty conscience has worn this bloke down and he wants to come clean and get a good night's sleep. Guilt can save us lots of bother. It makes some of them throw themselves into the net, like fish."

"Anyway, sounds pretty promising…" the presenter replied without enthusiasm. "But you keep saying 'him,' Kevin. Women can knock people over too. It's not a male preserve."

"Yes but…well, it takes a bit of explaining, this van being the only vehicle for miles around at the time this medic was dead, or dying, at the roadside."

The presenter drained her drink and got up, to show Kevin that it was time to go.

"Too right, Kevin," she said, shaking his hand. "An arrest would make an absolutely cracking item for next week."

35

One dull afternoon, with winter gathering at the window, Sniffer woke from a nap with a strange cry and Viv, who was talking herself through Eliza's lines in the My Fair Lady script in the living room, threw the sheaf of paper down and ran to his side.

Sniffer now had a bed in the front room, near the window. The positioning of the bed was at his request. He was increasingly anxious about darkness. He slept with the light on and craved light during the day.

By the time she reached him, to her surprise Sniffer was smiling benignly, head lolling forward off the pillow.

"Just a dream, Viv. Dickman again," he said. "But I got away. Granny Pud to the rescue!

Tucked me under her pinny."

"Like a swan with a cygnet under her wing were you, Sniff?"

"Just like that."

She cuddled him and said she would fetch tea and they would have a look at the local news. She knew that Posh had played the night before, and there had been renewed interest from Sniffer.

"I want to see what Swanny has to say about the new striker, Viv," he called out brightly. "The radio man said he had an absolute stinker." Sniffer knew that Swanny the columnist had a mind of his own and didn't mind if his match report needled the fans, or the club.

Viv rejoiced that Sniffer's old enthusiasm for Posh seemed to have resurfaced, giving her a glimpse of the man who over weeks now had been fading before her eyes.

Viv had taken to sitting on an upholstered stool beside Sniffer's bed, so their faces were level. They looked at each other more now than they had ever done and they were gentler with each other than they had ever been.

Ursula had called in twice recently and Sniffer always seemed less morose after she had been. Viv always left them alone and although she couldn't be certain of what they talked about, Viv guessed that Ursula was still trying to lead Sniffer to confront any inner conflict.

During one visit she overheard him say, as she approached the door with drinks: "Hang on Ursula, I might not get this dying thing right first time, you know. Remember, I've had absolutely no bloody practice."

Remarkable – the way they had laughed, about dying.

Once, when Viv was remaking the bed, and Sniffer was sitting in a chair, she had remarked, in a throwaway manner, that Ursula had been an absolute godsend. Sniffer said firmly: "More like God himself. No kidding. She's goodness on legs. No preaching, just pure truths, as she calls them. Things like: All you need is love."

He explained that lately she had told him about unconditional love, love that didn't depend on what you had or hadn't done, and that he was wrong to think he didn't deserve love, whatever dark sins he had committed.

Viv touched Sniffer's forearm and said: "I'd liked to think that's what I give you but I did have one condition, didn't I? That I wouldn't love you and share you."

"You're only human, Viv. You've been a saint. I wish I had been that good."

Suddenly discomfited by having been so tender, Sniffer asked for her to pass the paper so he could read about the match. Then she could pick out items that interested them both.

She was about to give a précis of the front page story when a thought came into Sniffer's head, a point that couldn't wait. "And there's another thing that Ursula's come up with. She thinks the people at Walpole Marsh, that family I used to go to on Sundays, sort of poisoned my mind. Indoctrination."

He had spilled out memories of the smart visitors his friend's family entertained each Sunday afternoon at the big house that had once been a farm.

The children were not allowed to play outside and this left Sniffer frustrated because in the barn there were l bantams and little gamecocks, like multi-coloured feather dusters. There was exciting rusted farm equipment, the decaying bales of straw. There was a pig somewhere round the back, you could hear it, sometimes.

"I used to walk past the place on the way to the house and it gave off a smell, of animals and hay and stuff. I was always dying to get in there and explore," Sniffer said. "But every time I was taken in and sent up to my mate, to do Meccano in his room while all the visitors sang and shouted and had some sort of ceremony."

Viv could tell that Sniffer felt a strong urge to talk about those Sunday afternoons.

"One day, my friend took me downstairs and I was saved," Sniffer said flatly, smiling at the thought.

"Saved? You've never told me that!" said Viv, widening her eyes.

"They were all sitting in a big ring and my mate took me in and his Dad said that he knew me and the boy had been talking, and that he felt I had been called. Well, I'd been called for my dinner a few times but not called to God or anything!

"Anyway, I was saved and touched on the head and then I went back to building the Meccano crane. All was fine but the lad began to go on a lot about God watching every move so he knew every act and every bad thought, saying there was always a penalty to pay. It spooked me because I couldn't be good. Beyond me."

"So that's where your guilt comes from, Sniff."

"From that – and the big bad things that came later."

He had laughed more today than for ages and as he was still in good spirits Viv thought it a good time to tell Sniffer the news she had kept from him – that she had a new and demanding role in My Fair Lady.

She hurriedly added that there was a proviso that if it all became too much, she would put his needs first, and that Frankie had found an understudy to cover if she had to drop out.

"Frankie had the idea of coming round here and I could practise the songs with him on the keyboard," she said tentatively. "But I wanted to make sure you didn't mind."

Sniffer thought for a moment, then said matter-of-factly: "Do it, love. I know you'll be safe with Frankie boy!" They laughed together, Viv mainly out of relief.

Sniffer folded the newspaper and laid it on the tray that spanned his bed.

"Sure it's not me being selfish?" she asked.

"Not at all. So what's that part you've got?"

"It's changed. I was Mrs Eynsford-Hill but there's been problems and now... I'm Eliza," she said sheepishly. "I've just about memorised my lines."

"Bloody hell. She's the main one isn't she? The lead?"

Viv regretted raising the subject – and of having been persuaded by Frankie to step in to the main role at this time.

"You'll be great," Sniffer said kindly. "Great."

She could see that he meant it.

Viv felt her eyes pricking but she resisted the urge to shed a tear and instead said lovingly: "But my number one priority is you."

o o o o o o o

Next afternoon, Frankie called. He was a fussy dresser but prone to put on weight and so he constantly struggled to show clothes off well. His paunch tended to disrupt the tailor's line and forced him to wear his belt low.

Today, he sported a dark, crisply-cut jacket and, covering the too-tight shirt collar, a large chunky-knit scarf in a shade of rust that echoed precisely the colour of his fine-leather boots. Matching had taken an absolute age, and involved visits to a dozen shops and an internet search. A charcoal beret and his favourite tortoiseshell-frame glasses with the large lenses completed his ensemble.

As Viv showed him in, he stopped stock still for a moment so that Viv could drink in the sartorial subtleties. She obliged.

It struck Viv (who had no interest in clothes) as sad to see people wearing characterful, big-city fashions away from big cities. She found there was something embarrassing about overt stylishness. She thought that today Frankie looked as if he had mistaken a Peterborough suburb for a Parisian arrondissement.

As she stepped forward to greet him, she could see faint traces of a coppery hair dye round his ears. An experiment perhaps? He was mid-fifties now and she knew he was the sort of man who would take desperate measures to preserve appearances.

"Alors! Tres smart, Frankie," she said kissing him on each of his puffy cheeks.

She'd noticed that she tended to use more exotic language when Frankie was about, as if to fit into the flamboyance that surrounded him. She took his folder of music from him and laid it beside the keyboard, then led him in to Sniffer.

They shook hands and Frankie was effusive and loud, to cover the shock, Viv suspected, of the change in Sniffer since they last met. As they left the room, Frankie put on an alarmed face to show Viv that the seriousness of it all had registered.

"Poor love," he said, reaching for her hand.

Frankie was running through Eliza's numbers when Viv came through with coffee. She called to Sniffer: "Door open or shut?"

"Open," he said. "Want to hear it."

So unlike the Sniffer of before, she said to herself. In the past he had shown only a passing interest in her theatrical activities, even though he acknowledged her passion. His after-show compliments amounted to variations of "You really did OK."

Frankie and Viv were soon locked in a wrangle over *Wouldn't It Be Loverly*. Viv wanted to do it little-girlish, wistful. Frankie favoured it being put over as a strong assertion of Eliza's ambition and demonstrated his point, singing in a warbling falsetto.

They sorted out what bits of simple choreography they might build round it, and then Frankie opened the sheet music for *Without You*.

"This is Eliza's celebration of release," said Frankie, striking chords to set the tone. "Give it some welly, Viv!"

She was well into the song when a part of the lyric caused her voice to crack and for her to struggle to hold herself together. It was an inner collapse that seemed to come from nowhere.

It came with the mention of future Springs arriving and there being no Professor Higgins.

She swallowed hard on the words and Frankie looked up, quizzically.

She tried to continue "I...can do bloody well... without you..." but put her head in her hands and began to sob.

Frankie hurried to close the door and then gathered her, wrapping his arm round Viv's head which heaved backwards and forwards. He slid her glasses away as she clung to him, as she tried to stifle the deep convulsions overtaking her.

"There," said Frankie. "Let it go."

He held her for perhaps a full minute before she looked up, her face streaked with mascara, and said: "I'll struggle on the night with that bit..."

"Time out!" Frankie said firmly, leading Viv to the small settee in the alcove of the window. They sat together, Frankie taking her hand and leaving a silence.

Finally, Viv said: "I'm so sorry. Don't know where that came from. I think that the reality of it...about Sniffer...has finally struck me. The prospect of him not being here."

Frankie replied: "Well you know what The Master said about cheap music being so potent. Coward was so right, love – it can catch you unawares. It churns up what's going on inside. As a kid, Judy Garland used to turn me into a bleeding jellyfish. "

Viv laughed, and then sniffled.

"I came out to Gloria Gaynor, snogging a warehouseman at my sister's twenty-first. Look – there's tears coming now at the thought of it!" He fluttered his hands in front of his eyes, as if he, too, had been wearing mascara that was in danger of running.

Viv stood up and went into the adjoining room, and was relieved to see that Sniffer had slept through her crisis. She would have had difficulty explaining that a handful of words of a simple song from a musical had torn her in two, and couldn't, wouldn't, have told him which words.

She also knew that there were other words in that song, words that before Sniffer's illness would have not inflicted such crushing poignancy.

Somehow it was all different, her and Sniffer.

How ironic, that they should have got it right just as it had to end.

36

"Tell me again, Wayne. Why exactly did you move to be near London so soon after getting settled out in the Fens?"

"Promotion," Wayne replied.

He hoped that the irritation in his voice would be picked up by the lanky sergeant straddled over the settee, nursing his notebook. The policeman had a skeletal face, close-cropped hair and his cunning showed in his features. He was enormously tall and to

Wayne he seemed to dominate the room.

"Promotion. I told you."

"You'll have to bear with me Wayne. This is a very serious business and we need to explore every avenue. By the look of it, you were the only one around when the chap was killed and so you're important."

The sergeant corrected himself: "You, that is, and the driver who wiped out the doctor and then left the scene."

The sergeant had arrived from Cambridgeshire an hour before and had accepted a cup of tea and exchanged pleasantries for a while before quite formally steering the conversation to the hit-and-run.

Wayne had become increasingly tense and he now felt anger welling inside as the sergeant reviewed the notes he'd taken, and then seemed determined to go over exactly the same ground.

"Now. Just to get this straight…" he said, looking intently at Wayne, who suspected the sergeant was watching for any reaction that might indicate guilt.

"You're sure you picked up the man. That he got in where you said? And that you didn't overshoot your turn-off that night, even though it would have been understandable as you were so exhausted, and didn't know the area too well?"

"I'm sure."

"Wayne…" he said very confidentially, "…you were very tired, it was getting late, it was pitch black. No one would blame you if you had overshot and your van had clipped this chap who, for all we know, was walking in the middle of the road. If it was a glancing blow, you might not even have felt it…"

Wayne stood up and said angrily: "Look! I gave the bloke a lift. He got out. I turned off. I went home."

"Steady Wayne," said the sergeant quietly, raising his eyebrows and putting on a face that showed slight surprise, as if to say: "Have I touched a raw nerve?"

Wayne sat down again, in the corner chair.

"Sorry," he said, wearily. "But don't you think I feel bad enough without you doubting everything I say? I let this poor sod walk off in the dark and he died. I feel terrible."

The sergeant, sounding conciliatory, said: "Look Wayne, there's no need to be so agitated. If you didn't hit this man in your van, you shouldn't feel bad. In fact I'm surprised how bad you feel. Because all you did, all you said you did, was give the bloke a bit of a lift."

He said that this was really kind, a nice gesture especially as Wayne must have felt half asleep after all that fetching and carrying.

Wayne's sense of outrage rose again but he stayed seated and said in a monotone: "Sergeant, I wasn't half asleep. I was very tired but I was alert. I knew I had a load of things waiting for me to sort out before I'd get to bed."

The sergeant waggled his pen and made a little hissing noise. Then he stared again at his notebook. He let a long time elapse before he picked up the thread of his questioning.

"So you had lots to do before the family could settle. I've moved five times so I know that feeling. No curtains, some lights not working, kettle buried in a box somewhere, beds to put up…that kind of thing."

Wayne and the sergeant exchanged nods.

"Could it be that you were rushing a bit, just a bit, to get home so you could get it all sorted for the night?"

"No, not rushing. No!"

"Look, Wayne. We're not accusing you, just wanting to get the full picture. Actually, one thing that has me flummoxed. Why didn't you know of the doctor's death?"

Wayne bridled. It was unfair that he should be criticised because two years ago, for a couple of days, he failed to keep up with the news.

"Well," said the sergeant "after all, the thing happened on your doorstep. We put a sign up at the roadside appealing for witnesses, and the newspaper was full of it for a couple of days. Then there was local radio and TV - and you didn't hear a dickybird?"

Wayne struggled to remember details of that couple of days.

He said: "If your sign was where you said it was, sergeant, I wouldn't have seen it. I used to take the other road to work, a bit longer but a better road. I remember there used to be signs saying 'Don't drown' or something, because of the deaths in the drains and the river. That's the only sort of sign I ever saw. But I was working nine hours a day and then sorting the house out. There was so much to do…"

The sergeant moved his gangly legs from one side of the settee to the other and flipped through his notes, giving himself time to frame another question.

"Now, the thing about the imaginary phone. That all seems very odd, although evidently that poor young lad was hearing voices in his head. Didn't you think it worth reporting, that there was this man yomping through the Fens at night, talking to himself?"

"I suppose I was too wrapped up in what I was tackling that day," Wayne replied. "You're making me feel even worse now. I have to live with the fact that I let him go, rather than take him further up the road. He said it was only a couple of hundred yards."

"It wasn't. In fact it was sixty-odd miles to where he was going, on the route he was on. He was headed for Norwich, Wayne. Not to a friend's just up the road. He had written a note in felt-tip on the table top in his room mentioning some mission there. At the cathedral."

Wayne was anguished at the thought of the man's plight.

"I could have taken him home, got help. If I'd known what was going to happen I would have even driven him to Norwich, there and back, tired as I was. If I'd thought about it, it was obvious he wasn't fit to be wandering around. I feel so guilty now."

"No, Wayne. You'd only need to feel that way if you'd overshot your turn-off, knocked him over, which would have been understandable in the dark when you were shattered, dropping with tiredness, and if you'd then driven off not knowing."

"Yes, but I didn't. Yet I feel responsible for letting him get killed."

The sergeant left an especially long pause. Then he alarmed Wayne when he said: "The van has been scrapped. The works van you borrowed."

So they've even been trying to track the van.

"But the manager of the vehicle pool, Mr Taylor is it?"

"Traylor. Bill Traylor."

"Mr Traylor. He remembered you having the van for something private. There was no damage. At the front. He always checked vans when staff used them. So that's a relief."

Why a relief, Wayne thought? It would have been a relief if he'd been the driver who ran the man down. But he was just the Good Samaritan who gave the poor chap a lift.

When the sergeant had left to drive back to the Fens, he felt frightened.

He couldn't rid his mind of the image of the sergeant's bony head, his great loping legs and the expectant way he peered when he put a question.

When Gemma came home with the children, he hugged her so hard she protested: "Hey – steady, tiger!" and then he wrapped an arm round each child and held them to him.

Over the next few days, Wayne began to become withdrawn, something that was noticed at work and by Gemma at home.

He was not sleeping and seemed disengaged from the children who normally took over every free minute with games, and cuddles and walks with the dog.

Gemma had become irritated because his restlessness was breaking her sleep.

Deep in the night she heard him ask something, so quietly that it was as if he needed to talk but simultaneously did not want to disturb her.

"Come on. What is it? Tell me, and then maybe you'll be able to sleep properly. And so will I."

Wayne lay on his back in the dark and said: "You know those films where people have blank spots, bits of their life they have no

205

memory of. Does that actually happen to people? Is it possible to lose a lump of memory of what's happened to you?"

"Possible, I suppose. Amnesia, but..."

"It's just that all this talking with the police has started to make me wonder..."

"Now stop this right now!" she shouted angrily. "You're not seriously going to say that you could have knocked somebody down, come up with a story that you'd given them a lift and then wiped your memory bank clean."

"It's stupid, I know. It's just that you start to doubt, Gem. I was exhausted, stressed, worried. I just wondered whether at times like that..."

"Well, don't wonder. Sleep, Wayne love, for God's sake."

Gemma refreshed her pillow with a couple of soft punches. She immediately regretted being dismissive but the road Wayne was stepping on led to madness.

She knew he'd be fine once the culprit was found.

She lay her arm over his head, as he always asked her to, whenever troubles robbed him of sleep.

o o o o o o o

Mad Mick was a terrifying sight when he was angry. It wasn't only his muscularity, and the wild mop of hair and the alarming black eyes but the way he barrelled about, like a rugby player looking for the man who'd just bitten him in the scrum.

He banged the sideboard with his fist and wheeled round to resume his tirade.

Pat stood by the window with tears streaming down her face. She was pitifully thin, wore no make-up and her hair was dry and neglected. Poverty had left its mark on her.

"Bastard blue-bottles!" Mick bellowed, and she grimaced and drew in her shoulders.

Mick's rage had been ignited earlier that afternoon when the police had come to the site where he was rendering a house side and fired a load of questions at him over the hit-and-run.

Police had been the bane of his life. Motoring stuff mostly but there were a couple of other things, incidents. He'd found that they didn't like it when people answered back. They couldn't tolerate a bit of chelp.

"So the crafty coppers called on us separately..." he said contemptuously.

Pat was used to having to absorb Mick's outbursts. But they still frightened her. They were like sudden storms that blew themselves out. Afterwards, he was tranquil but she was left feeling edgy and resentful.

The worst tantrums were usually over money, officialdom, scarcity of work. Mick and Pat had a knack of struggling ahead and simultaneously going backwards. Debt encroached like sour fen water, lapping at the door of the old rented cottage.

The children would scarper to a place of safety when Mick started to raise his voice. Not that he would harm them. It was just their natural reaction to feeling they were in the presence of a wild animal. After the worst of the rows, Pat would sometimes take an extra tablet but as she had told the doctor, she felt that it was Mick who should be having pills, then perhaps she could have coped without medication.

When Mick had spent his anger, he felt pity for Pat. This latest business wasn't her fault, and he knew she didn't like having to lie. And, overall, he could have done better, been better for her, he knew that. Sometimes he would look round the place, at the chipped and discoloured cooker, the steamy walls, the matted bit of carpet and despair.

He asked in a more controlled voice: "You're sure you didn't say anything that could drop us in it? They've got their claws into this one and they'll have somebody."

"Sure," Pat sniffled. "I just stuck to what we'd said. They seemed fine when they left. It's just a bit scary."

She could see that the storm had nearly passed. He walked over to her and put a beefy arm round her.

207

"You did well, Pat. Good girl," he said hoarsely, planting a kiss on her bony cheek.

∘ ∘ ∘ ∘ ∘ ∘ ∘

Lydia was carrying a bucket of feed out to the furthest troughs when she heard a commotion from the birds and saw the policeman at the door.

She filled the trough and returned to the house, lowered the bucket, and invited the officer in. She refrained from smiling to show that the call was an inconvenience.

The sergeant promised not to take up much time but he was looking into the hit-and-run accident that happened two years ago. Perhaps she'd seen the TV appeal on Close This Case?

Lydia said that she hadn't, and asked why on earth she had to answer questions she'd answered at the time.

"A new initiative. To make sure we hadn't missed anything," the sergeant said, noting Lydia's impatience, and her annoyance at having to keep the chickens waiting for their food.

The sergeant asked her to confirm that she had not been out in her car on the night of the accident. That she had not heard anything untoward that night. That she had not seen anything that might be related to the accident.

"I won't have seen anything or heard anything because I was inside the house," she said, without expression.

The sergeant said that he had noticed her car near the back door and that it had many deep dents, an especially large one on the left hand side above the front wheel.

Noting her unyielding manner he tentatively asked about how the damage had been caused.

"Bumping into things I suspect," said Lydia loftily. "But I do strive not to bump into people. And with the state of the car, I think if I did hit a person the car would come off worse."

He scribbled something in his notebook, and pondered. Here was a woman who was shabbily dressed and who lived in a crumbling damp dump, set in a morass of duck and chicken shit, and yet she had the air of a duchess.

He felt slightly enfeebled by her assumed authority and was a little ashamed of the fact.

Scrabbling round for something relevant and new to say, he spotted that there was no mention of family members in the notes of the investigating officer who had called just after the incident.

The question had to be asked. Lydia replied that she had a son and a daughter.

"Although you didn't leave the house in the car, is it possible someone else used your car that night? Your son, perhaps?"

"No, officer," Lydia said. "Not my son. I don't let him use the car."

Banned, maybe, thought the sergeant, hopefully.

"Is his licence suspended then?"

"No," replied Lydia. "He hasn't got a licence."

The sergeant waited for more details.

"But then he is only 12," she said.

Lydia made sure that the officer could see the contempt she felt for him.

○ ○ ○ ○ ○ ○ ○

The police sergeant was very sorry to bother Viv and Sniffer. He said so – and it was true. He didn't take any satisfaction at all from questioning a man who looked as if he might croak at any moment.

"This won't take a tick," he said briskly. "Just need you two to confirm what you told the officer who visited two years ago in connection with the hit-and-run, out where you used to live."

Viv replied that she quite understood. It was his job. But they'd nothing to add. They had been at home all evening.

The sergeant nodded; what he had in his record was confirmed.

Viv said that she remembered the night well because Sniffer and her had had a "bit of a domestic" over the noise her husband had been making with a screeching tool, and he'd eventually come to bed, after listening to a match commentary on the radio.

She thought this might lighten the conversation but the sergeant was unsmiling.

"I don't suppose you remember what the match was, sir?" said the officer, spacing out the words somewhat, as if Sniffer were a simpleton or stone deaf.

"Home to Walsall. Posh came back to draw 2-2."

The sergeant opened his eyes wide to show his amazement.

"Cor, what a memory!" Nevertheless, he thought to himself, he would check the match details later on the internet.

"One other thing you might not have been asked before," he said. "I know you didn't venture out but did you have any visitors that night, anyone arriving in a vehicle?"

Sniffer pulled a face that said: "Are you kidding? If they'd come they wouldn't have stayed long! No. No visitors. And just as well, from what Viv remembers. We were fighting like cat and dog around then. She was in the bath for a couple of hours, she says. All I remember is the match and my hands being covered in brown paint from finishing the gun."

"Gun, sir?"

"Yes, a gun for Annie."

"Annie?"

"The show. The one where Annie gets her gun. Except that she didn't have one to get. So I made one. She says that I still smelled of turps when I got into bed. I seem to remember her giving me a bit of chelp."

"Oh," said the sergeant, closing his notebook and sliding over the restraining elastic band. Perhaps the bloke's illness was the sort that affected the brain. He'd heard of the musical Annie but he could not for the life of him remember the orphan girl having a gun. Anyway, there was nothing new to be had from this pair, he thought.

He thanked Viv and Sniffer and said he would see himself out.

37

Sniffer's pain had been replaced by euphoria since the nurse had fitted the new drip. He knew in some rational but fuzzy way that he should be in terror, fighting the approach of death, and yet he was at peace.

Simple things had taken on special qualities. He had become filled with a child-like wonder. The world felt newer somehow.

He was comforted by the feel of cool cotton, when the bed sheets were changed. The sunlight falling to the room was as soothing as a warm bath after a long, hard day. Even a sip from his invalid's cup seemed like a first experience of drinking water. The very fact that it was colourless and tasteless seemed now to be remarkable.

Sniffer felt cleansed, and, when he talked with Viv, they were loving, respectful, gentle.

They had even spoken together, calmly and good-naturedly, about Lydia.

Viv had been generous, Sniffer concluded later.

She said that although she could find it in her heart to accept what had happened, it was only in an objective way. She still couldn't bear to think of Sniffer and Lydia together, of them talking intimately, of the deception. That was only natural, Sniffer, wasn't it? But she would keep trying.

Sniffer again implored Viv to forgive him but asked whether he could say something that Viv wouldn't want to hear but which was the truth.

Viv said: "Go ahead."

Sniffer hesitated. He touched his tray, looked away from Viv, preparing himself but in fact thinking of her, of the effect of what he was going to say; how what he said would stay with her when he had gone.

"It'd be easy for me to say that she was nothing to me. But she was."

"I know."

"Sorry Viv. But she still is."

"Oh."

Viv's chin dropped, she felt herself buckle inside, and she looked at the window, as if she wanted to be out, away from this room and a truth.

She took off her glasses, something she always did when she was emotional, or when they argued. She did not use this tactically but it always had the effect of making her appear more vulnerable to Sniffer.

"It's wrong. But I can't help it," Sniffer said. "Can we talk about it?"

"No, Sniffer. I need time to understand."

"If I could wipe it all out I would..." he began but Viv said: "Shush. Enough."

The sharp edge was back in her voice.

Viv disappeared and came with a mug of hot chocolate for him. He could see she'd been crying. She sat on the stool and said: "Can I ask you to be honest about something else?" Sniffer nodded.

"Well, when you sent Ursula away with that CD you did together, as your wife I can't tell you how hurtful that was, that what was on it couldn't be shared with me."

"Sorry about that too, Viv. You'll understand..."

Yes, I will know eventually, Viv said to herself. All will be revealed. But afterwards.

"But what I really want to know is about the candles. What were the candles about? Who were they for? Why can't I know? Sniffer –

I'm your wife."

"It's not really a secret. It just seemed so private at the time. It wasn't as if I wanted to shut you out, Viv. It's like praying. I've been finding that praying inside your head is fine but if you did it out loud it'd be embarrassing."

He stopped to think of another way of explaining.

"Say you were asking God for something, or frit shitless. You wouldn't want to be pleading out loud in front of somebody now would you?"

"It's your business," she said curtly. "But could it be you needed to say things silently because of who you were thinking of... because of hurting people. Hurting me. If one of them was for her."

"It's not my business, Viv, it's my...well my eternity. My last feelings. A bit like famous last words..."

"I'm wrong to want to know."

"No, Viv. You're not. I can tell you about the candles."

Viv could see that Sniffer was becoming agitated. How bad she felt, suddenly, of prodding and pushing a man who figuratively was on his knees.

"Right - number one. When I lit the candle at Ely it was for my daughter, whoever she is, whatever she's called, wherever she is. Just regret really, and the hope that her life is good."

He took a sip of hot chocolate.

"Now, the Clench candle, the one Pat took, looking as if I'd asked her to carry a bloody bomb, was for family, for the Clench days really - for mum, even though she never understood me but also for Granny Pud and Uncle Clarrie, and Terry and Sheryl."

He took another drink. Viv was amazed at the way he finding the words, at the flow of his thoughts. At that moment he didn't seem sick, certainly not on the verge of death.

He asked teasingly: "Right, Viv, who do you think the next was for, at Norwich, the one Mick lit?"

Viv didn't know what to think, or say. This could be a treacherous conversation. Please God not Lydia...

"Give in."

"It was for Ursula, Viv. Saint Ursula in my book. Explainer of everything. The person who rid me of the Dickman and the other fen spooks. The woman who showed me that there's still something worthwhile about me, and that I wasn't a total, 22-carat bastard…"

Sniffer suddenly looked tired. The words were drying up. Viv asked him if he wanted to rest.

"No," he said. "But I will in a minute."

He gathered his breath and got hold of Viv's hand.

"Anyway, the candle at Peterborough was for every single person I've ever hurt."

He laughed ruefully – "It should have been a humdinger! In a way, that candle was to gather all the regrets, to get all the bad shit into one place. Ursula called it my grand act of contrition."

"Clearing your conscience?"

"Yeah."

"And did it make you feel better, Sniff. Relieved?"

"Yea. Free. Light. And truly sorry about everything. Lighting that candle – and talking on that CD – made me feel, well, as if something had literally been lifted off my chest."

Sniffer shuffled down into the pillow that was propping him up, seeking comfort. He was drifting but said sleepily: "I lit a second one at Peterborough you know."

"Terry didn't tell me that."

He patted her hand. "One for you, Viv. For everything."

Viv gulped then kissed Sniffer's cheek.

She thought he would plummet into sleep as he had been doing; it was almost as if he was passing out. Although his eyes were closed he was still awake.

"By the way, it came to me this morning. The name that those weird people used, the people who used to come to Walpole Marsh on Sundays when I went to play with Gary. It was The Church of Imminent Arrival. I think it was Revelations they used to go on about. Must tell Ursula. Yes, Revelations."

Sniffer said that the visitors used to talk about God as if he'd got an overnight bag packed ready to drop down and start pointing at people and telling them whether they could go to heaven or hell. Gary had lived in a constant state of anxiety in case the arrival coincided with him doing something wicked.

"The cruel, silly buggers. They'll all have gone now, all probably died of boredom waiting. All except maybe Gary, who's my age. All those bloody years and Mr Big still hasn't arrived…"

o o o o o o o

Viv had to find things to do to occupy her as Sniffer slept, or when he was just resting, wanting her to be there.

Her head was still full of the show.

After weeks of learning lines, rehearsing and running through the choreography and shaping the songs, finally there had been four performances.

Then, suddenly, nothing. A big nothing. The photos and the local newspaper reviews were all that remained as evidence of all that dedication, that passion, that team work.

This time the post-show phase, the morning after feeling magnified many times, seemed more acute because she'd had the lead role. The adrenaline was still coursing through her but now she was back at Sniffer's bedside. It might as well have been a dream.

Viv got out her cuttings book and flipped through idly before turning to a blank page, taking the latest clipping and, having drawn the adhesive stick across the page, fixed it in place.

It was the cutting that made her feel proudest, the press review of her supreme night.

"Is your Eliza report in there?" said Sniffer, craning forward from his pillow.

His voice changed from day to day. She found it disturbing, just as she was pained by the way Sniffer's looks changed, the cheeks growing more sunken, the eyes more prominent, the hands softer now than they had ever been.

"I've just put it in," Viv said.

"Read it out again. You know the bit…"

Viv said: "Again Sniff? It's embarrassing!"

Viv relented and after skipping through the first paragraphs she read, almost bashfully…

"…but any doubts about Vivienne making a convincing Eliza vanished within minutes.

"She gave us just the right amount of naivety, she teased out the pathos, exploited the comedy and sang like an angel. Mercifully, there was less of the gorblimey-Cockney-sparrer-knockabout than is sometimes seen.

"When Eliza sang Without You, the number in which she girds herself up to tell Professor Higgins that she will manage very well without him in future, thank you very much, she stopped the show.

"And as she told him that he was 'not the beginning and the end' and that she would not feel alone after he'd gone, it was with the touching bravery of someone who is unsure but who is willing things to be all right.

"How often do we see a singer in a locally produced musical sing with such conviction that the audience is visibly moved? And how often do we see a singer shed tears in doing justice to lyrics?

"Vivienne lives it. And every second of the long ovation as Vivienne took her bow was thoroughly deserved."

Viv put down the scrapbook. Sniffer was pretending to be asleep but she knew he had heard it all.

She wondered whether he had made the connection between the song and the tears, and what was happening to them, and that's why he wanted her to read again from the cutting.

o o o o o o o

Viv could tell that Sniffer was failing and she said so, falteringly, in her phone bulletins to Terry, to Mick and to Sheryl.

She drew comfort from the new peace he seemed to have found. His waking days were untroubled and he no longer had tormenting

216

dreams.

Viv believed these changes had come before the morphine; also, he had been so different since he did the recording with Ursula.

The residual feeling of being excluded was countered by the heartening change in Sniffer. Now, calm showed in his face. His voice had softened. He showed concern and affection when they talked about the people he would leave behind.

He was especially concerned that Viv should keep in touch with Mick and his family and although she promised, she knew that she would not honour this and nor would they want her to.

That evening, when they had done so much talking that they had lost all track of time, as soon as he'd watched the early evening news on television, Sniffer seemed desperate for rest. He did not comment when on the regional sports round-up they showed the Posh goals from the weekend.

When he felt Viv tuck the duvet under his chin, he settled on the pillow and said: "I think I'll get off for the night now Viv. I'm beat."

She kissed his forehead and, immediately, in his mind he was back in the flat-bottomed boat that wildfowlers used to sit in. But this boat, the one he was lying in, belly down – paddling along with a hand at either side – was made of crystal. Pure and clear as polar ice.

The sun made every surface refract slivers of light; the sky was so bright he couldn't look up. If he gazed down, the sun was like floodlighting, sweeping the depths of the watercourse.

Through the clear crystal bottom of the boat he could see weeds undulating in grey-green swirls. And when he looked really carefully he could pick out sticklebacks, perfect like silvery jewels, some with a flash of orange on the underside.

The drain went straight as a train line, with bankside reeds so high that no-one could have seen the boat, except from up in the huge globe of the sky. Somewhere up there were skylarks – he could hear the trilling and a sweet burbling that reminded him of boyhood and summers and nests and the fragile remnants of eggshells.

The boat moved soundlessly. Birds clinging to the reeds were untroubled as he glided past them. Fascinated, he paddled backwards with his hands so that the boat almost stopped and he could stare, just inches away from birds that seemed to have assembled especially for him. Blackcap. Whitethroat. Bullfinch. Reed Warbler. There were birds everywhere, many gently swaying on the reeds.

Magically, when he looked down again through the crystal boat-bottom there was snow falling on a cottage, like in a shaken snow globe, and he could smell hot, sweet rice pudding.

He turned over, lay on his back, switched off his mind, and shut his eyes against the sun. He wondered whether he was the only man on earth; if he was, he did not feel alone, or afraid.

He felt that he was part of everything around him, and that all of it had always been as it was at that silent, sunlit moment.

The boat glided on soundlessly, and all Sniffer could hear were the skylarks.

38

I killed the man on the road.

Please, Sniffer. Not yet. One moment, dear.

I'm Ursula Elliott and I am a volunteer ecumenical chaplain, hospital visitor and befriender. I confirm that the following was recorded in my presence. Clarence asks specifically that I refer to him as Sniffer. We have gone through it and believe the events he describes is a true record of what happened.

So, Sniffer. From the very start...

I killed the man on the road.

I haven't got long to go. Ursula the chaplain is turning this into a CD and I have asked her to hand it to you. I want to make sure that nobody gets blamed for what I did, or punished if I dragged them into it in any way. Every single thing to do with the chap dying was my fault.

A couple of years ago my wife Viv found out that I had broken my promise to stop seeing a woman. She's called Lydia and she lives near where we used to live. Sells eggs.

Viv said to me that if I had any contact with Lydia again, our marriage was over.

I was very fond of Lydia, a lovely lady, but I couldn't live without Viv so I had to explain to Lydia why it had to end.

Early in November, I went to see my friend Mick O'Malley and borrowed his big Dodge.

I used to give Mick work when I could, and he'd let me have the Dodge if I had a load of stuff to take to a job, stuff too big for my van. He'd bought the Dodge from a USAF man. It's a Ramcharger. Had stuff done to it, customising.

That day I'd been to Johnsons building supplies to get plasterboard for a job out Eye way and when I got back I parked the Dodge next to the entrance to our drive ready for the next day.

After tea I went into my workshop to work on the wooden gun for Viv's show. It was Annie Get Your Gun but they had no gun and they were doing a full dress rehearsal the following night. A plastic one looked daft, Frankie said. I had to shape one like a Winchester. I often helped out with scenery and bits of carpentry for Viv's shows.

Viv and me were going through a bad time.

She always liked a long bath with a glass of wine and because we hadn't been speaking and she knew I'd be busy and listening to the Posh match commentary, she said she'd have a bath and an early night.

We'd sorted out the business over Lydia but I could see that Viv was still feeling it, and I don't blame her. She looked at me as if she hated me.

It must have been a still night, and my angle grinder made such a racket that she came down in her dressing gown to get me to stop using it. She was nasty. We had another argument because I was only making the noise to help her and the show.

I used a little saw instead, and a rasp, to finish the gun off and then I sanded it and painted it…

Stop a bit if you need to. Drink?

Sniffer, explain what you did then…

I was listening to the match against Walsall and when it was half-time, with Posh losing 2-0 I think it was, I got it into my head to slip off and tell Lydia about what Viv had threatened.

I didn't take the van. I took the Dodge because it was parked far enough from the house that Viv wouldn't hear it.

It only took minutes to get to Lydia's. I thought I could be back in half an hour or so and nobody would be any the wiser. But it turned out that when I told Lydia, she was heartbroken. Beside herself.

I couldn't get away. She's a strong woman, no self-pity usually, but she cried like a little girl. I didn't know how much I'd come to mean to her. I was very upset and I had to just about pull myself away from her in the end.

I started the engine and I could see her crying outside the back door so I left the engine running, went back and gave her a cuddle and then I piled into the Dodge, turned in the yard and then drove out on to the road…

OK? Have another drink. No rush. What happened then, Sniffer? When you tried to drive home?

As I remember it, I swung the Dodge round and pulled away quite fast because I was angry at Viv for making me break from Lydia and I was angry with Lydia for making me feel so bad about leaving her.

It was all my doing. And wasn't it typical of me that football came

into my mind minutes, minutes, after I'd left that lovely woman?

I'm not really sure exactly what happened next because it's been going round and round in my mind for two years.

You must have set off for home, Sniffer...

I did. I'll try to get it absolutely straight.

I remember I pulled at my seat belt to put it on and tried to switch the radio on with the other hand, so I could hear how the match was going. The Dodge was going straight enough then, I think, as I did that. But when I leaned forward it was revving, lurching forward.

Anyway, just as I was going to brake and get hold of the wheel again, suddenly I saw a strip of something. It was silvery. Just a flash in the dark. And then I felt a hell of a bang. A sickening bang, as if I'd hit a deer but there's no deer where we were.

I pulled up and reversed but couldn't see anything on the road. But when I wound the window down and got my head out, and reached as high as I could, and looked down to the water's edge, I could see from the light shining off the water a training shoe sticking up. I knew that I'd hit somebody. I knew that I'd hit them so hard they wouldn't have survived....

Do you want another rest Sniffer?

I want it finished, over with.

Just take your time...

I pulled up at the junction for Watersend where there's some decent lighting and I looked at the Dodge. It was covered with dents and scratches anyway. A proper rust bucket but Mick loved it. I could see that there weren't any new dents and there was no blood.

I found a bit of sacking in the back and wiped the front anyway. I was panicking and my head was filled with ideas for protecting myself. Same as always – not much feeling for the poor bugger dead on the bank of the drain.

I knew that if I owned up, never mind the police side of things, Viv would know that after she'd gone to bed I'd been out seeing Lydia. Where it happened was only a few hundred yards from her

house. I'd have lost Viv forever.

It was Mick's darts night, when he was always picked up and then dropped off by a team mate who didn't drink. Mick would have three pints before he threw a dart and he couldn't risk another driving case.

I rang Pat on my mobile and said that I was in a bit of trouble and that I needed help. I told her it was serious. Pat called me a bastard because she thought I was in some kind of bother involving a woman. She was always loyal to Viv.

I said I was going to drive the Dodge back to hers but I'd need a lift home, straight away. No messing. She said she'd just put the kids to bed. I told her that she was to be ready with them when I got there in ten minutes. I was bullying her.

I wanted the Dodge there overnight. I wanted it well away from our house and well away from where it happened. Bastard that I am, I didn't care that a good friend might end up in the shit.

I know you feel bad about getting friends involved and you want to make sure that there aren't any repercussions. Is that right Sniffer? Let's get it all on record...

Funny, that's what I feel worst about, and that's what's given me the torment.

I'd worked it out. Mick and Pat lived a bit off the beaten track and I knew that if the police did come round asking questions, Pat could say that Mick had been out darting and hadn't been on the road. The truth.

If they came to question me, I knew I could say that I hadn't been out in my van, which was true. Viv could tell them that I'd been busy in the workshop all evening and then come to bed, something she thought was true.

But what I can't forgive myself for is not that I knocked the lad over, I think that was just bad luck all round.

It was that I put Pat and Mick in danger of going to jail and if they had, the kids would have ended up in care. Because Pat had been told by Mick and me that if the police came she wasn't to mention

driving me home.

Mick was fine about it, but Pat was a bit arsy. She said why should she get into bother all because I couldn't keep my trousers zipped up. Poor girl had no idea that this was about death, not shagging.

I'm ashamed to say it but I'd warned her that if I got lifted and couldn't work, Mick wouldn't be earning. They were always elbows out, her and Mick. Never had a quid to spare.

In a roundabout way I threatened her, and put Mick in a sticky situation, my friend, who would have taken a bullet for me, killed for me. I'd reached a new low.

Here. Take a rest. Hanky. Let's leave it for today, Sniffer…

OK.

We are resuming but we might have to stop. Clarence is very weak this morning but wants to continue. So how did you leave things with your friends…?

Anyway, Pat was waiting for me with the kids. They had coats over their pyjamas. Pat looked at me as if I was something nasty that had stuck to her shoe. I got out of the Dodge and checked again under the house security light, where the impact must have been. There was nothing I could see.

"Bloke tried to cut me up," I said to her but she didn't believe a word. She just looked at me as if I was a piece of shit. And she was right about that.

I'll have to stop a minute. I want it right in my head.

Are you sure you're up to it?

I want to finish it.

You'd got to where you'd gone to your friend's house…

Pat dropped me off. I was in bed next to Viv ten minutes after that, as soon as I'd turned the radio on to hear the score. Posh got two in the second half to draw.

Funny what you remember. Funny how bloody football could come into it, at that time, with all that terrible stuff going on. Maybe it helped me keep sane.

I nudged Viv deliberately to disturb her, so she knew I was in bed, so she'd think I'd been around all the time, and I said to her "I've just finished the gun. The paint'll be dry by morning," and she got snappy. She said, "OK! Do you mind – I was asleep!"

She was still sulking. It was a bad time for us. I've been pretending that I don't remember anything about that time but I remember every bit.

I'll have to stop for a bit Ursula....

It is afternoon and we are resuming. Sniffer, you wanted to say something about Lydia. Did you think she'd tell the police you'd called on her just before the accident?

I wouldn't have blamed her letting on. I knew your lot, the police, would have to talk to her because she was so near to where it happened. But I never told her to deny I'd been to hers. We've never said a single word about it but for some reason I know damn well Lydia knew that I was the driver. And somehow I knew she knew.

Well, there's hardly any traffic along that road, especially at night, so when the police started appealing she will have known that it was odds on that it was me. Not only that, she knew I was in a bit of a state when I left.

I want to repeat. At no time did I tell her that I was the driver so there was no cover-up from her.

Is there anything else you need to say Sniffer to get it all off your chest?

I have to say what I did on Bonfire Night...

Go on Sniffer...

I moved him.

You hadn't told me that...

Because it haunts me. I can hardly say it.

I couldn't sleep when I got home after it first happened, just falling into nightmares then waking up terrified. The loneliness of it! I couldn't share it with Viv, or anybody.

I started thinking that maybe it was all a dream and so eventually I went back to check, to make sure that if it had actually happened.

If it had, and I knew it had really, I could hide him and let time pass and one day things would be like they'd been before.

I went out in the van in the dark, found the skid mark where I'd braked, and climbed part way down the bank. And it was true. He was there. Even in the dark I could see his training shoe.

There were little shelves down near the edge that the water had made, flat bits where the bank had been washed away. There was one just below him and I had this idea.

If I could get him on to one of them, he'd be just about invisible and just, you know, eventually waste away, and then when the high water came, one day when the water level was up, he… what was left would be washed off the shelf.

Then everything would be normal again.

Anyway, I couldn't touch him and so I lay on my side on the slope and pushed him hard with my feet until there was a horrible thump as he went down on to the packed mud of the shelf.

But I could still see the training shoes, orange ones, and his face had turned up as if he was looking at me. It was a terrible look so I started to push mud and soil down on to him with my feet but he wasn't getting covered so I went up to the van and then did a proper job with a shovel. Then I went home.

I just want to say sorry about the young chap and sorry to his mother. But bad luck came into it. Me getting in a tangle in the Dodge and him being where you'll never normally find anyone out at any time of the year. Just wrong time, wrong place.

But what I've really been broken up about was Viv, that I tricked her again, and then gave in to Lydia when she wanted to see me on the bike ride because she thought it would help me with the dying.

But there's that worst bit – that I'd been a coward and used my friends.

Me and Ursula have talked a lot about hell and punishment. If it's any consolation to anybody involved I can tell you that there is a hell, for me anyway. It's now, lying here with my ribs sticking out and pipes all over and my head full of nightmares.

But at long last I've said it all. I've come clean.

It feels good to know that for once in my life there's absolutely nothing I'm hiding from anybody. Maybe getting cancer is enough to clear the debt.

You've done it Sniffer. You've come clean. Believe me, God will love you for that. Love you even more.

39

The morning after Sniffer died, Viv was up long before dawn.

She had barely slept. She had gone into his room, put down the tray, and although it was still dark, she had opened the curtains as if to will the day to start. She was anxious to give him his extra medication.

She had said "Rise and shine" very softly in case Sniffer had gone into a deeper sleep than usual. It was what her mother had said to get her up for school.

She saw immediately that Sniffer had gone.

She had hurried to the phone in the hall and rung emergency services as if there was still hope but she knew it was pointless.

"Is there any pulse?" the emergency lady with the calm voice had asked. Viv had not needed to check.

"No," she had said. "Maybe. But I don't think so." She had included "maybe" so that the paramedics would have to come and make sure.

Although she had had many weeks to prepare for this moment,

she suddenly felt helpless. She needed to have someone to take charge of what was to come.

Terry and Jess and Sheryl and Dusty had arrived by lunchtime. They were now sleeping, as she made coffee and trudged around in her dressing gown as if in a drug-induced trance.

Sniffer must have known it was the end, she decided, hearing in her head their last conversation.

He had looked disarmed, bowed, beaten, and it felt to her as if every deceit, every scream of protest, every thrown plate, every broken promise was as nothing.

Death really did put things in perspective.

"It was for you, Viv. For everything."

Words she could tuck away and draw comfort from for years. The words had been on her lips when she had emerged today from the shallow nap, in the lonely darkness of what had been their bedroom.

The hardest part of yesterday had been telling Terry. She had left a message at the school asking him to ring her. She had been glad that he was in class. Viv knew he would have guessed the reason for her call. When she told him that Sniffer had died in his sleep, he didn't reply.

"Still there, Terry?" she had asked. There was a few second's delay and then he had said almost inaudibly: "My poor Viv. Hold on. We'll be with you soon."

Sheryl, who was all in black, called almost inaudibly from the front door as she came in, as if she was entering somewhere holy. She was in tears before she reached the kitchen.

Dusty, carrying an overnight bag and looking awkward, wore the eternal hint of a smile as usual but his eyes reflected sympathy for Sheryl, uncertainty as to how he should be, and sadness as he hugged Viv.

He had thought a lot in the car about Sniffer and the way they had irritated each other and decided that at the root of it was Sniffer's ego, not his own waspish way. He felt the loss mainly for

Sheryl.

He joined Terry and Jess, Sheryl and Viv and after sandwiches they sat is a desolate circle round the dining table.

The conversation was almost all about practicalities. Viv knew this was to keep the grief and loss away.

When at last she broke down and cried inconsolably, she felt she had breached the dam, making things more difficult for the others. It had. It had set off Sheryl, who from time to time made keening noises and hugged Dusty as if he was a teddy bear.

Terry had been a rock. He had held Viv hard. He had fetched pizzas that night, and some beer and a bottle of the Irish whiskey Viv always bought as a Christmas treat for herself but which Sniffer would always have seen off by New Year's Day.

They had eaten, chatted over a couple of drinks, and then gone to bed because there seemed little else to do except talk about Sniffer, something Viv wanted, but which the others seemed to be avoiding.

"They're trying to be strong for me," she said to herself. But why must we be strong? She looked forward to the time they could all cry, give in to grief, fume over the injustice of their loss, and finally tell the stories that made up Sniffer's life.

Light invading the room from the edges of the kitchen blinds showed that at long last the night was finally over, so she raised them, grateful that she could occupy herself by preparing breakfast for everybody.

She was at the sink when she saw a police car had pulled up outside. She wondered whether there had been another break-in along the road. But then she saw the two officers coming up the path.

"Sorry it's so early," said the older of the policemen. He held a clipboard. "This is 54 isn't it? I wondered whether we might have another quick word with your husband?"

He said that he was aware that he was ill but he believed he might be able to help with a pretty serious development concerning a major incident – "I know we've spoken about this before, at the previous address..."

"I'm afraid you can't speak to him," Viv said. "He has just died."

The older policeman tried not to appear shocked but Viv saw the fleeting change of expression and she could tell he was frantically assessing the consequence of what he'd been told.

"In that case, may we say how sorry we are. Oh dear. We'll be in touch but please don't worry yourself at this time."

So, thought Viv, reflecting on the officer's words, I mustn't worry at the moment but later they'll give me something to worry about.

She began to speculate but knowing Sniffer, any manner of minor law-breaking had been possible. But then they had said "pretty serious."

Viv knew that "pretty" was probably a substitute for what was really meant – "very." She knew that it would have been about the CD Sniffer had made with Ursula, about the horrible secret she knew Sniffer had been hiding from her.

° ° ° ° ° ° °

Mad Mick was doing a bit of sand and cement mix for his young nephew Darren when he got the call saying that Sniffer had died.

Darren had been trying, in an amateurish way, to render the inside of the crumbling brick wall in front of the tumbledown cottage he was buying.

For Mick, the project had little appeal. He saw many hours of unpaid work ahead. But you did things like this for family.

He could have made things easier by bringing the mixer in the Dodge but there was something satisfying about hand mixing, integrating the cement with the sand until they were blended into an even grey.

There was a rhythm you could get into, circling the board, swinging the shovel to the base of the pile, overturning the mix. You got a good feeling knowing that the stuff you were giving to the brickie would be still holding bricks together in a hundred years.

And anyway, he wanted something physically hard to do, to stop him thinking about Sniffer.

Mick had been steadily turning over the pyramid of sand and cement after showing Darren how to pin lathes at intervals along the wall, and demonstrating how to use the float boldly to make the mix defy gravity.

"Slap it on, man!" said Mick, taking the float and smearing the mix with flourishes, leaving the section of the wall smooth and sound.

"Bloody hell, Daz – you'll have as much on the bloody floor as on the wall!" he shouted, with more affection in his voice than criticism.

He loved Darren, his attitude, his youthful striving, and especially his manners, the way he still called him Uncle Michael. He loved being called Uncle Michael.

The phone was going. It was in his puffer jacket, which hung on a nail at the back of the cottage, where they'd been looking at the potential for French windows.

It had stopped ringing by the time he reached it.

"Shit," he said. There was a ping and he saw that there was a text message: "Please ring Viv."

Mick didn't like the look of this. He began to breathe heavily. Then he said to himself: "Don't fear the worst, Mick. She might just need some help. Or Sniffer might need something."

He went to the front of the house and saw that Darren was getting on well now, putting the mix to the wall with strong, arcing sweeps. He then went to the back of the house and rang Viv.

"It's Mick," he said, aware he must be sounding nervous.

"Mick," said Viv. "I'm sorry but he's gone."

"Gone?"

"This morning, when I went to wake him."

"Fucking hell, Viv. Sniffer. Gone?"

"I'll keep in touch," she said but Mick had unknowingly switched off the phone.

He put it in his pocket, then faced the cottage wall and raised his arms and spread his hands, leaning forward as if he had lost his balance.

Mick didn't want to cry, especially in front of Daz, but no matter how hard he swallowed and shook his head, he knew that there was no holding it all in. He concentrated hard on the crumbly brickwork in front of his eyes, and tried to think of things to distract him, but the tears came.

"Fucking hell. Sniffer. Gone?" he said.

He had to get away. Think about Sniffer. Find somewhere private to get to grips with the news. He'd known it was coming. He felt bad that he had not been there, that he might have made a difference.

Mick walked briskly back to the front rubbing an eye with the back of his hand. He paused to shout: "Are you OK with it now, Daz?"

"Cracking on well," he replied proudly, smearing more mix on to the wall with hefty sweeps of the float.

"I've gone and got a bit of mix in my eye so I'll have to pop off and get it washed out. You're OK? There a nice bit of stuff there," he said pointing to the mound on the mixing board. "Be back if I can get this eye clear. Stinging like hell."

"Cheers Uncle Michael," Darren called, as he worked. "No worries if you can't get back."

"Cheers, Daz," Mick said, getting into the sanctuary of the Dodge where he could hide and drive and cry as much as he liked, and try to start to come to terms with losing his best friend.

o o o o o o o

Lydia heard about Sniffer's death much later than most, two days after the event in fact, and then only by chance.

The pub crib team were playing away at The Eel Trap. She had picked up her friend Enid in the old 2CV and they had played, lost, put away the cards and boards and had stayed to watch the climax of the darts match.

Two or three of the Webbed Foot players were using the table Lydia and her friend sat at for their drinks.

As one of them picked up his drink, above the din she heard him ask his team mate if he'd read in the Telegraph that Sniffer the builder had gone.

The mate looked puzzled and shook his head, barely able to hear above the hubbub.

"You know him. Been working all over for years. Dark. Baldish. Bit wild. Right character. Loved the women. Used to really hammer the drink."

Lydia's hand tightened round her glass. Her eyes widened and her mouth formed an "o," and she consciously had to close it.

"Ah, yea! Used to see him in Johnsons. Used to be a regular, then he moved to Peterborough," the mate said, picking up his darts. "Bit of a lad in his time. Big Posh fan."

They were having to bawl at each other to be heard.

"Yea. That's him. Cancer."

"Cancer? Poor bugger."

Lydia felt the room moving round her. She leaned across so she was close to Enid but could not speak and hurried to the toilets, shut herself in a cubicle, sat on the closed lid and cried into the palms of her hands.

She stayed there until the deepest sobs had subsided and then sat staring at the door, trying to compose herself.

At last she got up, went out into the noisy bar and said in Enid's ear: "Do you mind if we go, love? I...don't feel well."

Enid looked concerned and mouthed "OK," and nodded but was puzzled by the suddenness of Lydia's request.

In the car park, as Lydia opened the car she said: "Sorry Enid, but I thought

I'd pass out in there. I think I'm getting something."

Once she was at the wheel, ready to drive off, she wondered whether she would be capable of driving. Enid was concerned.

"Are you sure you're OK?" she asked, searching her face in the weak light from the pub windows.

"I'll be fine," Lydia said, but knew she wouldn't, not for a long time.

o o o o o o o o

Jo Johnson hardly went into the showroom nowadays because Old Man Johnson was so unsteady on his feet that he had to stay in the bungalow most of the day.

She would pop across the yard whenever he was settled but his health was becoming a worry and she could see that she was now more of a carer than a helping hand for Brian.

She so missed the showroom work, the steady stream of tradesmen calling. She missed the teasing and the jokes but also seeing the customers going off with exactly what they needed for the jobs they had on.

Jo just happened to be going into the shop after giving her father his lunch when she caught the tail end of a conversation Brian was involved in.

"A real character. He was never out of here at one time," Brian was saying nostalgically. "All right, he wasn't everybody's cup of tea but he was right as ninepence with us. God, we had some laughs!"

She knew the man he was speaking to. Tony something, a plumber.

Tony said: "I hear it had spread everywhere." And then: "Always seemed to be embroiled with some woman or other..."

Bri noticed that Jo had come in. He made a sad face and called across the shop: "Jo – Sniffer's gone."

For Jo, there was a brutality in the way Brian announced this but she knew that was not intended. She could feel a strange tremor go though her.

Sniffer gone. How could he have gone? A bloke who had always been so brimful of life?

She decided that she had loved the man. Not in that way, of course, because that would be ridiculous. He had been ancient compared to her. But it was love of a sort, a special connection, friendship and yet as it registered with her now, more than friendship.

The rest of the customers were nice enough. But not one of them could hold a candle to Sniffer.

She thought again about the time he had asked to tell the bloke on the phone that he had fainted. How she loved being in that little conspiracy! It made her happy and sad to think of it.

The last time she had seen Sniffer was a few weeks after the ride when Dad and Sniffer and the other riders had posed together at the cancer charity office.

Sniffer was gaunt and, she thought, a strange colour beneath his tan. It made his eyes stand out and twinkle even more than usual.

He had been fooling around and at one point shouted "Cover for me Jo!" and pretended to be running off with the giant cheque which was out on show again after the final sponsorship figure had been sorted out.

Sniffer was pretending to look like a thief and his legs went up and down a few times on the spot as if he was running. She noticed that even with that little effort his breathing had become laboured.

Dad had asked the photographer to take an extra picture of him with just Sniffer, and they put their arms round each other's shoulders as if they were wartime army pals, or reunited brothers.

Jo decided she would go in now, tell Dad and then find the photo. She left the shop and headed across the car park for the bungalow.

Dad was going to be bitterly upset about the news. But not as much as she was.

o o o o o o o o

"You know what, Kathy", Doreen said zipping up her body-warmer.

"What?" said Kathy, settling at her desk, reluctant for the moment to take off her gloves and hang up her coat.

"I'd love to get the architect who designed this bloody great box and make him sit here for a day bollock naked."

"Doreen!"

"Well, we're either like chickens on a spit, or we're having our tits frozen off. I'm bloody sick of it."

"Doreen!"

Doreen fetched the work tray from the cosy admin office nearby. It was like a nest in there. Warmth, chatter, laughter. Lucky devils, she thought.

She took the tray, which was heavy with files, and put it between herself and Kathy, and they switched on their computers, and signed in, the ping of recognition echoing round the huge, cold office.

Kathy volunteered to go to the coffee machine and asked Doreen if she wanted anything other than the drink.

"Just a hot water bottle and a foil poncho," she said unsmilingly.

While Kathy was away, Doreen made a start, scrolling down lists of patients, noting actions required, listing appointment letters to be sent, phone calls to be made.

Kathy and the coffee had just arrived and she was handing Doreen a couple of squares of chocolate when she noticed that her eyes had widened, and her face had contorted.

"No! Oh no," she said and then held her breath.

"What, Doreen?"

"Nothing. Nothing, love."

Kathy snapped off a couple of chocolate squares for herself, and dipped into the pile of documents. She worked on, blithely unaware of the maelstrom of feelings that one word had stirred up in Doreen.

It was the word "Deceased" and it had come up on screen against the name of a man called Clarence.

o o o o o o o

A good part of Ursula's job was watching people die. Watching and waiting with them; soaking up their fear; giving her own hard-won view of God, of mercy, and love.

Sometimes being a chaplain made her feel small and ineffective; at other times she felt she had been the conduit for the most sublime feelings.

Ursula knew she had helped Sniffer, and it pleased her. He was a lovely, soft man beneath all the banter and the bluster, a pickle of a man. He was a charmer, of course, and he was also selfish, devious, a loveable manipulator.

He was also a man with a tortured conscience, although their talks, and doing the recording, seemed to have given him such solace. She would be building on that when she saw him next.

She was glad to have got to the bottom of that fire and brimstone nonsense. Sniffer's sister Sheryl had spoken to her about the strange people at some place called Pig Fen and their propensity for tales of eternal suffering. Ursula felt satisfied at having helped Sniffer over this nonsense and that she had acted properly over Sniffer's confession.

As he could not talk with Viv about the things that haunted him, about the accident, about resuming contact with Lydia, she had been his confessor.

Poor Viv must have felt redundant and had surely have resented her. But the priority, she had decided, was to help Sniffer to die, to ease his terror and the way to do that was for him to free himself of guilt.

When she had last seen him, when they made the recording that she had then put on to a disc to take to the police, he had looked much thinner but the morphine drip meant he had little pain. They had laughed over him getting a "fix" any time and all on the National Health.

It was time to see him again, especially as the end must be near now.

Ursula was about to hunt for her diary when the phone rang in her little book-lined study.

It was Viv saying that Sniffer had died.

Ursula was always upset to hear that those she had shared confidences with, those she had grown to love, had finally been snuffed out. But this was different.

"The poor, dear man," she said, sinking into her office chair. "And poor Viv. What a man you had!"

"Of course we all want you to do the honours – the service or whatever," Viv said. "You were his godsend."

"Dear man."

"He either called you that, or love on legs – or Saint Ursula."

How could have resisted helping him? And what was it about Sniffer that reached areas in her she had set on one side?

Ursula suspected that Sniffer had appealed directly to the femininity she had subdued, minimised over the years. Perhaps she had strived too hard to be what those who were suffering wanted her to be, a person they perceived as having gravitas, wisdom?

Stupid to think that make-up, or a smart skirt, was contrary to spirituality but that's how some would see it and perhaps she had fallen in with that.

Whatever this thing about Sniffer had been – this special thing – she knew he had invaded some remote part of her being, and that it had been a warm sensation now replaced with a gnawing feeling. Loss.

o o o o o o o

Kath McGill had watched her favourite TV serial and then turned off the set when she heard that awful, dramatic music that always announced the news headlines. There was nearly always something brutal on.

She hated the news. Strange, she hadn't felt like that before, before she lost Robert.

She was on her way up the stairs with her crossword book when the phone rang.

Kath chose not to answer it. It would be someone in India trying to hook her into something.

But then, she decided, she could always let the phone lie on the table in the hall. She'd read in her magazine that doing that deterred cold callers because they eventually twigged that no-one was listening. She went down and picked up the phone.

"So sorry to ring you late in the evening Mrs McGill." The voice was Scottish, rough but friendly, and had the ring of authority.

"DCI Barclay, Three Counties Police. We were sure you'd want to know straight away that the TV programme was a great success," he said kindly.

"I'm so pleased," said Kath. She was surprised at her lack of curiosity about what the caller had to say.

"We have identified the driver responsible. And we also located a young man who gave your son a lift just before the accident."

"How very kind of him," she said.

"Would you like you like to know more now, or could I arrange for one of our liaison ladies to visit you for a chat?"

"No. No thank-you. I'm in no hurry to know more. I feel no urge for vengeance, or justice really, although I don't want to seem ungrateful for your efforts. I will not dwell on the person who did it but I'll think often of the young man who bothered to stop."

None of this police business engaged her really. Just as the report from the health trust about Robert getting out of the unit seemed merely academic. Their official apology and promise to change procedures was of no interest.

People were people and things would go wrong. What none of it would do is bring Robert back. But what did touch her was the thought of that young man stopping to help Robert, pulling up to help.

"Yes, I really would like to get in touch with that kind chap to thank him," Kath said.

"I'm sure we can help with contact details. Meanwhile, goodnight. We'll be in touch."

DSI Barclay had broken a lot of shocking news in his time but he was glad that he hadn't to tell her that the man who had run her son down was now also dead. Disturbing for this really nice lady, on her own late at night.

As he drove home after his shift one question went over and over in his mind, a question still unanswered when he pulled into the drive. How could the mother of an innocent son killed by a coward not even be vaguely interested in the bastard's identity?

The answer dawned on him as he went into the home of his sleeping family and settled to watch a late night film.

The mother didn't want to know because it didn't matter a monkey's.

Her lad was dead, full stop. So it simply didn't matter whether it was this Sniffer character, or Bart Simpson or the Prime Minister who had knocked him over.

She was only interested in the chap who'd given her boy a lift. That was because that link took her back to when he was alive, and she could get a crumb of comfort from the thought of someone being nice to him.

40

The chief at Three Counties police – the proper chief, not the eager heir in waiting – had made a pre-retirement promise to herself. This was that in her last few months she would not be facing a press conference to say: "We're sorry. But lessons have been learned."

Her plan was to ease into retirement – to the countryside and her bit of greenery and her horse – rather than have to firefight right to the bitter end.

She was sick of the taste of humble pie, heartily sick of saying sorry on behalf of some dim greenhorn.

Two years ago, when she could have been hacking round the

lanes, she had instead been taking the flak on behalf of a bone-headed constable who had dragged them into the national papers by getting his retaliation in first, but, worse, stupidly doing it under a CCTV camera.

And then, last autumn, there was the case of the missing delivery man who was finally found lying, bloated beyond recognition, across the front seats of his van, which was almost covered by the waters of the River Nene.

Unfortunately, the force had still been looking for him days after the van had been "found" by constable who had declared the van empty.

She had made a mealy-mouthed apology to restore public confidence and had hurried forward the launch of the "Slow down, don't drown" campaign, that involved putting notices at bankside spots where drivers, most of them sober, had shot into one or other of the waterways.

So Helen was determined not to end what had been a good career with yet another embarrassment. And yet this hit-and-run business was shaping up that way...

The chief spread out the papers and copies from notebooks and decided that there had been bad mistakes, and if as result "it" hit the fan, she would be in her office listening to "it" splattering on Kevin, fouling those new designer glasses of his.

Lately he had been talking a good game but there had been slippage in his performance. She was appalled to hear he had been ingratiating himself with people beyond her rank in his quest for stardom.

That rankled. He needed bringing down to earth.

Helen rearranged the papers on her desk and set her forensic mind to work.

She could tell immediately that the fact-gathering had been poor. She played the CD again, with the confession and all the details of the offence, details that her force (with the help of millions of TV viewers) had failed to obtain. When she looked again at the notebooks she could see why.

Yes, Kevin could paddle his way through this particular stretch of Shit Creek, the chief decided.

After all, he had been running this inquiry.

"Right, Kevin. The hit-and-run," the chief said brusquely, having called him in later that day. "View?"

"It's sorted, chief. I take it you know that the driver, the one who sent the CD, has just popped his clogs? We're just looking at statements to see if there's any cases coming out of it all – conspiracy, obstructing the course…that sort of thing."

"And the van driver who came forward, the man who gave the victim a lift? Were we leaning on him too hard, considering it turned out there was precisely nothing linking him with what happened after he dropped the victim."

"No. Not really. Anyway, he doesn't figure any more."

"Thanks to the helpful confession. And I see the young chap does indeed still figure in the papers, Kevin. He comes over as a decent, truthful young man who, as a result of doing a good turn, has had his reputation ruined."

She leaned forward, put her elbows on the desk and rested her head on her hands.

"Very concerned that in the quotes, there's dangerous pre-judgment by you, something that would get a defence lawyer salivating. You virtually say in this paper: 'Got him!' You know it's best not to say that ever. But especially if it's the wrong man."

Kevin tilted his head as if to say: "Well, that's your opinion."

"OK, let's cut to the chase. Let me tell you I think that there are aspects of this inquiry that would make a Brian Rix farce."

"Brian Rix, ma'm?"

"Before your time. Anyway, let's look at some of the work that you've overseen, Kevin…"

Kevin's faced showed that he was needled. This seemed to him to be the final floundering of a dinosaur. He couldn't wait until it tottered off to oblivion.

God, Helen had really been up herself lately. But then she'd always been very private, almost standoffish. Impersonal, impervious to charm. No time for small talk. He had never really found a way past the façade.

"Now, take the interview with the lady Lydia…"

Helen was enjoying this. Kevin was looking piqued.

"It was a well-known fact that she was being pleasured regularly by the man popularly known as Sniffer. When asked about her movements on the night of the hit-and-run, at the first interview she said she had been at home all evening."

Helen noticed that Kevin had begun to clench his teeth.

"She had been in. But I see no one asked her whether she'd had a visitor. Nor did they ask in the subsequent interview. It is only now, when this Sniffer sends in his CD and ties up everything for us, that she says that yes, lover boy had called."

Helen said that when asked at this third interview why she hadn't told the police before, the lady Lydia had said, quite reasonably, that no one had asked.

"No-one had asked…" Helen said with a slow, shake of the head.

"I see, Kevin, that in the interview with Pat, the wife of the Dodge-owning Mick, she confirms that Mick had been picked up and returned from the pub by a friend, statements we corroborate. But at no time Kevin, do we ask whether she went out that night while he was out. We presumed that because she had kids to look after, she couldn't go out. And of course she did go out."

She made sure that Kevin met her gaze full on; she was looking for signs of discomfort.

"So this lady says 'But no-one asked me that. I just answered the questions.'"

The chief riffled through the papers to ensure that Kevin was kept expectant about what else might be said.

"And now we have this," she said. She held up a copy of the Telegraph and cuttings from the national press.

" 'My arrest hell over good turn,' this one says. So, the Good

Samaritan has been given a tough time. Result: Joe Public is behind him, and into us."

The chief went to the window, with the clippings from newspapers. She held another up.

"You'll probably have seen this from one of the nationals. 'I killed him – deathbed confession on CD' it says and describes us as 'baffled police' and points out gleefully that the cowardly killer of the young doctor lived, unsuspected, within a couple of miles of the incident. Hence the term 'police bungle.'"

The chief said that she wanted Kevin to go away and think about how the officers under his command had performed, and for him to come up with a form of words that he, Kevin, would use when he, Kevin, lead the press conference that would inevitably follow all that had gone on.

"Oh, and by the way, could I give you some advice about your approach to our masters? It's a saying. 'If your work speaks for itself, don't interrupt."

Again, Kevin was silent. As he reached the door, he put aside for a moment all his training in tolerance, equality at work, respect for sexual orientation, and said under his breath: "Butch bitch."

The chief looked quizzically at him wondering what words his mouth had formed knowing he would not have the courage to voice them.

Then she said: "By the way, Kevin. Hope you don't mind me asking. Are they new safety glasses you're trying out for us?"

41

"Well...that's got me beat. Just have a butchers, Piotr..." Gerald called to his junior colleague, at the Co-operative Chapel of Rest.

"Butchers?" Piotr replied, arriving at the other side of the table.

He had been in England two years now and yet these strange English words kept coming. Only the other day, Gerald had asked him to "pop up the apples and pears" and he had no idea what on earth he was supposed to do.

Now it was "Have a butcher's hook at this."

Gerald was saying. "Butcher's hook – a look. Cockney rhyming slang."

Piotr had not come across the words Cockney, rhyming or slang but guessed that Gerald was inviting him to offer an opinion about the strange tattoo on the marble-white bottom of the body.

"CHE... CHE..." Gerald said distantly to himself, as if by repeating the letters a solution would offer itself up.

Gerald had seen some weird tattoos in his time, of varieties and in places people would never believe. He would never forget the lovely young lass with the Bird of Paradise on her back, the head just below her waist, the long twin forks of its tail running down, parallel along either buttock.

"It is very...very..." Piotr began. He had found that if you left a gap for a word you didn't know, people filled it in for you.

"Strange. Mystifying. Bewildering, Piotr?"

They put the tattoo conundrum aside while they busied

themselves around the body.

"He looks like monk this man. He is bold," said Piotr pointing to Sniffer's circular bald patch.

"Bald, Piotr. Like a monk's tonsure. You'll have seen a lot of them in Poland. But this bloke wasn't a monk. Clarence here will once have been a strong chap, a manual worker."

"He is a Clarence? What is a Clarence?"

"His name, Piotr. It's an old sort of name, not popular now."

"I think it's cool name. Clarence…"

Piotr went to the far end of the room to bring the carrier bag that the dead man's wife had sent. Inside were items that were to go in the coffin. When he returned, he struck his forehead with the base of a hand and said: "I know it, Gerald!"

Gerald looked round quizzically.

"What do you know, Piotr?"

"The writing. It is for Chelsea. The football team."

"Well, possibly…" said Gerald, disappointed that Piotr's had beaten him in offering a solution but finding it less than convincing nevertheless. "Given where it is, I suppose it should have been Arsenal instead!"

Piotr frowned.

"Joke," Gerald explained, laughing. "Arsenal because it's on his arse. Understand, Piotr? Oh, please yourself." Gerald derived great joy from Piotr's constant state of incomprehension.

"I am sorry," Piotr said earnestly. Then he asked: "Gerald, why does the tattoo man not write it all, all the words? There is plenty paper on the other side of the butum."

"Skin, not paper, Piotr. And it's 'bottom.' I think you've come up with a word that combines bum and bottom."

Piotr nodded and pretended to take the point.

"What you're saying, Piotr, is that there was space for the whole word but for some reason the tattooist didn't do the LSEA on the end. Yes, weird."

Sharon shouted from reception to say that she'd poured the tea and that two more bodies would be arriving that afternoon.

Piotr declined the tea. He just broke off for a biscuit – and went back to the coffin with the carrier bag of items from the widow.

They had placed Sniffer on his back, his hands by his sides. Piotr put the tattered red exercise book on the chest of the corpse. He did it gently, then reverently laid the photo frame with the broken glass on top of it.

He was intrigued to pick out the face of the dead man in the picture, and touched to see the man so happy with his friends. For Piotr, dead people were still people. He sometimes felt himself shaking his head while looking at the body in front of him, feeling wonder and pity and incomprehension at the mystery of life and death.

Dipping into the bag, Piotr pulled out a scarf and a woolly hat and was delighted to find that they were blue and white. He was no football fan but he was certain that Chelsea played in blue and white.

"Gerald!" he called. "I am thinking I am right! Clarence is Chelsea man!"

Gerald arrived at the coffin side, once again feeling slightly miffed that Piotr had come up with an answer that had evaded him. But his dismay was short-lived.

"No, Piotr. Look," he said, pointing to the badge on the woolly hat. "Look – 'Upon this rock.' That's Peterborough United. Posh. Their coat of arms. Bloody hell, Piotr! This bloke would have spun in his grave if he heard you saying he supported Chelsea. Not that he's having a grave to spin in. He's gone for the hot option."

"OK, Gerald, but we do not explain still why he has butum writing."

Gerald consulted paperwork and ticked a box to show that they had fulfilled the widow's request that the deceased should be wearing the hat and the scarf when the coffin was sealed.

"Bottom writing, Piotr," he said with a hint of impatience. "Not butum."

Gerald flicked through his papers and seeing that everything was complete said: "But you're right. The Case of the Tattooed Butum remains unsolved. And we'll never know the answer now. After all, we can't ask the poor chap."

42

Terry was finding it hard to think of anything but Sniffer.

Jess had driven down to be with Viv for a few days but he had decided not to take time off before the funeral. It was a crucial time for the kids at school and he would have felt he was letting them down. But he could not concentrate for long.

He began to feel emotional about Sniffer as soon as he was away from people. The first couple of evenings had been quite difficult and he had drunk too much and fallen asleep in front of the TV.

Terry had not come across anyone who was openly critical of Sniffer and what he had done but he was sure that there was much talk out of earshot of the family. He knew that those who had always regarded Sniffer as a loveable rogue might now be castigating him as a callous coward.

He had come to terms with what had happened, and Sniffer's role, and had come to a conclusion, in what he was sure was an objective way.

Sniffer was guilty of betrayal but he had been right in his view of the accident – it really was an accident, an unfortunate confluence, the young doctor being there at the precise moment that Sniffer lost control of that beast of a vehicle.

He was then guilty of cowardice, most would say, and Terry agreed. But Sniffer had known that he was not leaving a dying man but a dead one – and that he would have lost Viv if she knew he had been visiting the Egg Woman.

The fear of losing Viv was the decider. And when that initial decision had been made, there was no option for Sniffer but to try to cover his tracks, and that's when, to his dying shame, he had implicated friends who were guiltless.

If those who were whispering now about his villainous brother ever confronted him, Terry would have reassured them that Sniffer had paid a fitting price for his behaviour. He had died believing that his cancer was the direct result of his action. Direct justice inflicted without mitigation – just as, once, the clips behind the ear from his mother had been in reaction to some misdeed.

Terry was sure that some out there – injured parties, cuckolded husbands, abandoned women – will have believed that dying from illness was too good for him. But unlike Terry, they had not seen the spirit of a man withering, a strong man turned to a skeleton, a hell-raiser reduced to a croaking, dependent child.

o o o o o o o

Dusty had rung to ask about the funeral and they had agreed to meet at the pub, and Malcolm promised to join them. Malcolm decided it would be good to hear Dusty's news and have a proper catch-up with Malcolm who rarely had time to chat during the working day at school.

First they talked about Sniffer's last days, about the trials and tribulations on the ride, and Terry described the cheque presentation at Posh, when Sniffer had been so proud.

There was no mention of Sniffer's confession. Terry was tempted to raise it because it seemed to demand attention, to be dealt with, but he sensed that Malcolm and Dusty were determined not to respond.

Terry wasn't sure whether it was grief, or just a sentimental feeling that came over him, but when part-way through the evening he stood to go and buy drinks he said: "Seriously, I want to thank you for what you did. On the ride. Sniffer would..." but couldn't finish the sentence and hurried to the bar.

When he returned Dusty said: "Now I feel bad about all the teasing about the Fens. I didn't mean it, you know Terry."

"Of course you did!" Terry said brightly. "Sniffer wouldn't have expected anything else from you."

"Actually I've got an idea about the Fens, and I need to talk." Dusty stopped when he noticed that Malcolm's wonky finger seemed to be back in place.

"It's about a project I've been working on."

Dusty described how he was finding that there was indeed life after Aardvark. During the meeting he had dreaded, he had said his piece. Embarrassingly, he had included a puerile meat-based jibe about scapegoats, one he regretted because it spoiled what he regarded as a plucky performance.

He had resigned, then enjoyed turning down pleas from his boss to stay.

"I thought, if he believes I'm good enough to be paid, then I'll be my own boss."

Malcolm and Terry nodded and made approving noises.

He described how he was going to use his marketing skills to market himself and his products – books he said, books that told the story of places.

"Places like the Fens, Terry. What I'd like to do, if it's all right, is to start by producing a book modelled on your mum's old jottings, topping it up with classy photos, and nice bits of history. I won't use her title – what was it 'Fen Water in my Blood'?

That's a bit too close in my mind to some medical problem, you know, Blood In My Fen Water."

He explained that he'd researched it. People liked books about the way places used to be.

They sold well. He was sure that Terry's photocopy of his mum's journal and characterful jottings would be a fascinating basis for a debut publication.

The trio talked companionably, showed each other photos taken on the ride.

Malcolm was passing one showing Sniffer holding up a sausage on a fork, beside the fire and with the expanse of the Fens behind him, when Dusty again noticed that Malcolm's finger had reverted to normal. Dusty pointed at it and raised his eyebrows inquiringly.

"Yes, went back into place," Malcolm said. "Tripped over Lucky one day and it hit the door jamb and, hey presto, it was straight again."

"Good. Maybe you're luck's changing," Dusty said.

"Maybe. The finger was fine but actually I hit a chair as I went down. Look."

He pulled up his top lip to reveal that part of a front tooth was missing.

ooooooo

"That was good what you said this morning, Ursula. One of your best."

As soon as she heard her name, Ursula paused near the bedside of a grey-haired, concave woman with a grey cap of wiry hair – a frequent patient in the renal ward. She was an unhealthy brown and was arched over a quizword book.

She waved a crinkly arm and called out: "It's all right people talking but they never know how they'll be if they're in a disaster. And we've all got a bit of shame inside somewhere."

Not many patients tuned into the hospital radio; feedback was scarce. So it was so rewarding when her regular Sunday morning Time To Think talk attracted interest.

Ursula was especially relieved today to have had a response because she had felt this morning's offering pushed at the boundaries. It was because of her upset over Sniffer, she knew, but she was disappointed to have yielded to emotion and let it inflame what was usually a cosy chat.

It had been altogether too powerful a theme, and she also knew she had chosen it in defence of Sniffer, because she felt he had been demonised in newspaper reports. She had not referred to the hit-and-run or to Sniffer but some listeners might have made the link.

She had spoken of courage and cowardice, remarking on how sometimes we bestow the quality of courage on those who are incapable of being brave.

"We talk of courageous sick babies, fighting their illness when the poor mites can have no concept of bravery. We sometimes have to play up the idea of courage, to inspire our soldiers."

And then she dwelt on cowardice, and how it is reviled, often by those whose own courage had not been tested. She asked how many people who seem plucky are quaking inside, resisting the urge to run but are prevented from doing so by their greater fear of being seen to be a coward.

Ursula realised now that the illustrations she used were far too graphic, far too powerful for the two dozen sick people passing ten minutes of the long day as nurses scurried around them.

"Maybe we ought to ask ourselves whether, in trying to escape from being crushed to death in a crowd, we would tread on someone lying beneath our feet to clear a barrier. How many of us would leave the welcome window in a smoke-filled room and go off in search of a figure coughing somewhere in the dark, beyond a wall of fire?"

She'd acknowledged that society had to have its moral boundaries, that examples – good and bad – guided us, helped us to aspire to what was best. But she had pleaded for those tempted to cast stones to put them down for a moment and to think.

As an example, she had said, people ought to ask themselves whether they could conceive of circumstances in which they would be so frightened, so petrified of consequences that they would run.

She was thinking of Sniffer and the terror he sometimes had in his eyes. Of him being – what was it he used to say? – being fritless, was it?

43

When Viv got over the initial shock of what the police had told her about Sniffer and the accident, Terry's words had come back to her – "When other people are putting the brakes on, Sniff will be tickling the accelerator."

That was Sniffer. And how strange that this had been literally true at that moment when the young man had died.

What was on the CD made her feel that she had not known Sniffer at all – and yet all that had happened, the meetings with Lydia, the deception, the self-preservation, it was pure Sniffer, on reflection, no more no less.

It was what you got if you loved him, and she had done, and still did. She had thought of that phrase about love being blind and had understood the meaning behind it.

Viv drew some comfort from the messages of sympathy arriving at the house.

Among the cards was an expensive, flowery sentimental one from Sniffer's estranged son.

In it he wrote loving words about a complete stranger, his father, and expressed regret that he hadn't been braver as he grew up, and defied his mother. She had banned all contact with Sniffer, when he was small and they were divorced, regarding him as the Devil incarnate.

This reminded Viv that there was a daughter somewhere, the product of some youthful coupling.

She recalled Sniffer had talked of the time he had been sent a note by the mother-to-be, saying that he "might" be the father. It was a girl he barely knew, he said.

She believed Sniffer had reasoned that this potential problem would go away so long as he showed no interest. He had said that he had not replied on the grounds that there was a chance that the child was not his.

That's what he said. But now Viv wondered whether the question mark over paternity had been placed there by Sniffer, as a salve to his conscience. Perhaps the note had even said he was the father and what was he going to do about it.

So somewhere, maybe within a few miles, there was a woman whose father had died, a stranger who might be the grandfather to her children. A woman who was unaware that he existed. For Viv, this possibility piled more sadness on top of sadness.

Frankie had sent a ridiculously extravagant bouquet. Attached was a card on which he had written – "Darling Viv – just remember, death cannot steal memories." There was a footnote saying that the society was planning to stage a songs-from-the-shows extravaganza and to keep the first week in October free. He wrote "This is to remind you at this terrible time that life will go on."

In fact, it was mainly to ensure he had a soprano for the line-up, Viv said to herself. Frankie's crass insensitivity prickled but she took heart from the prospect of another show.

Among cards from people Viv had never heard of, was one from a lady called Doreen who simply wrote: "He was the star we all followed when we were young." Viv tried to picture Sniffer as a teenager and understood.

Viv had cleared the mantelpiece of the photos – the Wembley picture, the pictures of herself in shows, and a group shot of the charity riders in a pub garden – so she could display the cards, but then had to use the windowsill and hearth. There were dozens.

○ ○ ○ ○ ○ ○ ○

But it was three, simple, unadorned notes that carried significant meaning, as Viv began to come to terms with the prospect of life without Sniffer...

One was from Ursula to Viv confirming that she would speak about Sniffer at the funeral.

The lilac ink and the sweeping cursive hand combined to enhance the warmth of the message written on ivory paper.

She offered comforting words, words heavy with meaning, not trite words people usually wrote in cards. They brought tears to Viv's eyes.

Ursula also said that she was sorry that in seeking to help Sniffer she had invaded the intimacy that a husband and wife share at critical moments of their lives.

She only hoped that Viv's love for Sniffer enabled her to accommodate the closeness that had developed, and that any feeling she had of having been excluded was surely outweighed by the blessed relief Sniffer had experienced when he faced down his demons.

"Sniffer so loved you that he couldn't lay his shame in front of you. It had to be revealed to a stranger. He so wanted to have your approval. He was full of regret that it was only when he was preparing to die that he realised the depth of his love for you.

"He was a rascal of course, and often let his appetites overrule his decency and loyalty. But in case he didn't tell you properly, now I'm free of the constraints of confidentiality I want you to know that he often told me that you were the love of his life."

◦ ◦ ◦ ◦ ◦ ◦ ◦

The second note was from Pat.

It was scrawled on the back of a brown envelope – one of many scattered around, each containing a threat relating to debts. The note was propped up on top of the coffee jar. She knew that is where Mick would see it as soon as he came in.

The note said:

"That's it Mick. No more.

Did you know it was Sniffer who killed that poor doctor?

I'm sure you did but muggins here didn't of course. I'm only your wife.

This afternoon the police were round again, this time to lecture me, ME mind you about how serious it is if people help to cover up a crime. They were asking me to confirm all sorts of stuff that Sniffer mentioned in some recording he left.

They're not going to do anything. I think they just wanted to scare me with words like conspiracy and it worked. But all I ever did was to give a lift to a selfish little creep. Your so-called friend.

So it turns out you risked ME going to jail to cover up for HIM. You put that coward before me and the kids, to keep him out of the shit.

I want you to keep this note so you'll remember what I've said and I hope what you've done stays with you.

The kids are at Ken and Sandra's where they're always happy unlike here.

There's papers inc. birth certificates etc. in the biscuit tin (red one Scotch shortbread) under the bed.

I'm in the garage."

o o o o o o o

Mick thought first of the blue nylon tow rope.

Then of the girder he had threaded through the old brickwork at ceiling height, ready to make an upper floor, once they had the money.

Then he thought of the stepladder he kept in there.

He could envisage the scene without going into the garage, see it as clear as a photograph, and he knew the image would always be with him.

There was no going back, nothing to be lost by going out there and confronting the terrible reality. He dropped the note and went out to the garage.

o o o o o o o

The third note was written by Viv. It was to Lydia.

She had been trying to pick herself up and be brave for the

funeral, but had just been thrown headlong back into the black abyss when the news of Pat's death reached her.

She had thought immediately about Ursula, and the way she talked about love and how she showed it. She thought about the brevity of life and about her own feeling of isolation, of being orphaned.

She drove from the city with the note, out into the fens and past the ramshackle house, checking that the 2CV was not there. She turned and then pulled up near the gate and walked into the yard and up to the door with its rotting panels.

The noise from the chickens was alarming, and behind the house a dog was barking and ducks quacking in alarm. She pushed the envelope through the wonky flap in the door and hurried back to the car.

When, that afternoon, Lydia bounced down the yard in the 2CV and took in the shopping she spotted the envelope in the hall.

The house was chilled. Without taking off her waxed jacket or fingerless mittens she began to stow the groceries as she waited for the kettle to boil.

She was about to sit at the table with her coffee when she remembered the note. She fetched it and opened it.

She did not recognise the hand.

The note began "Dear Lydia…"

(As Viv had begun to write she had paused at the thought that this was the first time she had written the name that she once could not bear to hear).

Viv said that if Lydia had not got details of the funeral arrangements and the evening to celebrate Sniffer's life she would find them on the slip she'd attached.

She would be very grateful if Lydia could come. Sniffer would have wanted it. The thought would have given him such pleasure and peace of mind.

She added that she did not have much in the way of family, and believed that Lydia was in the same position.

Life was short, as she had learned lately, she wrote. There had been a terrible tragedy involving someone close, straight after Sniffer's passing.

"It would be so good for me to know that we could support each other on the day, when we both say goodbye to Sniffer," she had written, and ended the note "Viv X."

She had immediately regretted the kiss and had reached for paper so she could re-write the note; scribbling the kiss out would send a confusing message.

Yes, a kiss for a stranger, once the enemy, was a step too far.

Or was it?

If there was to be some sort of reconciliation, some way of making the past less painful and future less bleak, she had to trust her instincts and follow them.

She had thought of Ursula, then of dear Sniffer.

She had folded the note, complete with its X, and set off to deliver it.

Thanks to...

...my family for text-checks, feedback and for playing devil's advocate.

Sharon Reid for design, support and technical input and Chris Munden for the cover photo of a fen sunset.

Veteran Posh supporter Robert Whitehead for reminders of past heroes, and to Brian Marshall for suggestions concerning vehicles

About the author...

Neil Patrick is a retired journalist and former editor of the national magazine Yours. He has written thousands of articles in a career covering 50 years and is now a columnist for Choice magazine. He was co-author, with Edmund Hockridge, of Hey There, the biography of the Canadian star of West End musicals.

Just Dying To Tell is Neil's second novel. His first, The Healing Hut, is a funny, heartwarming story of loss, hope, romance and family conflict.

The Healing Hut has been hailed as a brilliant debut novel.

It is both funny and sad but most of all it's compelling reading. Many readers have said they struggled to put it down once they entered the world of Kyff Pugh, a man who lost his wife and thought he'd also lost his future.

Much of the action takes place on ancient allotments where Kyff tries to rebuild his life, having taken over the hut where his late father spent most of his days.

The book teems with colourful characters who befriend Kyff and draw him into their community.

Although not a gardening book, The Healing Hut was chosen by the Garden Media Guild as one of the five most inspiring books of 2013.

• *The Healing Hut by Neil Patrick is published by Touching Tales (ISBN 9780957608306) at £7 99. It's available through any bookshop, or via Amazon (Kindle version available).*

What readers have said about The Healing Hut...
"A debut novel that is a revelation"...
"A novel, heartwarming book"...
"Witty and perceptive"....
"Brilliant! Both funny and sad"...
"A delight"